Cacy & Kiara
and the
CURSE OF THE KI'I

Sophia! Aloha. Enjoy the adventure!

Cacy & Kiara and the CURSE OF THE KI'I

an adventure story set in Hawai'i

written and illustrated by
Roy Chang

BEACHHOUSE
Publishing

The events and characters in this book are entirely fictional.
Any similarity to actual persons or occurrences is purely
coincidental.

ISBN-10: 1-933067-47-0
ISBN-13: 978-1-933067-47-6
Library of Congress Control Number: 2012943070

Design by Jane Gillespie
First Printing, October 2012

BeachHouse Publishing, LLC
PO Box 5464
Kāneʻohe, Hawaiʻi 96744
email: info@beachhousepublishing.com
www.beachhousepublishing.com

Printed in Korea

Contents

Acknowledgments

Writing and drawing this book has been a labor of love for a decade. It would not have been possible without the vision and support of Jane Gillespie of BeachHouse Publishing to "go for it" even at just the idea stage.

Also, much appreciation to both the professional editors and the special friends who volunteered to read developing chapters and give their honest feedback (and listening patiently over and over about my crazy dream of writing a novel and the story ideas.)

Thanks especially to Shaun for taking the trip with me to Hawai'i Island in 2003, and to Linda for critiquing the summaries of each chapter. The Park Rangers and staff at both Hawai'i Volcanoes National Park and Pu'uhonua o Hōnaunau were a big help with information and for being good sports.

In the final stages, the G.T. Language Arts students and teacher at Mililani 'Ike Elementary School really contributed with their reviews and suggestions. Your feedback was great (and my revised cover looks a lot more cooler than the first version)!

Lastly, thank you to Ke Akua above for His aloha and blessings and also to all my teachers and students and family and friends. To the readers, I hope you enjoy this book. Even though this story is fictitious, visit the real locations where the story takes place and you're sure to have your own adventure!

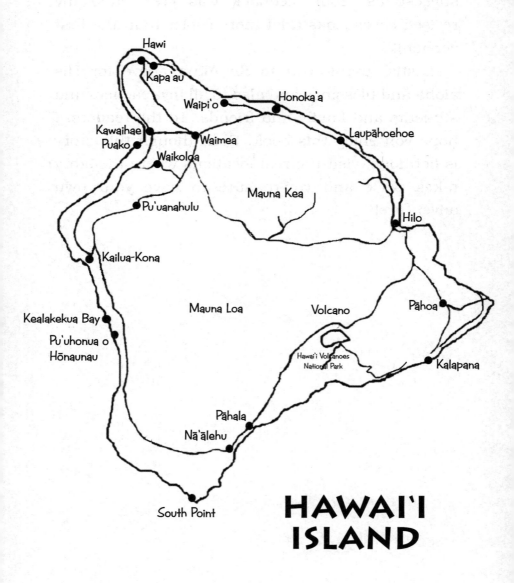

Hawi

Kapa'au

Waipi'o

Honoka'a

Kawaihae
Puako

Waimea

Laupāhoehoe

Waikoloa

Pu'uanahulu

Mauna Kea

Hilo

Kailua-Kona

Mauna Loa

Volcano

Pāhoa

Kealakekua Bay

Pu'uhonua o
Hōnaunau

Hawai'i Volcanoes
National Park

Kalapana

Pāhala

Nā'ālehu

South Point

HAWAI'I
ISLAND

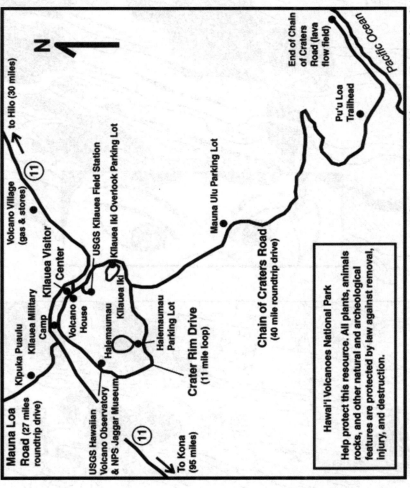

Courtesy Hawai'i Volcanoes National Park

N

to Hilo (30 miles)

Volcano Village
(gas & stores)

11

Mauna Loa
Road (27 miles
roundtrip drive)

Kipuka Puaulu

Kilauea Military
Camp

Kilauea Visitor
Center

USGS Kilauea Field Station

Kilauea Iki Overlook Parking Lot

Volcano
House

Kilauea Iki

Halemaumau

Halemaumau
Parking Lot

Crater Rim Drive
(11 mile loop)

USGS Hawaiian
Volcano Observatory
& NPS Jaggar Museum

11

To Kona
(95 miles)

Mauna Ulu Parking Lot

Chain of Craters Road
(40 mile roundtrip drive)

End of Chain
of Craters
Road (lava
flow field)

Pu'u Loa
Trailhead

Pacific Ocean

Hawai'i Volcanoes National Park

Help protect this resource. All plants, animals
rocks, and other natural and archeological
features are protected by law against removal,
injury, and destruction.

Chapter 1

Cacy's New Friends and the Bullies

"**I** hope I get to see real lava and how hot it really is!" Cacy Dang shared to the sea turtles as she was about to reach down to touch them. It was early morning past sunrise, yet still dark and chilly. The entire Island of Hawai'i was covered by layers of thick rain clouds. No one else staying at the Hilo hotel was around its popular live honu pool this early. A large sign at the pool stated "Please Do Not Touch the Sea Turtles. Thank you." So she kept her hands to herself, still leaning over the two-foot-high rock wall surrounding the sea turtle exhibit. On the other side of the pool was an artificial island of sand and lava rocks where the sea turtles could rest. A motorized waterfall created bubbles, and waves rippled over the surface of the pool as the sea turtles frolicked and flapped around in the shallow water. Their dark shells and bobbing heads looked like little islands moving in slow circular patterns. Some of the turtles swam right up to Cacy to look at her with equal curiosity and interest clearly wanting her to play with them. "I'm sorry," Cacy explained with slight embarrassment, "but the sign says I'm not supposed to touch you."

Later that morning Cacy and the rest of her sixth-grade class from Malulani Elementary School on Oʻahu would be visiting the world-famous Hawaiʻi Volcanoes National Park. This wasn't her first time away from home and her parents, but it was her first time visiting the Island of Hawaiʻi, the largest yet youngest island in the Hawaiian chain. The students had arrived in Kona the night before and rode an old charter bus across the island to the quiet town of Hilo. A silly idea, since Hilo has its own airport, and it was just a few minutes' drive from there to the Honu Bay Hotel where they were staying. Their teacher, Ms. Windbagg, felt it would be more beneficial for the students to enjoy a leisurely view of the island on the way to the hotel. After arriving in Kona, though, there was nothing to see but black clouds, fog, and pounding rain outside the bus. The drive from the Kona airport heading northeast through Kohala, Waimea, Hāmākua, and into Hilo took three long, nauseating, shi-shi-holding hours and 102 miles for the students. They now knew why it was called the "BIG Island." Arriving late at the hotel—past 10 p.m.—all anyone could think of doing was to go straight to their rooms to sleep.

On this morning, Cacy was first to wake up, first to be in the breakfast line in the hotel restaurant, and first to have free time before the charter bus would arrive to take everyone to see the volcanoes. In preparation for this interisland field trip, her class had spent weeks studying volcanoes, Hawaiian ecosystems, and ancient Hawaiian practices. Learning about legends and myths like Pele, the Hawaiian Fire Goddess who lived in the volcanoes, really interested Cacy. She herself was part-Hawaiian, but it was hard to notice with her round Chinese features.

The serenity of watching the sea turtles was broken when a big splash of icy water doused her from the left. She squinted and recoiled, all wet and surprised. At first, Cacy thought it was just a playful slap on the water's surface from one of the large adult turtles. Instead, it was a harassing slap by three of her classmates. It was Tiana Crown, Momi Momona, and Shaun Lackey. Tiana and Momi were the two most popular and bratty girls in school who relished spreading gossip, igniting arguments, and especially agitating Cacy. Shaun was mostly a follower who hung out with the two girls. He often got into trouble doing the naughty things Momi or Tiana asked him to do. This time, Momi had told him to sneak up next to Cacy and splash her with pool water.

The cold water was still running down Cacy's pigtailed hair and down her neck when Momi tried to scoop water and splash Cacy as well. Instead, Cacy ducked quickly out of the way. Most of the water splashed on Tiana, who was sneaking up on Cacy's right side. Tiana shrieked from the cold water and in disgust. She swung her arm into the pool and splashed both Momi and Shaun.

"Ha!" Cacy burst. "Serves you right!" She stepped several feet away from the exhibit to keep an eye on all three of them.

"What, Cacy?!" Tiana teased while tossing back her damp, long auburn hair. "Trying to make friends with the turtles? You don't have ANY friends, you know that!"

In a way, Tiana was correct. No one else in school really wanted anything to do with Cacy. She was seen as either an oddball or a loner, mainly because she didn't like trying to fit in with others just to be accepted. Plus, the baseball bat that always stuck out of her pink backpack scared away most troublemakers. She first used it to help a younger student who was often being bullied after school. Every student in the school knew about this, but didn't want to speak up and tell a teacher. On that day, the retiring P.E. teacher was throwing away old sports equipment but gave Cacy the very wooden bat she had successfully learned to hit a ball with. After school, Cacy witnessed three older boys bullying the much smaller and younger student while others stood at a distance watching in amusement. Angered by this, she went up to the boys and used what she describes as her ninja moves. For a girl with her chubby frame and frumpy clothes, she had quick reflexes. All who saw the fight between her and the three bullies were amazed at how fast she could move and use her baseball bat to defend herself. It wasn't a pretty fight to watch, but it certainly was a brave one. After the principal's investigation, the three boys were expelled, and Cacy was given detention for fighting. She learned that sometimes there are no rewards for helping those in trouble.

With the bullies gone, both Tiana and Momi felt they could now rule the school, and Cacy the do-gooder was the only one in their way. In this situation, it was at the sea turtle exhibit. Shaun ignored all three of the girls, reached deep into the icy cold pool water, and snatched up a baby sea turtle. It flapped its tiny flippers in panic. All the other sea turtles in the pool began to react with agitation. Other baby turtles swam to the sand island for protection.

"Yeee-oooooo! It's cold!" Shaun shouted as he shook water off his pale skinny arm. The little turtle in his hand was being shaken around as well.

"Put it down! The sign says don't touch them!" Cacy scolded, pointing to the clearly posted sign. Tiana and Momi turned to glance over at the sign and laughed. Shaun copied them.

Both Tiana and Momi were known by other students to be mean and nasty at times, but they exceeded their reputations when they both began repeating Cacy's words in a high-pitched, babylike whine.

"Aw, poot it down! The sign says don't touch them! Aw, poot it down!" the two girls teased over and over.

Cacy's eyes burned with both hurt feelings and anger. She was ready to reach back for the baseball bat, but knew that if she got into a fight, she would end up being sent back home to O'ahu. This was what Tiana and Momi wanted to see happen.

"Eh," Momi said to Shaun. "Let me see the turtle."

"Here, catch!" Shaun bursted with laughter as he quickly tossed it over to her.

Momi shrieked and backed up, holding her hands out. The little turtle landed clumsily in one hand and, like a juggling ball, was tossed into her other hand, back and forth several times as she tried to get a solid hold of the wet, slippery creature. Both

Tiana and Shaun laughed hysterically as Momi tried to hold on to the writhing baby turtle. Suddenly, she got a sharp poke on her palm by either the turtle's pincher-tipped mouth or its pointy flippers.

"Ouch!" she screamed, throwing her hands up in the air and sending the baby turtle spinning recklessly in a high arc. Everyone's eyes followed the turtle, watching it spin and peak just before descending.

It was going to land several feet from Cacy. With ninja moves, she followed the fast descent of the baby turtle, and with a quick leap forward, dove full throttle. Cacy landed hard on her chest and stomach with the whole weight of her backpack on top of her. A loud slap and thud echoed with the crunching sound of gravel. The wind was knocked out of her lungs with the crushing blow, and she grimaced from the sharp stinging in her rib cage. Cacy squeezed her eyes tight, trying to soak up the initial pain. She slowly opened her eyes and looked at her outstretched arms. In her cupped hands, the baby turtle was lying upright and staring at her with its shiny black eyes.

"Hey, what are you kids doing?!!" yelled a loud adult male voice the kids didn't recognize.

All four students froze and looked directly at the stout, dark-skinned man wearing a straw pith helmet, dressy aloha shirt, and white pants, standing on top of the nearby marble steps. At first, they thought he was a mainland tourist, but he looked local. And, he looked angry. The shiny silver Honu Bay Hotel Security badge on his aloha shirt said it all.

"Eh! You damn kids no can read da sign, or what?!" he pointed out in a deep pidgin English all of them could understand. He glared at the three dumb, wet kids standing at the edge of the pool exhibit and the one poor kid lying flat on her stomach cradling a baby sea turtle in her hands. He pointed his finger at Cacy. "Put dat turtle back in da water now, or I going tell your teacher fo' take you damn kids back to O'ahu. Das why I hate when you folks do field trips to da Big Island! Always gotta go act stupid wen you come stay in da hotel. Hurry up!"

Momi, Tiana, and Shaun didn't miss a beat. Taking the opportunity to humiliate Cacy, they began scolding her as well, and reprimanded out loud, "Yeah, WE told you not to take the turtles from the pool. Put it back!"

"But...but...," Cacy tried to explain to the security guard. It was no use. She numbly walked back to the turtle pool, tenderly carrying her little friend under the strict and seething eyes of the guard, as well as the sly and slithering eyes of her classmates. She felt like drawing out her bat to teach them a lesson, even if it meant being sent back home. Again, she controlled her feelings and thoughts and obeyed the security guard. Besides, all school year, she had been looking forward to visiting Hawaiʻi Volcanoes National Park and didn't want to miss the chance to see real molten lava, no matter what happened.

"Don't worry," she said softly to the baby turtle as it calmed down in her gentle hands. "You're safe now. I won't let them harm you or your friends."

She lowered the little sea creature back into its aquatic home. Slowly and happily it wiggled and flipped its fins in the rushing flows of the water and swam off on its own. For a moment, it looked as if all the other turtles were smiling as they gathered around the baby and circled together. Tiana, Momi, and Shaun sat on the pool edge silently watching Cacy. Yet on the inside, they were still laughing and mocking her. Oh, how they wished cell phones were not banned on the field trip so they could've filmed Cacy being busted. The guard's fiery stare still burned on Cacy. She figured that trying to explain her side would result only in a back and forth she-said-they-said type of argument, going nowhere.

"I...uh...I'm sorry, sir," Cacy said, looking down. Not waiting for anything else, she turned and slowly walked away along the narrow pathway, past sagging palm trees, cold metal torches, and leering tiki statues, to the empty swimming pool area. Nobody was around to see the hot tears flowing down her face.

Waiting a few seconds longer, the security guard turned to the other three and gave them a stern look of disapproval. His stink eye look was, indeed, a noisome glare. Momi, Tiana, and Shaun looked back at the hotel officer as innocently as they could. A walkie-talkie call broke the silent tension, and the disembodied static voice of someone from the front desk asked the guard to report to the hotel driveway to supervise another group of arriving school kids. For an instant, he stared blank-faced in disbelief, then gave a deep sigh of exhaustion.

"Ten-four," he responded. "Man, I'm getting too old fo' dis!" he muttered to himself, shaking his head and walking off.

The turtles bobbed their heads above the water surface to make sure the guard was finally gone. Three of the biggest adult sea turtles in the pool nodded to each other and submerged. They slowly swam to the edge of the pool just below where Tiana, Momi, and Shaun were still sitting and giggling to themselves with delight. With the speed and stealth worthy of ninjas, the three big turtles used their mighty front flippers to thrust swiftly up from the water and snapped the students sharply on their butts.

Chapter 2

Kiara Arrives with Her School

While the other sixth-grade students of Central Academy on Oʻahu looked outside their air-conditioned luxury tour bus at the somber gray morning of Hilo, Kiara Yoon could tell the exact temperature, humidity, precipitation, and more just from the readouts on her Digital Data Pad. Throughout the short bus ride from the Hilo airport to the driveway of the Honu Bay Hotel, little Kiara sat alone in the back, totally engrossed in her handheld electronic invention. The device looked like a cross between a large cell phone, an electrical metronome, a calculator, and a stun gun. All the students in her school were known to be the best and brightest of Hawaiʻi's private elementary schools, and Kiara was not just a star pupil, but a genius as well. She was planning to test her high-tech creation during her class visit to Hawaiʻi Volcanoes National Park later in the day. The Digital Data Pad would collect her own raw data on volcanic activities for her school science project. Most of the other students settled for making a simple papier mâché model of a volcano.

"Looks like Hilo is having another cloudy day," said Ms. Fitzgerald, the sixth-grade teacher at the academy, as she gazed out from her seat in the front of the bus. "This sort of weather reminds me of the Windward side back on Oʻahu."

"Ms. Fitzgerald!" Kiara called, raising her hand out of habit. "Windward Oʻahu and Hilo are similar in both precipitation levels and rain frequency since both land masses face obstructed westerly clouds. As a result, both the Leeward side of Oʻahu and the Kailua-Kona side of Hawaiʻi Island tend to be drier and sunnier than their respective Windward counterparts."

The entire class turned their heads to the back of the bus to look at Kiara. With their eyes, all the students seemed to express, "Who cares?!!!" Then they resumed looking out at the sights of the tiny town. One student pointed out a colorful restaurant advertising that they exclusively served pancakes. It instantly attracted everyone else's attention as they saw a long line of hungry diners waiting outside the restaurant for available tables.

"Pancakes," Kiara snickered to herself as she scrolled the menu on the Digital Data Pad screen. "What's so special about a pancake house in Hilo?"

While most teachers would praise and appreciate a student like Kiara for possessing such high academic abilities and critical thinking skills, Ms. Fitzgerald had become rather worn and jaded by it. Kiara was respected in the academy, but nobody really wanted to associate with her. She had a lot of head knowledge, but most felt she lacked heart knowledge. Though Kiara never teased others or misbehaved, she often made those around her feel inferior and intimidated by her intellectual acuteness. Even previous teachers feared being embarrassed in front of the class if Kiara had to correct them. The academic standards of Central Academy were already high, and Kiara liked raising the bar even higher in class subjects. It made her feel superior and she liked to look down on others. If there ever was an intellectual version of a school bully, it was found in a thin, frail little Japanese, Chinese, Korean, and Hawaiian girl with large-rimmed glasses. While other students chose to forgo wearing their formal school uniform for this class trip, Kiara still wore the standard white collared shirt, red bow, blue vest, and pleated skirt. Her teacher had warned all the students that hiking the rocky fields to see the lava flows would require rugged walking shoes. Kiara had her hiking shoes covered in shiny black patent leather so as not to clash with the school uniform. When the weather got cooler, she had her blue and white varsity-style jacket with her school's emblem embroidered in gold over the chest pocket. If fashion was a statement, Kiara stated very clearly that she was one of the elite students enrolled in Central Academy.

The bus made a turn past the pancake house and down a narrow road. Enormous banyan trees towered high on both sides of the road, their thick ancient branches twisting and fusing into each other and forming a vaulted ceiling over the bus. As the bus passed each sacred banyan tree, students began calling out historical names as if playing a game. Kiara looked outside her window and noticed that a name plaque stood before each tree. The plaques identified the famous American or member of Hawaiian royalty who had planted the tree. As each name was read out loud by a student, Kiara shouted a quick description of the person's biography. By the time the bus passed the tree labeled "Mark Twain," the students were no longer interested in playing, but Kiara went ahead and gave a long speech about his visits to the "Sandwich Islands." Only Ms. Fitzgerald acted as if she was listening to her with the big generic smile she had mastered from being in beauty pageants.

To the delight and excitement of the rest of the students, the bus turned a corner into the busy driveway of the Honu Bay Hotel. The gray morning didn't stop the colorful action at the hotel as luggage porters, guides in bright muʻumuʻu, lei greeters, and tourists rushed about their business. The students in the bus noticed that there were kids from another school roaming about outside.

"Hey, what school is that?" shouted Jae, one of Kiara's classmates, as she pointed to the red-shirted kids standing near the hotel entrance and looking curiously back at them.

"I hope they're leaving!" Victor, another classmate, declared. "I thought only OUR school was going to be at this hotel." The rest of the students began groaning.

Ms. Fitzgerald and her fellow chaperones quieted the students down and explained that other schools were probably interested in visiting Hawaiʻi Volcanoes National Park as well. In truth, it wasn't just schools. Recent news and video footage of active lava flows from the Puʻu ʻŌʻō vent on the eastern side of the 4,000-feet-high Kīlauea volcano had attracted an incredible increase of tourists, photographers, and scientists from around the world. Last night Ms. Fitzgerald called the park's 1-800 phone number to hear eruption updates. It was the perfect time to visit. Fountains of lava were reaching heights over 1,000 feet in the air, and glowing red-hot rivers of molten lava oozed down toward the ocean where surging waves mixed and exploded into billowing acidic smoke clouds.

As the students and adults disembarked the bus, porters and other hotel workers had already begun unloading the luggage and setting them in neat rows along the sidewalk area. A young, pretty woman wearing a floral muʻumuʻu and a lei greeted the students and directed them to the hotel ballroom where they were treated to a sumptuous late breakfast buffet. All the students stuffed their bellies. The day called for a fifty-minute hike in the park to reach the lava flows, and Ms. Fitzgerald encouraged the students to eat as much as possible for energy. As the rest of the students gorged, Kiara sat prim and proper in her seat with her napkin laid on her lap, chewing her food properly the way her parents had taught her. During the meal, a porter from the hotel informed Ms. Fitzgerald that all the luggage was checked in and had been sent to their assigned rooms. Already some of the students were full and wanted to go to their rooms to get ready.

Ms. Fitzgerald had the entire trip outlined and planned like clockwork. She tapped her water glass and got the students' attention. In one hour, another charter bus would pick them up and take them all on the sixty-minute, thirty-mile drive to the volcano park. She reiterated the rules and policies of the hotel and the plan for visiting the park. Each student monitor was given a hotel room card and a lanyard. As a group, the students left the ballroom and eagerly made their way through the lobby area to their rooms to change and gather their gear for the day. Ms. Fitzgerald and the chaperones remained to have a short meeting. Kiara took her Digital Data Pad off the table and clipped it back onto her waist. She followed the huddled mass of students from a distance. Without any adult in the lead, the students walked silently and respectfully through the lobby, garnering the smiles of hotel staff and tourists. Even a certain security guard gave them a look of approval as the students made their way past the kitschy tiki-adorned cocktail lounge and tacky gift shop.

Just as the Central Academy students were reaching the elevators, a young loud voice boomed and resonated through the promenade, causing passing hotel guests to look around.

"KIARA!!!!...HEY! KIARA!!!!!...OVER HERE!!!!!"

For a moment, Kiara thought she heard her name amongst all the bustle in the lobby, and ignored it.

"HEY!! KIARA!!!!!"

All the students turned around to look at Kiara, who stood looking blankly back at all of them. Her thoughts raced like the spinning wheels on a jackpot machine and stopped at wondering which idiot was yelling for someone with the same name. Realizing that the voice was coming from far behind her, Kiara raised her eyebrow in curiosity and turned around. Off in the distance, amid passing hotel guests, stood another little girl. She was wearing an oversized scruffy red T-shirt, baggy blue jeans rolled at the cuffs, pigtails in her hair, and had what looked like the handle of a baseball bat sticking from her pink backpack. Kiara's eyes widened and her lower lip sank lower. It was her way of showing surprise and disgust at the same time.

"Hey, she must be a student form that other school we saw this morning," Jae said, trying to peek above the shoulders of the other academy students. She was the tiniest and most vocal of the sixth-grade class.

Victor walked up to Kiara and asked if she recognized the other girl. Kiara didn't take her silent focus off the girl, who was now walking toward her and the group. Some of the hotel guests who had been startled by the shouting of this brash child continued to watch her as she walked past them. In fact, all eyes were upon this girl as she strutted up, smiling at Kiara.

"Hi, Kiara. What are you doing on the Big Island? Are you here to see the volcanoes today just like our school?!" the girl asked.

The academy students were surprised and stunned that someone all the way in Hilo not only knew Kiara, but was actually excited to see her. Who was this loud girl, they wondered. She was obviously not as well mannered as they were, nor did she look like the type smart enough to be accepted into the academy. Her dusty red T-shirt read "Malulani Elementary School," which wasn't one of the most prestigious of the public schools on Oʻahu. Looking at her and Kiara was like looking at direct opposites. It seemed like a very long pause, but Kiara finally spoke.

"Oh...hello, Cacy," she said blandly. Kiara then turned around to her classmates. "Everyone...this is my cousin from Oʻahu, Cacy."

The students waved hello with artificial politeness and didn't return Cacy's smile.

"Yes," Kiara continued, turning to her cousin. "Our academy class arrived in Hilo this morning to visit Hawaiʻi Volcanoes National Park today." It pained Kiara to admit to her classmates that this so-different girl was related to her. Cacy easily sensed this but didn't care. She was happy to see a familiar face on this trip, even though it had to be "know-it-all snob" Kiara, and it helped her to get over the earlier incident with the security guard.

As Cacy began asking more questions, Kiara looked squarely at her through her large-framed glasses and stopped her coldly. "Listen, I have to make preparations for my excursion and data collecting. You should go back ...and remain with YOUR school group. Goodbye."

Everyone, especially Cacy, felt the icy tone in Kiara's voice. She knew that this was just Kiara's way of disassociating from Cacy and putting her down in front of others. As the academy students waited for the first elevator to arrive, Cacy turned around and started to walk off. Looking back over her shoulder toward Kiara, she shouted, "See you later at the volcano park...Kiki!!!!!!"

Kiara's back was turned toward Cacy. Those in front of Kiara had the misfortune of seeing her nonchalant face slowly change. Her lips crunched into a protruding frown and her brows raised and arched downward as the color of her cheeks and forehead reddened. Keeping her arms stiffly at her sides, her shoulders rose up and her fists clenched. Students stepped back in fear as Kiara's mouth snarled back and she hissed through her gritted teeth. It was like a scene in some horror film when a person is taken over by a savage spirit. Even Kiara's perfectly brushed hairdo showed signs of splitting. Just at the point when she looked like steam was going to shoot out her ears, Kiara swung around and roared at the top of her lungs.

"DON'T CALL ME KIKI!!!!!" she erupted. "My name is NOT Ki-Ki!!!! Argh!! I HATE THAT NICKNAME!!! MY NAME IS KI-A-RA, NOT Ki-Ki!! ARGH-UHHH!!!"

Everyone. Every student, every tourist, every hotel employee, every guest, and everyone as far off as the hotel driveway all the way up to the fifth floor (there were seven floors) all heard Kiara yell. People's heads were popping up from behind tikis, shrubs, columns, lounge seats, phone booths, cleaning carts, balconies, and corners, all curious to see who in the world could have yelled at such a volume! After the shocking outburst, Kiara realized that Cacy had gotten back at, and, once again, got the best of her. In fact, both girls now seemed embarrassed by all the attracted attention.

Cacy and Kiara always had their private share of cousin rivalry and bickered over any matter. One of the most significantly insignificant and unresolved issues between them was that even though they were both eleven years old, Kiara was six months older. In Kiara's mind, this qualified her to boss her younger cousin around. Cacy's constant rebuttal to this was that she was stronger and carried a baseball bat. Most of the time, especially at family gatherings, they couldn't stand being together and they both knew how to make the worst out of an already lousy situation. Both girls would never treat others that poorly, but because they were related, they felt it was acceptable. They enjoyed doing so.

Kiara regained her calm composure and wished that her Digital Data Pad had a button that would make her invisible as she quietly and swiftly slipped into an open elevator to go up to her room. All the students already in the elevator nervously pressed their backs hard against the walls. They were afraid this Cacy cousin might call out "that" nickname again, causing Kiara to blow her temper one more time just when the elevator doors closed. Cacy did.

Chapter 3

Evil Enters the Park

Even at ten a.m., thick and heavy clouds suppressed the Hawaiian sunshine. Only a faint glowing spot showed the sun's location. The Hilo air was wet and sticky. Despite the melancholy weather, the adults and students from Malulani Elementary School and Central Academy of Hawai'i were bright and energized as they boarded their respective charter buses, both heading to the same destination. The news got around fast among the students that Cacy had a cousin in the other school and that Kiara had her cousin in the other. Both girls tried to keep occupied looking out their windows.

After several minutes on the road, the Central Academy students felt like the hour-long drive was taking forever. Highway 11 out of Hilo was busier than usual. The southbound lane was nearly bumper to bumper with rental cars, tour buses, and SUVs, all heading to Hawai'i Volcanoes National Park. The only volcano to see so far had been the majestic

As a duo, Bishop planned out new assignments and secret negotiations with clients while Rook "eliminated" any problems.

Joining them today and sleeping in the back of the Hummer—hidden under a sheet—were Rook's shepherd dogs, Falchion and Gladius. They were small, but when hunting or tracking targets, they were as sharp and deadly as the ancient Roman and Greek swords they were named after. In addition to pets, the park banned firearms and weapons, so the men had their items secretly hidden in the Hummer.

Today, Hawai'i Volcanoes National Park was to serve as a meeting location between them and Dr. Petris Pōhaku, an archeologist and Pacific anthropologist from the University of Hawai'i on O'ahu. He recently discovered a very rare and unique ancient Hawaiian artifact that could sell pretty high on the black market rather than being kept and displayed in a museum of natural history. Pōhaku had not informed the University of his discovery, but instead contacted colleagues from Europe who had previously done secret business with the Queen's organization. Now they were retired and living luxuriously in Cuba.

"Aha!" Bishop said loudly, taking the cigarette out of his mouth. "The game is afoot, my friend." He pointed his cigarette to the upcoming large, dark, wooden road sign with white letters spelling out HAWAII VOLCANOES NATIONAL PARK. Traffic slowed as the stream of vehicles made the same left turn toward the entrance. Rook tapped his fat fingertips impatiently on the steering wheel as he waited for vehicles to move into the multilane entrance. He honked the piercing horn, startling the Japanese tourists in the van that cut in front of them.

"Oh, geez, my friend, why don't you just reach under for your gun and put a few shots in the air," teased Bishop sarcastically as he made a quick simple gesture of apology to the tourists who were looking back at them. For a moment, Rook paused to look at Bishop and began reaching under the driver's seat before they both broke out in a fit of wicked laughter.

Of the several lanes available for vehicles to pay the entrance fee at the entrance station, the Hummer ended up waiting in the one with two school buses. They held up the line. A park ranger had to board both buses and take a head count of all adults and children to make sure the pre-collected money amount was accurate. The young redheaded ranger with the stiff ranger hat and gray and green uniform on Cacy's bus noticed the bat sticking out of her pink backpack.

"Hey, this is a volcano park, not a ball park," the ranger said, half laughing at her own joke. Cacy couldn't help but giggle as well. This put off Tiana, Momi, and Shaun. Just before stepping out of the bus, the ranger turned to the group and wished them a pleasant adventure. "By the way," she added, "I'm sure all you kids learned about Pele ʻai honua: ʻPele who eats the land.' The volcano deity is very active today. Remember this; show her your respect when you see her."

With a sly grin, the ranger left the bus, which had turned silent. It was almost as if she was giving a bedtime warning to kids at camp to watch out for the boogey man. Some of the students snickered nervously. Cacy pondered if there was any truth to all the legends and Hawaiian ghost stories she learned back on Oʻahu about Pele, who lived in the active volcano.

She remembered lessons about the early Hawaiians and their Kumulipo chant, which tells how the earth, oceans, and islands were created. They had many gods and demigods. Pele was the vengeful and hot-tempered goddess of fire, lightning, and volcanoes. When she paddled to Hawaiʻi with her family from Tahiti, the islands were still being formed. Legends spoke of her landing on Niʻihau and using her mighty digging stick, Paoa, to find a new home. She dug to find intense heat and lava. If she hit underground water, the steam created would make her move elsewhere. Slowly she worked her way down the chain of islands, ending on Hawai'i Island where she finally made her home in Kīlauea. Many still believed that volcanic eruptions occurred whenever she was angered or troubled. Those who had taken home pieces of lava rock as souvenirs were said to encounter painful misfortunes. For years, hundreds of rocks had been mailed back to the park with letters apologizing to Pele. To this day, Pele worshippers came to the sacred grounds of Kīlauea to give reverence and offerings to the Fire Goddess.

As the buses and vehicles entered the park, it was like driving through a small town in the country. Cheerful direction signs and 'ōhi'a lehua lined the roads. The students from both schools were erupting with excitement and anticipation. They thought that at any second they would see huge boiling fountains spewing red-hot molten lava and flowing over the ground, engulfing all the trees in flames. Even Kiara had her Digital Data Pad in hand to take seismic recordings. To the students' disappointment, the teachers reminded them that the nearest lava flow was several miles away, eastward beyond the Chain of Craters Road where they would do their hike

grounds. Once safe, fugitives gave thanks to a god for their deliverance. Later, they were declared sanctified and free to return to their homes and families, with the protection of the gods.'" After reading the back, she looked at the picture again. This time it no longer looked fearful, but serene and kind.

Cacy rarely shopped for anything. Her parents usually got her anything she needed, if it was necessary—and better yet, on sale. But seeing all the adults and tourists piling the register counters with souvenir books, DVDs, posters, T-shirts, and caps made her want to join in on the buying action. It took awhile waiting in line, but Cacy proudly paid the full price for her ninety-nine-cents postcard. Once again she read the back of it. She placed it carefully into the smaller pouch of her backpack so it could not get bent. Just as she slung her hefty backpack on, she had to join the rest of the students in the visitor center's theater to watch their twenty-minute video about the park and hear the day's eruption forecast from one of the park rangers.

Using a map projection, the ranger explained the various sites within the park and the location to park vehicles to hike to the lava flows. She continued to talk about the ecosystem of the park as well as its wildlife and archeological features. The audience was surprised to learn that the park is in a tropical rain forest and that the park is like an island within an island because many species of plants and creatures were found nowhere else on Hawai'i, or anywhere else in the world.

During the questions from tourists, many of the students started getting agitated and began thinking more about seeing the real lava instead of endemic species.

Ms. Fitzgerald, Ms. Windbagg, and all the chaperones sat in the back row. They were quietly discussing and conspiring over their maps and schedules. Both teachers decided to combine schools and go as one group and visit each site together, saying that it would be good for the social interaction among the kids. In actuality, both teachers had never been to Hawai'i Volcanoes National Park and assumed that the other person already knew her way around. When told the news after the ranger's presentation, the only thing the students agreed on—in their minds—was that both teachers should go jump in a volcano. Cacy looked to where Kiara was seated, and Kiara slowly turned to look back at her as well. They exchanged disappointed expressions. Now not only were they on the same field trip; they would have to be together all day. Kiara turned away with a sarcastic look. It was time again to make the worst out of an already lousy situation.

Chapter 4

The Mysterious Little Man Driving the Big Nēnē Goose

"**I**t's your turn to pay." Bishop dabbed the sides of his lips with his table napkin. "I already took care of breakfast back at that pancake house in Hilo."

Both Rook and Bishop finished dining in the open-air restaurant at the Volcano House hotel. Just outside the dining area was a spectacular panoramic view of Kīlauea Caldera. Far off in the distance, at its bottom, the dense sulfur dioxide gas clouds from Halemaʻumaʻu Crater rose to the sky.

"You know, Rook," Bishop quickly added to change the subject, "this Volcano House was first built in 1846 as a thatched structure for early tourists. It was replaced in 1877 and made out of lumber, wooden doors, and windows till 1941 when it was designed like a Victorian-style mansion. This is the only hotel in the park."

"You learned this just for today's assignment?" Rook inquired.

"No, I just read it on the back of our menus. C'mon, let's move to the cocktail lounge for some drinks."

After leaving a measly tip on the table, the two ambled to the bar and ordered ice-cold longneck bottles of Hawaiian ale and toasted their new mission. Rook looked down at his watch, keeping track of time. It was already after eleven thirty a.m. Bishop fished out his map of the park and was busy tracing his finger along the path to take for their meeting with Dr. Pōhaku. Rook downed a deep sip and watched as Bishop stopped his finger over a spot labeled "Thurston Lava Tube." Bishop looked at his partner, tapping the spot.

"See here," Bishop said, "Dr. Pōhaku made his startling discovery deep inside the tube."

"Tube? Lava? What is it, a volcano or a tunnel?"

"It's supposed to be some sort of long giant tunnel made when lava once flowed there," Bishop began to elucidate as Rook took a another deep gulp. "The top part of the flow cools and hardens while underneath, a river of molten lava continues downhill. Over time, the lava drains out and leaves a cavelike shell. They say this island is full of secret lava tubes. Ancient Hawaiians used them to bury the bones of their dead and store things."

Rook leaned back on his stool and ran his hand over his prickly crew cut.

"How in the world do you know all these facts, Bishop?" asked Rook. "Now, I know you didn't read this on the bar menu!"

"It's all part of my job, partner," Bishop replied, giving a smug and sly look. "Anyway, this doctor fellow has found an ancient Hawaiian carving known as a ki'i. In your terms, it looks sort of like a tiki doll. This image is of a head and chest and is about eight inches high."

"Okay, you unibloke, here's the big question," Rook said, leaning forward and gripping his bottle as if picturing the size of the ki'i. "What's so special about it, other than it being another relic piece, and how come nobody found it in this tube thing all these years if you got tourists going through it?!" He slammed the bottle on the bar for emphasis.

"Well, from what I understand—as the doctor explained," Bishop replied as if speaking to a college class, "there's a far part in the cave that's not lighted for visitors and it's usually closed off with a gate. Most tourists won't continue on through that part because it's pitch-black and too dangerous without a really strong flashlight. Anyway, you're right, Rook, everyone seemed to have thought that the entire tube was completely explored. But deep within the

blackened part of the tube, Pōhaku stumbled upon some small secret niche in the tube's wall that was covered up by something called pulu grass. It was used to embalm the dead. He claims the centuries-old stuff was formed like a thin solid plastering, blending over the opening in the wall. Inside the narrow space, in near perfection, was this ki'i, wrapped in tapa cloth.

"Back in the 1800s when missionaries were converting the Hawaiians, there was a big effort to cast away all the graven images of the Hawaiian gods. At the same time, many wealthy British and American families had hundreds of these carved and feather-covered images, ancient weapons, and tools that had been taken away and shipped to them. Over time, museums of natural history were able to trace and get back most of these artifacts, but many are still missing to this day. In a way, these early collectors helped to preserve what might have been destroyed if they remained in the islands."

Rook looked at him quietly and then said, "Good on ya! An artifact like this...ki'i would get worldwide attention and could be worth millions." He drank down the rest of his ale and concluded, "But if Pōhaku went public with this discovery, the park could claim ownership of it instead. How much moolah does this Pōhaku guy want flick it on the Queen for?"

"Chump change," Bishop said, motioning the bartender for another round of ale. "He's a scholar, not a dealer. He's such an amateur the Queen is only paying him an economical finder's fee of two hundred grand. Shoots! You can't even buy a house with that in this state. But you know the business; we buy low and sell high to others. Already the Queen has interests coming in from private collectors in Saudi Arabia, Australia, Italy, and Hong Kong. I think our client in Hong Kong will outbid the rest, though."

"So, almost noon," Rook said, looking at the bar clock. "How are we on time?"

"We don't meet for another hour," Bishop replied, bringing his bottle to his lips. "It's only a mile drive from here. All we gotta do is follow him into the tube, retrieve the ki'i, pay him half up front, and then give him the access code to the overseas bank account the Queen set up for him so he can get the other half. By two p.m., we'll be back in Hilo and it's ZIP! BANG! And PAU HANA, bruddah! We be outta here! Helly onward! Aloooha!"

Rook chuckled at the way Bishop tried to speak the local lingo called pidgin English. Even laughing, he still looked sinister. Together they toasted to the job ahead.

"Yeah," continued Bishop, licking his lips, "I don't think Pōhaku will give us any trouble. If he does, you know how to...how shall I say...eliminate the trouble. Anyway, most of these university eggheads are always too eager to get money on the side, since they have low salaries and grants are hard to come by. Today should be a breeze for a change. What could possibly screw this assignment?"

Cacy popped her head around the corner and peeked into the cocktail lounge. Soon after leaving the visitor center, the combined schools had walked the short distance across the parking lot to the Volcano House Hotel. Once inside, the students from both schools seemed to have forgotten the main idea of "staying together as a group" and took off excitedly into different areas of the first floor. Some ran to the lookout spot to see the caldera, others scampered to the gift shop or to check out the burning fireplace constructed of lava rocks.

Cacy was alone and noticed Rook and Bishop sitting at the bar. Both caught a glimpse of Cacy in the corner of their eyes and quickly turned to stare at her. Rook's brutish glare startled her and she quickly hid behind the corner and ran back to the lobby area. Passing the gift shop, Cacy saw a bunch of students running in to look at merchandise and buy snacks. She saw Kiara inside standing in front of a mirror considering whether or not to buy one of the cool-looking yellow miner's hats for exploring the Thurston Lava Tube. Kiara thought it would flatten her hairdo so she placed it back on the shelf and stood in line to buy candy.

Cacy went to look at the fireplace up close. This was her first time seeing a real one.

"Excuse me," said Ms. Fitzgerald, "are you Cacy, Kiara's cousin?"

Surprised, Cacy turned around and faced the beautiful young teacher from Central Academy. She was holding a plastic shopping bag brightly labeled "Volcano House." Ms. Fitzgerald had purchased a T-shirt for her husband and one of the yellow miner's hats for herself.

"Yes, ma'am," Cacy answered quietly. "Is something wrong?"

"Oh, no. Not at all. Not at all," she answered with her glowing pageant-like smile. "I'm Ms. Fitzgerald, Kiara's school teacher, and I heard a lot of talk that her cousin was here with the other school."

Ms. Fitzgerald looked at Cacy from head to toe and back up again with keen interest, mentally comparing her to Kiara. The two cousins were very opposite. Kiara was like a prim, well-groomed Pomeranian who loved attention. Cacy looked more like a floppy eared mutt who wanders alone.

"Are you two close?" asked Ms. Fitzgerald. She took notice that the girls hadn't hung together since arriving in the park. It was a question Cacy was often asked by adults, and she never really knew what to say.

"Uh, well," Cacy began slowly, "not really. I mean we talk, but we mostly like to argue and fight. We're very different. Right now she's kind of mad at me for teasing her this morning. I know which nickname she really hates."

Ms. Fitzgerald admired and acknowledged Cacy's honesty and even mentioned that she had heard Kiara's voice yelling in the hotel, which was really a shock. "Well, you know something, Cacy?" the young teacher began to gently explain. "When I was a child, I used to fight a lot with my cousins. It's normal. And even though we were different, we were still related to each other. That meant we were all family. I'm sure both you and Kiara would stand up for each other when needed. Both of you are very bright."

Cacy's face beamed with delight. It wasn't so much that she was looking forward to being close to Kiara. Hardly that. Instead, she was thrilled at being considered intelligent and on the same level as her cousin. Ms. Fitzgerald excused herself to go round up the wandering students in the hotel and get everyone ready for lunch. The hotel had made box lunches and drinks for the schools to take and picnic on the park grounds outside the hotel.

Not wanting to miss a chance to look outside at the caldera, Cacy raced through the lobby, through the second gift shop, and outside to the lookout area. A long rock wall and safety rail stretched across the length of the viewing deck. Just on the other side of the wall were thick rows of bright green ferns. No one dared to climb beyond the railing because they could see that the ferns were growing from the edge of a steep cliff.

Below, a dark, lush forest lead toward the distant rim of the caldera. From left to right, the view was like a vast canyon, and far off in the middle of the barren lunar-like landscape was the smoky crater.

At this moment a new crowd of adult tourists began streaming out to the lookout spot. Cacy was too small to go against the tide of visitors coming toward her, so she walked along the length of viewing area. Hoping to sneak back into the hotel from some side door, she walked farther down along the length of the building and came to what looked like the back delivery door for the hotel. It was open and she could see that inside was a large kitchen full of huge metal bowls, pans, and hanging utensils. It reminded her of her school's cafeteria, but this one was much larger and cleaner.

On a large steel table, Cacy saw several cardboard crates full of boxed lunches and juice cans. She knew that this must be the lunches for the schools. Seeing them made her feel relieved that the schools hadn't left the hotel yet. She quietly walked into the kitchen and stood on tip toes next to the table, trying to look into the crates to see what was for lunch. If she stayed too long, she thought, the staff person might come in and scold her, just like the Honu Bay guard this morning. She quickly looked for the door leading back to the public part of the hotel. Just as she saw the door and made her way for it, something, or rather someone, caught her attention.

Cacy looked to the right, thinking it might be a chef. Instead, she saw what looked like a little two-year-old child standing in the corner of the kitchen just below a countertop. The startled being looked back at Cacy and earnestly began shaking his head left to right, both surprised and looking for a way to run. She took a double take herself and rubbed her eyes as if making sure she was really seeing this mysterious little stranger. On closer look, Cacy became even more surprised and shocked. It wasn't a little child, but a tiny man. He wasn't a dwarf or a midget; Cacy had seen both. This person was smaller than the average preschooler, but looked like an adult. He had smooth dark skin, thick black sprouty hair, large expressive brown eyes, a wide round nose, and the cheeks of a cherub. His mouth hung wide open in fear. He wore an adult small sized "Kīlauea Crater" T-shirt, which fit loosely over his tiny body and reached his ankles like a nightgown.

After what seemed like an eternity of just staring at each other, Cacy regained her composure. She didn't feel like she was in any danger discovering this mysterious little person. In fact, she was more concerned that this person might think she would harm him. Cacy swallowed and cleared her throat before trying to speak.

"Ah...hello," she whispered calmly. "My name is Cacy. I'm from O'ahu. What's your name?"

The little imp continued to stare back at her with his wide eyes and open jaw. At first he was terribly frightened to be seen, but soon his expression turned to embarrassment. Then, like a sad pouting child told to go sit in a corner for being naughty, the stranger turned away and quickly walked toward the exit door Cacy had just come in through. His little bare feet made a loud pitter-patter on the cold tiled floor.

Once outside, he turned back to look at Cacy, bit his lower lip, and then took off running.

"Hey, wait a minute!" Cacy called out, running after the stranger. "What's wrong? Where are you going?!" She was careful not to run too fast and to keep a safe distance in case the stranger suddenly turned and became aggressive. He leapt over a row of trash bins and ran under a gate that led around the corner of the hotel to an area not meant for the public or guests. Cacy was amazed at his agility and kept in pursuit.

When she passed the gate and rounded the corner, she nearly froze. Before her, the little man was climbing up inside the body of a huge nēnē goose. It was enormous! She knew that these Hawai'i state birds were not only endemic, endangered, and a common sight in the park, but that they were not five feet high and six feet long as this one was. The stranger turned back to see Cacy watching him. He gave a high-pitched whine of terror and looked both tremendously ashamed and teary-eyed for even being seen with the bird. The left wing of the nēnē was raised upright like the gull-wings on certain sports cars and revealed that the bird was mechanical.

Inside its body was a small single seat with a periscope and several joysticks. She couldn't understand who, or what this person was, and why he seemed so distraught. The weird goose-mobile made even less sense to her. The stranger's legs kicked wildly outside the bird's body till he was able to sit up and adjust himself in the seat and buckle

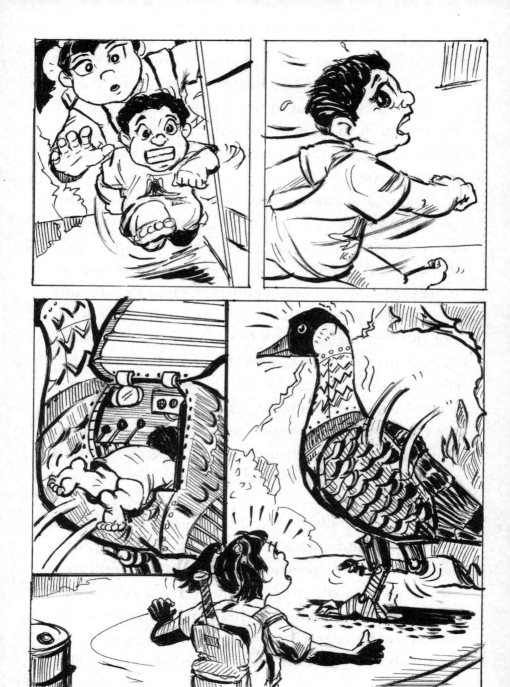

As he turned to lead the way, Rook tapped Bishop on the shoulder, held up his open right palm, and gave a warning wink. Bishop knew that Rook had picked up something about the doctor. Both men's eyelids lowered into dark frowns as they watched the doctor walking ahead.

"Well, Rook," Bishop quipped dryly, "I suppose there might be some trouble for you to take care of later."

As the three men went up to the paved trail at the entrance, the buses for Kiara's and Cacy's schools careened into the large parking lot. Everyone had finished their boxed lunch and drink on the spacious picnic area across the street from the Volcano House Hotel. Only Cacy still had a musubi and some other unfinished lunch items stuffed into her backpack. She hadn't finished eating it in time because she was late getting back to the group after seeing the mysterious little man in the nēnē-goose-mobile. It was an embarrassing scene when Cacy rejoined the group. Everyone else was already sitting on the grassy lawn eating their lunch when Cacy came running frantically out of the hotel's front entrance, screaming and waving her arms in the air as she looked for the group. Everyone, including some of the hotel guests, stared at this crazy little girl running around shouting about some tiny little man, a giant robot goose, and if anyone ate her lunch. Kiara was sitting in a circle of her classmates, eating and trying to hide her face behind the lid of her boxed lunch.

"Hey, Kiara!" said little Jae, who was sitting cross-legged next to her. "Isn't that your cousin running around screaming?"

"Don't remind me," Kiara replied stoically as she took another large bite of her musubi. "And I really think she was adopted."

After getting a long and demeaning lecture from Ms. Windbagg, Cacy was loudly warned that any more stupid behavior in public would mean she would have to sit out the rest of the field trip, meaning NO LAVA FLOW VIEWING!! Cacy could hear the students from both schools laughing, and she knew why. The sound of it instantly made her reevaluate her self-perception. To her, this whole field trip had been full of bad events outweighing the pleasant. Everything from the long bus ride the night before from Kona, to the turtle incident with the hotel guard, to seeing Kiara on the same trip, to not having any close friends, to not knowing whether or not she really had seen a little guy driving a goose, and to being scolded in front of all the children, made Cacy heave a big, depressed sigh. She made no eye contact with anyone, including Ms. Fitzgerald, who felt really bad for her but didn't want to overstep Ms. Windbagg's

authority. Cacy was halfway through her lunch when the bus drivers came to the large group and said it was time to go to the Thurston Lava Tube. It took only a few minutes for the students to properly trash their empty lunch boxes and juice cans. Some had to use the bathroom just before boarding. Cacy walked closely in the back of her class, carrying her boxed lunch and eating as fast as she could.

Once the buses were parked, the teachers stood up and led their classes safely across the lot and up to the entrance leading into the rain forest. Students anticipated seeing the gaping entrance of a bat-cave but were greeted by a park ranger standing in the middle of a modern, paved walking trail. The trail forked into two directions: one led uphill and those who passed through the tube route took that trail. Thin metal handrails kept hikers from plummeting into a gorge. The other was a downward trail cut at a steep slant into the side of a cliff. Surrounding them all was a vast tropical rain forest seemingly untouched by both time and humans. It was chilly and damp. A ghostly mist filled the lower regions and students ran to a ledge, leaning over the safety rails to see the abundant varieties of gigantic ferns and fruit trees more than a hundred feet below them. They looked up and marveled at the dense canopy of trees towering surprise and disbelief. It was her against the entire class from the other school. The park ranger noticed Cacy in the back of the crowd and pointed to her.

"Okay, dear!" the park ranger called over the students, "What's the answer?"

All eyes focused on Cacy. The silence was deafening. Even the birds hiding away up in the tree canopy stopped their singing to listen.

"It's named after that millionaire on *Gilligan's Island*," she answered proudly.

Ms. Windbagg wanted to run and jump over the metal railings and off the steep cliff. Ms. Fitzgerald quickly broke into a cough, covering her mouth with her hand to hold in her chuckle. All the other students weren't so subtle. They broke out into fits of laughter; only Kiara didn't join in. She looked at Cacy, who was now showing signs of embarrassment on her reddened cheeks and downcast face.

One of Kiara's classmates nudged her and said, "I can't believe she's your cousin."

"Don't remind me," she murmured. Kiara always believed that Cacy watched too many old television shows.

The park ranger knew that the little girl was sincere and felt sorry for her. To help defuse the situation, she smiled and pointed back at Cacy, exclaiming with a loud laugh, "Ha! Ha! That was a good joke. I gotta remember that one!" She clapped her hands and again asked for the answer.

Kiara raised her hand and was called on. She gave a small adjustment to her square glasses and gently tugged on her pleated skirt. It was her normal routine before speaking in front of an audience.

"Thurston Lava Tube," she began, "is also known as Nāhuku in Hawaiian. It was named in honor of Hawai'i newspaper publisher Lorrin Thurston. He discovered this lava tube while exploring the volcanic lands. It was he and Dr. Thomas A. Jaggar who petitioned the United States government to have the volcanoes preserved as a national park. It was President Woodrow Wilson who made it official in 1916."

Ms. Fitzgerald beamed with pride. Most of her students passed it off as another example of Kiara showing off. The students from Cacy's school were astonished yet secretly jealous. The park ranger was greatly impressed and congratulated her on the right answer and more. One of Cacy's classmates nudged her, saying that he couldn't believe that girl was her cousin.

"Yeah, she's also a Vulcan," Cacy said with no admiration.

Chapter 6

The Girls Take the Dark Path

The hike down to the lava tube wasn't too difficult thanks to the modern trail and metal railings. Moisture collected on the stone steps, making some parts slippery. As the groups descended in single file, many of the students began to identify some of the unique Hawaiian flora they had learned about in school. The rain forest was rich in diversity of plant life. Some plants had leaves as big as an adult and some as small as a fingernail. Deep green wet moss and fuzzy lichen clothed most of the tree trunks. At some points, low branches made the adults stoop under to pass. A boy called out and pointed to a distant bird zooming from tree to tree. Its bright red color was easy to see: a stark contrast to the background greenery.

"Hey, it's an 'i'iwi bird!" shouted a girl. "I can see its long curved beak!" Cameras went off wildly as students hoped to get a perfect photo. They all paused to watch as the endemic creature perched next to a curved flower and sunk its long sickle beak into it to reach the nectar. In a moment, the bird zoomed away and out of sight. Those with digital cameras began showing off whatever they had managed to get.

As the group moved onward, Cacy followed from behind, deep in her thoughts. She brushed a large, low-hanging leaf away from her face. To her surprise, she saw a tiny yellow face smiling at her. It was a happy-face spider. Realizing her little find, she carefully held the leaf steady for a closer look. The spider was less than one-quarter-inch long and pale yellow. The balloon-shaped back had the distinctive markings of two tiny black dots for eyes and the red and black colored crescent that looked like a smiling mouth. She wanted to call the others back, but they were moving farther down the trail.

"You're so cute," she said, smiling at the little crawler. "Hope I didn't disturb you."

Carefully she released the leaf back into its hanging position. She ran on happily, almost slipping on the stones, in order to catch up with the group. Fortunately a group of tourists were coming up the same trail, so the schools had to pause and press against the cliff walls to let them pass. This allowed Cacy to catch up before she was noticed as missing from her class. Soon, both of the schools reached the forest floor. Hāpuʻu trees and vines towered over them, and low-growing ferns were even more abundant. Within a short walk the group stopped at a bridge connecting to the entrance of the long dark lava tube.

The gigantic black hole was framed by thick hanging foliage and clumps of stringy moss ready to fall on someone. The bridge seemed out of place in this natural environment, but everyone crossing looked over the railing where there was a drop of over seventy-five feet into a ravine. Decayed branches at the wet rocky bottom looked like the bones of people who had fallen to their death. The sight sent chills through some of the students as they imagined what would happen if the narrow bridge gave out. One by one they moved onward and into mouth of the lava tube.

Darkness and excitement. It filled the hearts and imaginations of all the students. Ms. Fitzgerald carefully placed her new miner's hat on her head and pressed the lamp button. Those without their own lights struggled to adjust to the dark realm, where shadows seemed to have their own lives and echoes returned as ghostly whispers. The tube had formed about three to five hundred years ago from a thirty-foot-wide channel of lava, leaving an eerie open passageway to the past. Students patted and rubbed the soggy plant growth on the walls. It felt like clinging seaweed on ocean rocks. Thick electrical wires ran along the bottom, running the dim amber lights that hung every sixty paces through the tube and gave just a little illumination at every curve. Everyone felt cold and damp as water dripped from the tree roots hanging through the ceiling like stalactites. Cacy paused to take out her flashlight and put on her red hooded sweatshirt from her backpack. Shining the light onto the walls, she saw all the vivid colors and textures the darkness concealed.

There were minute sparkles on the walls. It can't be diamonds, she thought.

She rubbed the wet lumpy surface and realized they were tiny bits and thin threads of glassy pāhoehoe lava. The rock was gritty and reddish brown with shiny gray smooth spots. Others began moving farther ahead, keeping close attention to the guiding light beam from Ms. Fitzgerald's miner's hat. The path was full of large water puddles that ran in a downward direction with the tube. Walking too fast meant breaking into running mode, or worse, slipping and getting lost in the dark.

As the students moved along, they noticed that the height of the ceiling and the width of the walls kept changing every few feet and with every turn. At one part the path became nine feet wide and only

six feet high, and in just of few steps it was twice as wide and about thirty feet high. Deeper and deeper into the tube the air got stale and the gravity pull from the downward slope made them feel like they were walking with a backward lean. Even though some of the students had to keep their hands along the wall to keep steady, everyone seemed excited, as demonstrated by the loud chatter, silly screams, and the sloshing of wet shoes. Cacy's light beam illuminated the thin smoky haze that lingered and hung still since there was no breeze.

Up ahead, Cacy spotted a tall, stocky Asian male closely examining the walls and examining some of the exposed roots. He wore a baggy photojournalist-style vest full of pockets, and a large camera hung around his neck. On his head was a yellow hard hat with a powerful light attached to it. Everything the light shone on looked as clear as it was in daylight. Curious, Cacy went up to the man and asked if he was either a scientist or a miner. He stopped and turned to look down at the little girl. The sudden blast of bright light in Cacy's eyes made her shout and step backward, shielding her face with her hands.

"Oh, sorry!" he said, adjusting his light beam up toward the ceiling, "Actually I'm here from Oʻahu to do research for an adventure novel I want to write."

smashed into the neighbor's bushes. Now only the horn works."

"Yeah, but even your mom and dad thought it was too dangerous for you to ride, so I might have saved your life by wrecking it myself!" Cacy countered, trying to sound logical.

Kiara just stared back incredulously at Cacy, wishing her Digital Data Pad had a built-in function that could make her cousin disappear. She then looked over Cacy's shoulder into the deep darkness. Through the line of the electric lights, she could see that everyone in their schools was too far ahead to be seen. In fact, the rest of the tube looked empty.

"Cacy, look!" she said nervously. "Everyone's gone already. C'mon you mango head!" Kiara clipped the Digital Data Pad back on to the waist of her skirt, grabbed Cacy by the shoulder strap of her backpack, and started running. She continued, "Hurry before you and I get in trouble with our teachers."

"Owee!" Cacy cried as the sudden jerk on her backpack made the handle of her bat konk her on the back of her head. The two girls raced and skidded down the corridors of the tube. The outlines of the walls and ceiling looked like surreal waves flowing around them. The rest of the tube was indeed empty of other children and adults. Suddenly, they reached another opening and stopped.

It wasn't the actual end, but in reality, a break within the length of the tube. They paused to catch their breaths. Kiara was panting more because she was much thinner and more frail. The two girls looked at each other and noticed that they were still in the tube but stood in daylight. High above them was a wide-open skylight that had been made long ago when a portion of the top layer of the tube collapsed in. The lava stones scattered and piled on the floor were the remains of the ceiling. Leading up to the top was a narrow stairwell carved into the walls. A safety rail ran along the steps with a metal gate midway up. Cacy turned off her flashlight to save battery power. Kiara did the same for her device. Directly in front of them the tube continued in the same downward direction. There was another gate placed at its opening. Beyond the gate, the rest of the tube's length had no more electric lights to guide the way. This second phase of the tube was so dark, the rays of the skylight didn't penetrate into it. It was like a gate had been placed in front of an enormous void. Both girls slowly walked to the ominous entrance. They stretched their arms over the gate and watched the darkness slowly consume their hands. If the first part of the tube felt exciting, this second part was fearsome. They quickly yanked back their hands as a deep chill ran along their arms.

"Good thing you got your flashlight, Cacy," Kiara said, warming up to her cousin all of a sudden.

"H-how do you know everyone went down there?" Cacy asked. "Maybe they all went up the stairs and back up the trail."

For a moment both girls didn't know what to do or which way to go. They noticed that the gate on the stairwell was shut. The gate leading into the pitch-black continuation of the lava tube was unhooked and slightly ajar. Maybe the stairwell exit was there for people who didn't want to go farther, they thought. Plus, they didn't hear any sounds of students or teachers coming from above. Kiara took the Digital Data Pad from her waist and pressed the power button. Instantly a yellow glow appeared on the keypad. She typed in her four-digit password and icons appeared on the small display screen. With her thumb on the center red button, Kiara scrolled down the on-screen menu to "sound." A short red antenna telescoped out of the top of the device. Cacy watched with deep amazement as Kiara pointed the antenna into the darkness and pressed some buttons on the keypad. Wavy lines appeared to flow across the screen at different frequencies.

"I pick up peoples' voices down there," Kiara said with relief. "They're not too far. If we're lucky, we can catch up and no one would have seen that we got separated from them since it's so dark."

Cacy pushed the creaky gate all the way open and the two girls carefully walked down several rocks that had been cut and arranged as steps. The floor of the tube was four feet below the gate entrance. Cacy quickly turned on her flashlight again. The steady beam seemed shorter and weaker in this new darker realm. A sudden breeze blew down the skylight and curved into this portion of the tube. The wind made a mournful long moan as bits of fallen leaves rolled like little tumbleweeds past their shoes and disappeared under the curtain of utter darkness. Kiara found herself standing closer to her cousin. Cacy reached behind her head to reassure herself that the bat was still there.

"I hope we don't have to go too far to reach them," Kiara whispered.

"Me too," Cacy replied as they took careful footsteps down the blind path. "I wouldn't want to be by ourselves in this part of the tube."

And they were not alone in the deeper and unlit part of the Thurston Lava Tube. Rook, Bishop, and Dr. Pōhaku were in there as well.

Chapter 7

The Power of the Ki'i

"**W**atch out, gentlemen, for this large rock here," Dr. Pōhaku said, waving the beam of his flashlight around its massive size. It lay there, about three feet wide, right in the middle of the pathway. The three men walked around it and continued on. As if the darkness could not get any deeper, Rook and Bishop had to strain their eyes to follow the line of their flashlights. They swung their lights along the ground like blind people tapping out their walking canes. The air was stagnant and smelly and the sudden fear of banging into a low ceiling kept Bishop holding his duffel bag high in front of him lest he messed his hairdo.

Dr. Pōhaku waited up ahead patiently. When the two caught up he called them to halt and not walk ahead. The doctor shined his light along the edge of a pit. It was like a small round crater four feet deep and about thirty feet in diameter. The rim of the pit reached across both walls, so the only way to continue on was to jump into it and climb out on the far end. Sharp rocks the size of cinder blocks were strewn about the base. The doctor shined his light to a clear spot and jumped into the pit. He then motioned for the others to come in. Rook stepped in with ease while Bishop slipped upon landing and fell on his rear.

"Are you okay, Mr. Bishop?" Dr. Pōhaku said, reaching his hand to Bishop's arm to help him stand.

"Fine, doctor," he replied, dusting himself. "I hope my hair isn't messed up. Rook, shut up!"

"I didn't say anything," Rook responded while grinning.

The doctor's mind was filling with both eagerness and avarice. He quickly ran to the other side of the pit and scampered out, standing back on the path. A few steps behind him, the tube became too low and narrow to go on. A pile of large rocks blocked the opening so tourists would not venture farther. Rook and Bishop made their way across the pit and stood at the edge watching the doctor shine his light to a high spot on the wall. He took out a small pick from his shoulder bag and used it to slowly peel away a portion that blended perfectly with the rest of the surface. The doctor took a deep breath to calm his nerves and carefully reached into the small opening behind the pulu wall. All lights were focused on the spot as the doctor gently pulled out what looked like a dirty worn towel wrapped up in a bulky mass. He then placed the bundle on the ground right at the edge of the pit's rim in front of Rook and Bishop, and knelt down. As they kept their lights steadily on the bundle, the doctor twitched his neck and cracked his fingers before slowly unraveling the tapa cloth like he was taking away the bandages on a mummy. The two moved in closer as the last layer came off.

The ki'i stood before them. Even as grown men, they felt a spinal chill seeing its fearsome and grotesque appearance under light and shadows. The ancient relic stood about eight inches high. A crest was carved over its head in the same style of the feathered helmets worn by the Hawaiian kings and chiefs. Its eyes were serpent-like and seemed to be staring angrily at them for being disturbed after centuries of rest. The most gruesome feature of all was its gaping mouth, which seemed to be snarling and laughing hideously at the same time, as if at any moment it would shriek with evil delight.

"Gentlemen," the doctor suddenly began, startling the two men as he raised his flashlight to his face. The glow from below made the doctor appear ghostly and formidable as he looked down on the men in the pit. "As a longtime researcher in both archaeology and anthropology, I've done some of my own extensive work into learning more about the Queen's illegal operations."

"Is that so," Bishop said calmly.

The doctor's voice cracked and began to sound dry from hiding his fear and nervousness. He continued to speak as boldly as he could, but his flashlight was quivering under his face. With his other hand he pulled out an envelope from his shirt pocket and tossed it into the pit. "This contract here is an amendment, in writing, that my payment increases to five hundred thousand dollars. In good faith, I am showing you the ki'i now so you can examine, photograph, and attest to its authenticity. Once full payment is made into an overseas bank account, then, and only then, will I give the Queen her item. I'm sure she can afford this new amount and these new terms. Besides, the information I have could become even more costly to her organization. Oh, don't be startled at this brazen turn, gentlemen. I'm sure you are already used to cutthroats in your line of work."

The men were silent. All of sudden, Rook began to laugh. He laughed loud and long. He laughed so hard he had to drop his flashlight and duffel bag on the pit floor to grab his chest. Inside his flak jacket, he unsheathed the long kukri knife he kept at his left side. In one blinding swing, slicing upward and across in the dark, Rook killed the kneeling doctor. In a moment his body fell backward, flat on the floor.

Bishop lit a cigarette and shined his light over the rim, looking at the body of Dr. Pōhaku.

"Hey, at least he didn't scream," Rook commented as he wiped the curved blade with a table napkin he had stolen from the Volcano House restaurant. "See? I was right again. This chump wanted to rip us off. If he had more than just academic brains, he would've waited till after he got paid as agreed to before trying to blackmail the Queen for more money."

"He was a scholar," Bishop said, placing his hand solemnly on his heart. "But he was no gentleman. Greedy fool. Instead of being satisfied with what he agreed to, he wanted a bigger piece of the pie. Huh! Threatening us with going to the law and exposing the Queen's operations was definitely a dumb idea on his part. C'mon. If we leave him lying here, he might be found by some curious tourists."

The men placed their duffel bags and flashlights on the rim and pulled themselves out of the pit. Standing over the body, they shined their lights on the doctor's face. His eyes were still open and frozen with a look of shock.

"Well, this job didn't turn out as simple as I thought," Bishop whined, tossing his finished cigarette into the pit and lighting another one.

light beam shake and waver as Cacy pulled herself out of the pit. The light then shone on her hand, signaling Kiara to take hold of it. Both struggled, but Cacy managed to help Kiara squiggle out of the pit and back onto the path.

"It looks like some tiki doll like they sell in all the Waikiki gift shops" Cacy said, holding the ki'i and scrutinizing it in the light.

By now, both girls were no longer scared by this object. Kiara took hold of the little sculpture to look at it also. She noticed that the wood appeared too old and the carving was more stylized and archaic-looking than a recently made souvenir.

"Cacy, I think is a real Hawaiian sculpture."

"There's no sticker on the bottom that says 'Made in China'?"

Kiara ignored her cousin and found the strips of tapa cloth on ground right in front of them. She put down the ki'i, held a strip to the light, and watched the delicate fibers break apart from getting wet in a puddle. "I bet this ancient tiki was wrapped in this," Kiara deducted. "But who left it all here sitting like this?"

Cacy noticed the reflection of puddles from the light and that it seemed to lead to the low continuation of the tube. Taking the flashlight from Kiara, Cacy shined it on the wet surfaces. There were large spots of fluid that did not look like clear water and seemed dark. She reached down out of curiosity and placed her fingers into it. Kiara was usually more cautious, but found herself doing the same as well. It was warm. They held their hands under the flashlight, making the horrible discovery. Human blood.

Their piercing screams echoed and were magnified through the long hollow tube. The outburst reached the ears of Rook and Bishop as the last stone was placed over Dr. Pōhaku's corpse. The men looked at each other in surprise. They quickly killed their lights and quietly crawled their way back to the entrance without being seen. Bishop's neck and back were hurting from being bent over throughout the whole time packing stones over the doctor's body. His arms felt weak as he kept his body supported.

Cacy and Kiara breathed heavily, still looking with disbelief and terror at the sight of their bloodstained fingers. Cacy immediately tried wiping it off on the ground, as well as splashing it into a clean water puddle. Kiara did the same thing but the blood would not remove itself. The stains were as red and fresh looking as if nothing changed. They both had had enough of being in the tube and began to leave before Cacy decided to reach down for the ki'i to take back with them. She thought it would be best to show the others and tell what happened. With her bloodstained hand, she grabbed the ki'i to place inside her backpack. Kiara protested and took hold of the ki'i with her bloody fingers as well. Just as the blood touched the ki'i, the Digital Data Pad began buzzing like an alarm and its lights pulsated erratically on its own. Its screen flashed "seismic energy" and "electromagnetic waves" on and off. Kiara didn't think that all this was some sudden malfunction, and didn't want to risk being in the tube any longer.

At first they thought the other was playing tug-of-war with the other over the ki'i, but to their surprise, the ancient object began to vibrate on its own. Its wooden form suddenly blasted into a blinding glow of light. The girls covered their eyes with their other hands as whips of white and yellow light rays shot from the ki'i like cracks of lightning in the night. They screamed again but could not free their hands that held the ki'i. The lights zigzagged and bounced against the walls and high ceiling, creating a wild strobe effect where portions of the tube were completely lit and then pitch-black again the next instant. As they tried to stand up, a massive rush of wind blew down the distant skylight and into the dark portion of the tube, sending a howl and roar like an oncoming rail train in a tunnel. It

carried loose sticks, dead leaves, and anything else not attached to the tube. The girls were thrown off their feet by the wind as it formed into a cyclone of debris over the pit. Stronger gusts entered the tube like ocean waves pounding the shore in powerful successions. Cacy's flashlight flew out of her hand and spun through the air and back out of the tube. Kiara managed to rise back up, pulling Cacy off the floor. They shrieked for help as the slippery ground began shifting under them, causing them to fall down again. Kiara's bloodied hand suddenly became free of the ki'i, which shined brighter with each stronger wind gust. The bolts of light began zapping toward the exit of the tube like laser beams fired into deep space. Kiara felt the pull of the wind flow begin to drag her to the edge of the pit. She cried out for Cacy to grab her hand. Cacy couldn't free her hand from the ki'i, but she was able to anchor her foot to some stable rocks and reach out with her free hand and take hold of her cousin.

Bishop and Rook made it back to the low entrance, fearing that there was not just other people in the tube, but an earthquake as well. They were about to turn on their flashlights, but the scene was lit enough to watch in dismay as the two girls were pulled into a vicious cyclone. The puddles on the ground were removed by the winds, but the surface remained wet. Cacy's foot slipped away from the rocks and she suddenly found herself being dragged toward the pit with Kiara. The whirling winds accelerated and lifted Kiara off the ground. She kicked in midair as both hands held on to Cacy's free hand. The wind forced Cacy to sit upright with her knees bent and feet digging into the ground.

"That's her!" Rook shouted over the loud winds to his partner. "That's the kid we saw at the bar! She's got our ki'i!! We gotta get it back!!"

Kiara could see the two men slowly come out of the small entrance and rise up to their feet, careful not to get pushed down by the winds. "Behind you!!" Kiara screamed as loud as she could, looking past her cousin.

Cacy ached holding on to her cousin, and it felt like her shoulder would dislocate. She groaned as she tried to slam her bloodstained hand on the ground to shake off the ki'i, but it remained stuck. Slowly she turned around to look behind her. She saw Rook and Bishop and called upon them to help her and Kiara.

The men stared with awe seeing the supernatural force emanating from the ki'i.

They instantly realized from the winds, the quake, and the lights that this relic possessed real power. All these years they had worked around the globe collecting ancient artifacts said to have this power, or that curse attached to it. And each time, these old objects of historical or religious significance turned out to be just another inanimate thing with a myth behind it. Not now, though, they thought. Not with this ki'i. Whatever its original significance was, what they were seeing was real: incredibly real. They had to get it back at any cost.

Cacy was being dragged closer to the pit and Kiara was soon losing her strength to hold on. Bishop couldn't wait any longer and staggered toward Cacy with one hand on his head to keep his hairdo steady. Instead of grabbing either Cacy's shoulders or help hold on to Kiara, he reached for the ki'i.

"Give it to me, or else!" he shouted into her ear. "C'mon, you stupid girl!!"

As his hand almost neared the ki'i, its glowing color turned bright red and an unseen force made Cacy clutch it close her chest. A side gust of the cyclone smacked Bishop in the face, sending him back against his partner.

"Cacy, look out!!" Kiara called out.

Rook moved Bishop out of the way and used his body weight to fight against the push of the wind. He reached into his flak jacket and drew out the kukri knife, preparing to swing down at Cacy. She turned and saw the blade coming down at her head.

Kiara screamed and tried to pull Cacy with her. As the kukri swung, Cacy used her ninja speed to tuck her head down and roll forward, dodging it. The problem with that move was that she accidentally let go of Kiara and was scooped up by the wind herself. Both girls spun in a circular motion as they floated over the pit. The ki'i remained in Cacy's bloodstained hand and changed to a greenish glow. Rook tried grabbing either Cacy or Kiara with each pass as they spun round and round with the cyclone like a chaotic merry-go-round. Bishop noticed that their duffel bags remained unmoved on the ground and had not lifted with the winds, nor had the tapa wrappings. It was as if the girls and the ki'i were deliberately being kept away from them.

With a sharp cracking sound like a bullwhip, the centrifugal force changed. The girls floated toward each other in the center of the cyclone and were whisked off together through the air and back out the tube, spinning and yelling. The winds ceased as the men watched the glow and the girls speed around a corner and disappear. Again they stood in complete darkness. For a few seconds they just remained speechless, listening to their breathing speed slow to normal.

"Yeah, I can't believe what I just saw, either!!" Bishop suddenly yelled, assuming Rook was thinking the exact same thing. "Hurry! Let's find our stuff and go after them before we lose them!"

Adrenaline kicked in, running so high and fast that in one continuous move they turned on their lights, grabbed their duffel bags, and were in and out of the pit in no time lost. They raced down the tube and leapt over the long large stone like it was a hurdle on a running track. As they rounded a corner, they could see the light up ahead and hear the girls screaming. The girls were back at the gate and the winds carried them over it. When Rook and Bishop reached it, the winds picked up into a cyclone again and more gusts rushed down the skylight. The force pushed back on the men as they gripped the bars of the gate and tried reaching over it to snatch away the ki'i as Cacy flew passed them. Again the girls floated on the air in a circular direction, but on opposite sides from each other. They both managed to look across the center of the cyclone and see that the other was just as terrified. Slowly they moved toward each other, reaching the center of the spin. Kiara grabbed Cacy by the arms like a skydiver during a free fall. Despite their fear, they were glad to be out of the tube together and they looked up at the skylight. The churning winds accelerated and began to lift them. Higher and higher the two went. They lifted higher than the nearby stairwell, which they both regretted not taking. With a mighty blast from below, the two girls shot up from the lava tube and several hundred feet above the canopy of the rain forest. A few tourists down below thought they were a pair of red and blue helium balloons someone let go of.

The wind in the lava tube once again subsided and Rook and Bishop kicked the gate open. They raced up the stairwell and back to the surface. Bishop took his binoculars from his duffel bag and was able to follow the two girls in the sky. They seemed to float eastward. Rook watched along with his binoculars and estimated that they were moving about a mile and a half away and that they were making a slow descent into the forest. The view to see exactly where the girls were landing was blocked by the tall 'ōhi'a lehua trees.

"Let's go back to the Hummer and contact the Queen," Bishop said, calming his nerves with another cigarette and combing his hair. "We gotta tell her everything that has happened!" He soon felt giddy with excitement over what they had witnessed. "This is so incredible! Rook, can you believe it?! A relic that really has power! This is bigger than... than...than...finding the Holy Grail!! We gotta get back that ki'i from those stupid girls. How are we gonna find them in the rain forest?"

"Relax and leave that to me," Rook said, grinning to his zealous partner. He held up a sliced-off hood from a red sweatshirt. "I think the dogs are ready for some exercise right about now."

Chapter 8

The Sanctuary of Hi'iaka

Kiara's grip on Cacy's hands tightened with each whirlwind thrust sailing them farther from the lava tube and higher over the vast canopy of the rain forest. Cacy found it almost comical seeing her cousin's hair blowing wildly and her screaming with her eyes shut like someone about to get sick on a roller coaster. *Just don't barf in my face*, she thought as the winds decreased and for a second they were in a stomach-churning free fall. Suddenly, the cyclone of air tightened around them and the girls felt the strong invisible grip of a giant hand holding them securely.

Cacy focused her attention downward, ignoring Kiara's piercing cries, which were now reaching the annoying shrill level of a car alarm that won't stop. Cacy initially thought the dense forest was getting larger. But she soon realized they were now falling at a high rate of speed. Cacy began screaming also. The girls' fingers dug deeper into each other's hands.

They began to plummet from nine hundred feet in the air.

"We're gonna die! We're gonna die! It's all your fault!!" Kiara wailed as the girls descended to eight hundred feet. In a fraction of a second, Kiara pictured the two of them being impaled on treetops or shredded apart by sharp branches.

Four hundred feet. What happened to the winds that carried us away from those two men in the cave? Cacy thought. Three hundred. The dense greenery of the rain forest canopy was clearer and Cacy could make out black pockets of space between some of the koa trees. One hundred feet and falling. The final second was the most terrible, but they kept their eyes wide open. Then, just at the point of hitting the top branches, everything went black.

Enveloped in darkness, the girls could hear their screams followed by echoes. Their grasps let go and in the darkness they desperately waved their arms to find each other again. Cacy felt a hard thin object hit her on the arm. She thought it was Kiara's arm or leg. Kiara could also feel sudden bumps on her sides and legs like quick taps of a long wooden yardstick. Falling in the darkness, both girls felt their bodies slowly spinning, and an occasional soft rap on their limbs. This went on for what seemed like a weird long dream they couldn't wake from. Only their senses of touch and sound seemed to work.

A firm force hit the girls out of nowhere. For an instant, their bodies jolted as though from an electric shock and then came to rest on a firm solid surface. The girls couldn't move their bodies or even open their eyes. They felt the soft, cool, prickly feel of grass beneath them. The crisp scent of dew, ferns, and flowers reached their noses. Cacy lay on her stomach with her cheek pressed against a pillow of thick grass. A few feet away from her, Kiara was on her back, asleep. High above, native birds chirped and fluttered between branches, eyeing the strange sight of two little girls lying at the bottom of the 'ōhi'a lehua trees.

"Kiara...?" Cacy murmured, slowly opening her eyes. Everything seemed like a spinning blur of shadows. She remained prostrate on her stomach and soon felt her eyelids getting heavy. "Ki...," she softly whispered before drifting into a deep sleep.

The girls were lying on a hidden patch of ground about two miles from the lava tube and deep within the wild rain forests of Kīlauea, where no humans ever ventured. A brief rain shower spread through parts of the park. Water droplets rolled and bounced from leaf to leaf through the canopy of the rain forest to the understory of ferns and flowering plants. The cool raindrops tickled the girls' faces. What was only a few minutes of sleep felt like a whole night of rest. The girls awoke slowly. They both felt groggy and entirely confused.

"What happened?! Where are we?!" they said in unison.

"Are we dead?" Cacy asked. The girls patted their faces and bodies, tugged their clothes, and looked wildly around them. High above they saw an opening to the gray sky. Looking up at the raindrops coming straight toward them reminded them of the fall.

"The lava tube!" Kiara shouted. "We were in the Thurston lava tube looking for our schools. You spotted that tiki, and...there it is over there!" Kiara pointed at Cacy's feet. The ki'i was standing up on the grass.

Cacy reached out for it but paused with her hand just barely touching it. She then poked it, and when it seemed safe, she picked it up. "Everything that's happened so far must be because of this tiki," she said, bringing it closer. "I'll bet those two men in the cave will come for this."

Kiara shivered at the thought. She could still picture the menacing image of Rook trying to kill Cacy with that giant knife. Kiara sat up on her knees and grabbed for her Digital Data Pad to make sure it was there. The device had no weapons built

in, but it gave Kiara a sense of security. Suddenly, Kiara's eyes widened. This was a surprise to Cacy because her cousin was so often stoic and without facial emotion.

"I think we're being watched," Kiara whispered, trying to stay calm.

"What?!! Where?!!!" Cacy yelled excitedly, spinning her ahead around and reaching for her bat.

A little ways away, among moss covered rocks and lichen-dressed trees stood a human silhouette. The being wasn't tall, but thick and feminine. The contour of a large crown sat on her head, and long, thick, flowing hair framed her torso. There was a reddish sheen to her hair, which reached down to her thighs. Her face and robe remained in shadow from the 'ōhi'a trees arching above her. Her right hand was placed on her waist in a fist. As the sun broke through the gray sky, light sprayed down into the rain forest like hundreds of moving spotlights. Beams passed over the mysterious stranger and reflected the bright yellow kīhei she wore and the royal purple wrapping around her shoulder and waist. Her head and wrists were adorned by lei of fresh maile and fern. Oh, but her face, the girls noticed. Her face was that of a young girl, perhaps twelve to fourteen. Young, brown, strong, Hawaiian features. She exuded strength in posture and beauty in form, but there was sadness in her eyes. In her left hand she held up a bunch of large ti leaves. Cacy and Kiara sat upright in silence, looking at the stranger. The birds above stopped their singing. The majestic girl stood motionless, staring straight back at the cousins.

Cacy's eyes widened and she glanced over to Kiara, who looked like she couldn't handle any more surprises in one day. Cacy quickly studied the strange girl. She didn't feel the stranger would harm them. Instead, Cacy hoped that this person would help make sense of what had brought her and her cousin here in the first place. The stranger stepped forward and spoke in a language the girls easily recognized but could not understand: Hawaiian.

Both girls sat dumbfounded, but did recognize something. Kiara mouthed the word that sounded familiar. "Hee-ee-yah-kah." Cacy did the same. This time she pronounced it more like how the stranger spoke.

"He-ee-ah-ka."

As if a lightbulb went on over their heads, they remembered what the park ranger at the lava tube talked about. The stranger before them was Hi'iaka, younger sister of Pele and the Goddess of the Forests. And this was her sanctuary.

Chapter 9

The Queen Makes the First Move

It didn't take long for Rook and Bishop to race back up the narrow trail from the lava tube. Rook was in front and pushed some of the tourists coming single-file down the rock steps. Bishop followed just a few feet behind and sneered at the tourists for being in the way. Back at the top where the park ranger had spoken to the schools, the two men suddenly stopped to catch their breath. Bishop wanted to light another cigarette.

He refrained not because of the many tourists herding in from the parking lot, but because the entrance area was now swarming with park rangers and school students. There was a sense of panic and urgency in their voices. It was apparent to the men that the schools were describing two missing girls last seen in the lava tube. They overheard the names "Cacy" and "Kiara." Rook tapped his partner, who was trying to avoid being approached with questions by park rangers. The two slowly slipped through a crowd of incoming Japanese tourists and left the rain forest area.

Once in the parking lot, the two sprinted straight to the Hummer. "I'll call the Queen! You go get the dogs!" Bishop yelled. Rook reached the Hummer first and headed beyond it to the dense forest. The dogs were sleeping in the shade next to empty trays and bowls. With a sharp command from Rook, the dogs shot to attention and bared their white fangs. Back at the Hummer, Bishop dumped the duffel bags and flashlights in the backseat. He reached over the driver's seat and under the passenger's side to withdraw a satellite phone. He pulled out its antenna. Shifting himself into the passenger seat, Bishop opened the glove compartment and broke another pack of cigarettes from his carton. After a deep long puff, exhaling a cloud of smoke that fogged the interior of the vehicle, he dialed a secret code and was immediately connected to a female voice.

Eleven miles off the eastern coastline of Hilo, a pristine white and gold luxury ship named *Chaturanga* cruised slowly. A crew of thirty men hired from around the world took care of specific duties on the three-hundred-foot long vessel with six decks and a helicopter pad. Each crew member wore a black and white tunic uniform with a red and gold-embroidered pawn chess piece on the breast pocket. The ship's captain was an old, gray-whiskered salty dog of the sea, uniformed in a white captain's hat and black pea coat. A large bent briar pipe hung from his chapped lips. The deep creases in his brow and the calluses on his hands exhibited both character and a long life working at sea. At the moment he wasn't at the bridge, but smoking a bowl of pungent English tobacco in the exotic trophy lounge, across from the female owner of the ship. He was deeply involved in pondering his next move on the large jade and ivory chessboard between them.

"How did the deal go with Dr. Pōhaku?" the woman said on the other end of the call while she tapped a chess piece with one of her long French-manicured fingernails.

"Uh, your Highness...Rook had to set him straight and we did some cleanup deep in the lava tube. We still got the payment money," Bishop responded.

"And the ki'i. Do you have it? I don't like disappointing our client in Hong Kong."

"Your Highness," Bishop intoned with deeper effect, "I...uh, Rook can testify also that, that...ah, hell! That ki'i has real power!!! You know how every holy relic our organization acquires has some story of a curse or power attached to it? Well, this piece is the real deal! Somehow two little girls came into the tube where we were and picked up the ki'i while Rook and I were hiding the doc's body after the deal went bust. We saw these girls holding it in their hands and the wooden thing was blasting lightning and glowing like fire! Rook and I tried grabbing it back, but some strange wind came in like a tornado and just scooped the girls off with the ki'i—out of the tube, up into the sky, and somewhere deep in the forest. Rook managed to get a piece of one of the girl's sweater and we're gonna use Falchion and Gladius to hunt them down." When he finished speaking, Bishop took a deep drag on his cigarette, waiting for an answer.

After a pause, the woman's voice calmly said, "Well, Bishop, at first I thought you might have been smoking something else besides cigarettes, but I do know that every legend is based on some fact. You and Rook weren't promoted just to tell me tall tales." She reached down to the chessboard, picked up two little pawn pieces, and crunched them tightly in her hand like dice about to be thrown. The captain watched the woman's narrow brow arch and her deep ruby lips crease. "Find the girls, bring them and the ki'i to me. I want to see this power in the ki'i, and perhaps those girls are a part of it. As for our client,

we can arrange a substitute relic if needed and keep this ki'i for my collection. If there IS supernatural power involved, then it can only have one purpose: to be USED by me. And Bishop, make sure Rook knows I want them ALIVE...for now. Use harm with caution."

She hung up her modified Tiffany-era phone and rose from her large Victorian throne seat. The captain stood immediately and asked if anything was wrong. "No. We'll continue our game later," the woman said. "Go back to the bridge and get us closer to the coastline of Kīlauea, but not close enough for the Coast Guard or any other ship to notice us. I'm going down to my bedchambers for a short nap."

The woman picked up her silk shawl and wrapped it around her exotic royal dress as she descended the marbled spiral staircase leading to the master bedroom. The captain bowed his head at the exit door in his usual manner and hailed, "Aye-aye, Queen!"

"Captain is coming!" the ship's yeoman yelled at the entrance of the bridge. Everyone aboard the Queen's ship knew when the captain was nearby just by the strong woody aroma of his pipe smoke. The *Chaturanga's* officers could now hear the captain's footsteps coming up the staircase. Each member stood sharp and attentive once the captain entered.

The first officer placed his espresso cup down.

"Set course for the south coast of Hawai'i Island," the captain ordered while tapping out the gray dottle from his pipe into his brass ashtray. "But stay in international waters. A stealth ship may be able to hide from radars, but the vessel can still be seen by day. When we reach Kīlauea prepare to receive others on board besides the Queen's operatives. I've known that calculating wench for many years and I can tell when she's up to something. Aye, you all know whenever she invites guests on board..."

The captain paused to place his briar pipe back on his pipe collection rack to cool, and picked up his long thin churchwarden to smoke. He continued with a grave look, "...they never leave alive."

Chapter 10

The Language of the Land

Cacy stood up and brushed some of the moist grass off her sweater. Kiara followed her cousin and readjusted her red bow and pleated skirt. Hiʻiaka approached them and once again spoke.

"Do you know Hawaiian?" Cacy turned to Kiara.

"No. Do you?" she retorted with annoyance. Kiara never liked admitting to a skill she did not know or have mastered.

Hiʻiaka spoke again, this time with a sense of impatience as she moved closer to the girls. Though her language was unclear, she expressed full emotions in her voice and eyes. She pointed to the kiʻi on the ground and again made an impassioned plea in Hawaiian. The two cousins stood confused and looked silently at Hiʻiaka, then to each other, and back to Hiʻiaka. Finally, Cacy did what she thought was the right thing to say at the moment.

"We come in peace." Cacy raised her open hands. "Do you have a cell phone we can borrow?"

"Auwē!!" Hi'iaka roared in anger. The 'apapane, mamo, and 'i'iwi birds above took off from their high branches in fear. For a moment, even the trees shuddered. The Forest Goddess shoved her ti leaves into her sash, grabbed the two girls by their upper arms, and marched them away from the clearing. Hi'iaka stood just slightly taller than both Cacy and Kiara, but her strength was enormous. Even Cacy couldn't wrestle out of the painful grip and was almost lifted off the ground. It was the type of feeling she remembered when her dad grabbed her arm and marched her to her bedroom whenever she got in trouble and was given a time out. Kiara had to break into a quick shuffle to avoid being dragged by Hi'iaka. Both girls screamed in pain and protested with each step.

Nearby, a small stream flowed peacefully, teeming with fallen leaves that looked like a parade of miniature rafts. Its source from one end and its direction in the other were blocked off by dark green curtains of thick trees and vines. Hi'iaka brought the girls to the edge of the stream and let go of them. They grimaced and rubbed their sore arms. Cacy felt like grabbing her bat, but realized that the Hawaiian goddess paid no attention to them, even though Kiara was complaining loudly and started quoting school laws prohibiting harassment and physical abuse.

"Shh! Quiet! " Cacy barked to Kiara. "Look, she's kneeling and praying at the river!"

"Stream, mango head," Kiara replied tersely as she continued to massage her sore upper arm. "It's a stream. Rivers are wider and come from a larger source of water. Plus, she's not praying. Look, she's processing mud."

After a few moments of squishing and wedging fresh mud at the edge of the stream, Hi'iaka rose and turned to the girls. In her left hand, she held a scoop of fresh, wet earth, and with her right hand, she motioned for the two girls to come forward. Out of curiosity, they approached. Hi'iaka beckoned them closer and they came obediently. Then, without warning, Hi'iaka swiped the mud from her left hand and wiped it on both Cacy's and Kiara's lips. Before they could react to the shock of this, Hi'iaka took both hands and patted more mud on the ears of both girls.

"Ewwww!!" the girls yelled, and spat the mud from their lips. They ran past Hi'iaka and dove to the edge of the running stream. Kiara took off her large glasses and tucked them into her vest. Cacy was already splashing water onto her face and wiping her mouth and ears. The girls' faces and hair were all wet and running when they were done. Cacy pulled up her sweater to pat her face and used her

sleeves to wipe her ears dry. Kiara used the packet of facial tissues she kept inside her vest and placed her glasses back on. Cacy looked at her cousin and giggled.

"Ha-ha! You should've seen the look on your face with mud on your lips."

"Oh, yeah? Well on you it was an improvement," Kiara sang sourly.

"Both of you! Stop your nonsense. You cannot waste any time if you wish to live!" shouted the Hawaiian goddess.

The girls looked over to Hi'iaka in shock! They heard her speak again in Hawaiian, but in their heads it was clear English.

"You could not understand me before," Hi'iaka said as she walked past the girls to rinse her hands in the stream. "I have blessed the earth with my mana, formed it into mud, and touched it to your lips and ears. Now you will be able to understand and speak the Language of the Land, ka 'ōlelo o ka 'āina. Listen carefully and wisely as you both make your journey."

"Journey? What journey?! We have to get back to our schools..." Kiara paused, realizing that her thoughts were in English, but her spoken words were in Hawaiian. Cacy jumped in, almost completing Kiara's statement.

"Yeah, and WHO are you and what are we doing in the middle of nowhere? And what's with that tiki doll?! Is this some curse?" Cacy rattled as she easily got used to hearing the Language of the Land flowing effortlessly from her lips.

"Come. Let us sit together and I will tell you about how you two came to be here, and the mission you must take." Hi'iaka motioned with her hand to a dry shaded spot where they could all sit.

Cacy went to pick up the ki'i and then joined Kiara and Hi'iaka, who were both sitting cross-legged on the fluffy grass. It was warm and Cacy removed her red sweater and straightened out her red T-shirt underneath. As she rolled up her sweater, she noticed that the hood was missing. Kiara noticed it, too, and in a sudden flashback she recalled the blinding lights in the lava tube and the ferocious large man with the goatee holding the giant curved knife and swinging it down at Cacy's head. Chills went up Kiara's spine.

"That man sliced off your hood just when you rolled off the edge of the pit and we were lifted in the air!" Kiara spoke with concern. "Are they after this tiki?"

"It is called a ki'i," Hi'iaka answered. "And it is cursed because the blood of a dishonorable maka'āinana has touched it. His greed blinded him and his life was ended by two other men who seek the ki'i. You two touched the shed blood and then touched the ki'i. Both of you have some Hawaiian blood in your families. It is little, but I could sense that. It saved you both from instant death, but a curse of dying before the next sunrise still remains on both of you."

A jolt of fear hit the girls at the thought of being cursed to die.

"See," Hi'ikaka continued, taking their trembling hands into hers. "The bloodstains on your fingertips remain. Only the kahuna at the heiau of Pu'uhonua o Hōnaunau can purify the ki'i and wash away the blood stains and cleanse US of the curse."

"Us? You as well? What is the curse, Hi'iaka?" Kiara asked bravely.

Hi'iaka looked down. Her thick, reddish locks of hair and head lei blocked her face. Her shoulders began to tremble as if the weight of her heart was getting heavy. Then, to the girls' surprise, the Goddess began sobbing uncontrollably.

Chapter 11

Into the Woods

With both dogs back in the Hummer and sniffing the red hood sliced from Cacy's sweater, Bishop began assembling the net bazooka outside the Hummer.

"You know, mate, there's too much underbrush and trees in the way to really snag the girls with a clear shot," Rook intoned, wiping sweat from his massive forehead and large neck with his shirtsleeve. Mixed with the humid air, his sweat smelled like burnt pepperoni. "Better off using tranquilizer darts."

Bishop threw the bazooka in the backseat and climbed back into the front passenger side and slammed the door. "Great minds do think alike." Bishop grinned with his snake eyes. From the glove compartment he pulled a bolt action handgun loaded with tranquilizer darts used to knock out large animals. "I hate kids. There's enough juice in this baby to keep them asleep till they're twenty-one!"

The Hummer was equipped with a special global positioning system that gave them a 3-D map of roads, hills, rock formations, and trees. Both Falchion and Gladius had homing implants in their necks. Wherever the dogs were—within a three mile radius of the Hummer—the men would be able to follow their movements. As Bishop was about to touch the end of a cigarette with his lighter, Rook pulled out of the parking stall, causing his partner to drop the flaming tool into his lap. He liked doing that as a prank. Bishop cussed and fidgeted as the Hummer made a sharp turn and roared out of the parking lot, sending tourists leaping out the way. Some yelled as the Hummer sped off. Rook stuck out his left arm and gave them all his version of the Hawaiian shaka sign—showing just one finger.

Within five minutes of barreling down the narrow road, they came to thick forest where they thought the girls might have descended. Immediately the dogs began barking, causing Bishop to jump in his seat. The men looked around the perimeter of the road and trees, thinking that the girls were in sight. An easy chase, they hoped.

"Shoot!" Bishop spat and pointed to large bird off in the distance. "It's just a nēnē goose crossing the road. Geez, look at the size of that thing. I didn't know they grew that big."

"Crikes! Look at its walk." Rook stared at the giant bird. "It's almost mechanical the way its legs move and head bobs. Never seen any bird that silly looking in any country."

Inside the nēnē goose, the little man Cacy had seen back at the Volcano House was looking back at the Hummer through the bird's periscope head. He was still a little shaken from being seen by the girl and felt like the two men might also know about him. The little man stepped on the accelerator pedal and the nēnē goose ran ostrich-like down the other side of the road till it reached an open spot in the thick wall of trees and disappeared from view.

The men's attention went back to the task at hand. Rook carefully took the Hummer into the woods, breaking down high fern leaves and low tree branches. He followed the 3-D monitor on the dashboard to find the path of least resistance—and far less traveled—to drive deeper into the rain forest. Finally, he stopped in a clearing and both men went to the back of the Hummer and released the dogs. By this time, Cacy's hood was practically ripped to shreds by razor sharp canine teeth, and soaked with thick saliva.

The dogs took off deeper into the rain forest, barking in excitement. In no time, both Rook and Bishop were sitting in the their seats watching

the red dots maneuver along the computerized topography of their screen. Falchion was faster, but Gladius was more brutal. One red dot stopped and was rejoined by the other. Both zigged and zagged around outlines of trees and rocks. Suddenly, both red dots came to a standing halt on the monitor screen. Then they began to move slowly, very slowly, heading toward an area symbolizing a clearing. Rook knew they were onto the scent, and instead of racing in, the dogs were slowly stalking their prey while they waited for their master to come up.

"You want to go hunting?" Rook said, looking over to his partner and stepping down on the gas pedal. "Get your gun!"

Chapter 12

Ti for Two

"**S**o you see," Hi'iaka concluded, "it was also a blessing that you two stumbled upon that section of the lava tube so you could take the ki'i to the kahuna spirits of Pu'uhonua o Hōnaunau before my sister, Pele, destroys the entire park with earthquakes and lava flows at sunrise." Her eyes were still moist and red long after she had stopped crying.

"Wait a minute!" Cacy blurted out. "You mean your sister, Pele, will destroy this whole entire park just because this ki'i was taken out of its burial spot? That's so silly; let's just go put it back and apologize to her."

Kiara looked over at her cousin and actually found herself in agreement. "Yes, it was all a misunderstanding, and isn't it well known that many tourists take lava rocks home as souvenirs even though they are not allowed to?" she added.

Hi'iaka replied, "My sister creates the land. Every little act of stealing what she creates is like a thousand little cuts in her. This ki'i is the last of its kind and was buried by the Ancients long before Kīlauea became part of a national park. It helped to establish a harmony between the Ancients and how I provided the forests over each new lava flow. Now the ki'i must be purified by a kahuna and transported into the realm of the spirits before the next sunrise. It cannot be returned to Nāhuku as you say."

A bright red flash appeared above the three. It startled Cacy and she instinctively reached for the handle of her bat.

"No!" Hi'iaka motioned her to stop. "Look. It is a Kamehameha butterfly. See the beauty of her red and black wings. Without the harmony, all this, the rain forests, her home, will be engulfed by the raging lava flows of the Fire Goddess." Again, the Forest Goddess lowered her head in sadness. This made Cacy remember how barren and desolate the land was along the highway heading into Hawai'i Volcanoes National Park. It frightened her to think of a volcanic eruption powerful enough to wipe out the entire park and all its rain forests, roads, and buildings!

Cacy held out her palm and the butterfly fluttered down to rest in it. She thought of Snow White and all the cute animals of the forest coming to her. Kiara

rose up like a race car doing a wheelie. The girls screamed and leaned back. Kiara wrapped her arms around Cacy's backpack. With a loud blast, the ti leaf and the girls shot off at high speed, just missing the snap of the first dog's jaw as he sprang at them. He slammed headfirst into the ground. The other dog came up behind his partner, who was already shaking the dirt off his face. They howled loudly to alert Rook and Bishop and then raced off together to chase the girls. Speeding wildly and recklessly through the rain forest on a giant hovering magic ti leaf, Cacy and Kiara began their journey to save themselves and the entire park.

Chapter 13

On a Magic Carpet Ride

R ook turned on the radio while watching the two red dots on the tracking screen move about. "Hey, mate! Have a look! Gladius and Falchion are running ragged all over the screen!" Rook hollered to Bishop, who was standing on the passenger footrest. He leaned between the vehicle and his open door to peer around all the trees.

"Hey, turn up the radio. I like that song." Bishop ignored what was going on on the screen. Rook liked the classic rock tune as well. It was called "Magic Carpet Ride" by Steppenwolf. Together they found themselves singing along and drumming their hands on the car, not noticing that the dots were heading in a fast arc back to the Hummer.

Just as they sang the lines:

"Well, you don't know what we could find
Why don't you come with me, little girl,
On a magic carpet ride?"

Cacy and Kiara came zipping right in front of the Hummer on the ti leaf. Both Rook and Bishop turned their heads left to right, following the sight of the two girls. Just behind them, Falchion and Gladius came running past the Hummer. Again, Rook and Bishop followed with their heads.

"What the...!" Rook yelled, snapping back to the mission at hand. He stomped down hard on the gas pedal and swerved the Hummer to the right, bouncing over a mound of rocks. Bishop nearly fell out of the Hummer but held on to the door and swung back into his seat.

"Geez! Watch how you drive!! I nearly messed up my hair!" Bishop yelled as he fumbled for his dart pistol.

"Did you see that?" screamed Kiara as the wind blew her hair wildly. "It was those two men from the lava tube!"

"I saw! I saw!" Cacy shouted and tried to steer the speeding ti leaf around each oncoming tree trunk and large boulder. They could hear the dogs barking close behind and the sound of the Hummer smashing through low branches and breaking down young koa trees.

"Cacy, slow down! You're going too fast! Ahhh!" Kiara shrieked as they made a sharp turn in front of a massive koa tree and a sudden jump over a fallen tree trunk. The fast landing on the other side sent the bottom of the ti leaf scraping the earth. They slowed down and floated midair as Cacy quickly analyzed the stem.

"I got it figured out! Yank the stem left or right and we turn that direction. Pull it toward me and we go forward! The harder I pull, the faster it goes! This is easier than driving a car!" Cacy said with satisfaction.

Without warning, the dogs leaped over the tree trunk together. The shock made Kiara grab and yank Cacy's backpack, which yanked Cacy, who was still holding the stem. In a flash, the front of the ti leaf rose up and they shot off again, leaving the two dogs in a blast of wind and leaves. Looking behind them, both Kiara and Cacy found themselves laughing at the sight of the two dogs far away in the distance.

Suddenly, the leaf was thrown off balance and the girls were struck by low branches and tall blades of grass that stung as they scraped by. Like a wrecking ball smashing through a building, the Hummer demolished a row of trees from out of nowhere and narrowly missed running over the girls. Shredded ferns, tree branches, and colorful berries flew everywhere.

"There!" yelled Bishop, pointing toward the girls as they screeched to a halt. The Hummer's dashboard was too high to see the girls, so Bishop leaned out of the window and gave Rook directions. "Straight ahead! I think I got a good shot."

They girls saw Bishop pull out a large gun and aim it right at them. With a hard yank on the stem, the ti leaf wobbled and took off. It seemed like there was less power in it now, and Kiara looked down and noticed that the tip, or tail end, was shredded. A sharp zipping sound whizzed past Kiara's ear and ended with a loud pop! A long tranquilizer dart was embedded in Cacy's backpack. Kiara looked in horror at the dangling projectile that had missed Cacy's neck by inches.

"What was that sound?" Cacy shouted, steering the ti leaf toward a ravine.

"You don't want to know!" Kiara replied. She grabbed the dart from the backpack and tossed it behind her. "Look out for that crevice!"

Up ahead was a deep, jagged crevice of dried lava that had cracked and split open like a long fault line. Rook gave too much acceleration and moved up close behind the rear of the ti leaf. Kiara was close enough to reach up and actually touch the front fender of the Hummer. If they went any faster, she would be pushed under its engine. Just a little farther and the girls would reach the crevice.

"Pull back! I can't see them!" Bishop warned. The Hummer dropped speed and the girls were visible

again. "There's some sort of drop up ahead! I think we've got 'em trapped, Rook!"

Instead of turning at the edge, Cacy pushed the stem forward. The girls plummeted down the jagged black sides of the crevice, dipped sharply at its nadir, and shot upward along the other wall and back out on the other side. Rook accelerated the Hummer, sending Bishop back into his seat. With a load roar, the Hummer jumped the entire distance across and landed recklessly on the other side with an impact that shook and cracked more of the hard lava field. Again, they continued after their prey. In all the excitement, both men forgot about the dogs. Their signals appeared on the tracking screen again. This time they were heading into what appeared to be a large field.

In a large field of grass that was tall enough to hide them, the girls waited still. Cacy's hands were numb and stiff from gripping the stem for so long. Kiara breathed heavily, hoping that this was all a nightmare and any moment she would wake up in her own comfortable bed in her own comfortable home back on Oʻahu. Realizing that this was all real, she let out a deep miserable sigh.

"Okay," Cacy whispered, "we'll sneak up on the Hummer and I'll hit their tires with my baseball bat. Ready?"

Kiara grabbed Cacy's bat handle as if to take it from her. "Oh, no WE ARE NOT!" she protested. "If they don't kill us first, YOU will! In fact, I don't think Hiʻiaka has to worry about Pele destroying the park. I think you've been creating enough damage in this forest. Why don't you let me...drive...or, whatever, for a change!"

Cacy relented and began to slide off the ti leaf so her cousin could take the stem. Suddenly, from among the thick grass, Falchion and Gladius charged at the girls.

"Hold on!" Cacy yelled, moving back into her original position. With a yank on the stem, the ti leaf shook and jerked until it could zoom forward again. As they traveled through the dense field, the blades of grass parted like waves around the ti leaf, creating a wide and flat pathway behind them. If one could see an aerial view above the field, the girls were going in circles and intersecting loops, being chased by the dogs. On the view screen, Rook and Bishop stared at the image of the field and the two red dots running round and round in a crazy maze formation.

As Cacy steered through the field, Kiara noticed that they would repeatedly pass over flattened trails. Eventually, the dogs figured this out as well and stopped running. They split apart and positioned themselves to lunge out and attack at a point when the ti leaf would zip by. Looking behind, Kiara saw that that dogs were off their trail and surmised that they were planning a surprise attack. At any moment, one might spring out! she thought. Then, for the first time that day, she smiled. Kiara unclipped her Digital Data Pad, and with her free hand she pressed the keys to take her to the section on analyzing wave frequencies. By readjusting the commands and making a few computations, she modified hertz ranges to create a combination of low infrasound below 20 Hz and highly intense ultrasound above 20,000 Hz. Both sound waves were out of the range of the human ear.

As if on cue, one of the dogs came out suddenly on the right side of the ti leaf. Kiara pointed the Digital Data Pad at the dog and pressed the red center button. The dog immediately jerked onto its back as if kicked hard in the face. It whined and shook. Cacy stopped the ti leaf. The girls looked at the dog to see if it was dead. In seconds, it rose back onto its legs and staggered in disorientation. The second dog was silently creeping up to Cacy and was about to pounce, until Kiara spotted it in her peripheral vision. She immediately swung her arm to the left and shot another inaudible blast from the Digital Data Pad. The other dog flew backward and tensed up as if lightning had passed through its body. Cacy turned to look at her cousin in amazement. Kiara leaked a sly smirk and clipped the Digital Data Pad back on her waist. Cacy started up the ti leaf and they moved on. They didn't say a word, but inside they both felt that somehow things were starting to look better.

Finally, Cacy spoke. "It's nothing but tall grass everywhere. I wonder where this field finally ends."

As they continued just a little farther, the field suddenly disappeared and they flew beyond the edge of a cliff. In front of them was a vast panoramic view of black lava fields, smoking craters, and deep green valleys. Directly underneath them was a drop of about three hundred feet to the bottom of a pool. They looked down, looked at each other, looked behind at the grassy field and how it ended at the edge of the cliff several feet away. Again, they looked down at the enormous drop, looked back at each other, and screamed in terror as the ti leaf stopped hovering and plummeted downward.

Chapter 14

Down in the Valley

The leaf and the two girls spun in a vertical nosedive. Hues of blue, green, and black blended like a kaleidoscope as they zoomed closer to the bottom of the cliff. Cacy managed to inhale quickly after her initial scream. In doing so, she jerked hard on the ti leaf stem and stopped the spiraling. Kiara focused her eyes to see that they were riding parallel with the side of the cliff. Only three feet of air space separated them and protruding rocks and cascading water. She leaned to the side to see beyond Cacy's head.

"Pull up!" Kiara yelled in her cousin's right ear. Their fall was slower than the pull of gravity, yet it was clear that they were heading into the base of a waterfall and large rocks. "Pull up!" This time Kiara let go of the sides of the ti leaf and grabbed Cacy's upper arms. It broke Cacy out of her fixed stare.

The ti leaf changed its course just before striking the surface of the water. The sudden air thrust

created a huge splash around the ti leaf as it turned horizontal and accelerated over the large pool, which flowed into several smaller ones. The magic ti leaf could not stay afloat over the water and it began to dip and strike the pool surface like a smooth stone skipping over a pond. The girls shrieked with each sudden bounce. Little by little the tips of the wet, sharp rocks rising above the surface began to shred the ti leaf.

With a hard bounce and splash, the girls swerved to avoid a large oncoming rock. It sent them sliding into the shoreline, which was made up of stones, black mud, and fern trees. The ti leaf ride came to a sudden halt. Cacy tumbled forward and nearly twisted her arm from being thrown with her backpack on. Her bat lay several feet away from her. For a moment, she shivered from both the fear of falling to her death and the exhilaration of riding the magic ti leaf. Slowly, she sat up and brushed the wet dirt and pebbles off her face and shirt. There, just several yards away, was the edge of the first pool. The ti leaf floated in the shallow waves coming along the shore. It was now the size of a normal leaf and torn to shreds. Cacy watched silently as the severely abused but useful gift was picked up by the rapids, carried off down the rushing white waters, and disappeared into the next pool. She couldn't

help but wipe her eyes out of sadness for what the leaf went through.

Looking up high above, Cacy could see the top of the cliff. The waterfall began off to the side from where they had gone over. It was hard to see clearly with the cool sprays of water raining down. She carefully estimated the spot from where they fell and could see some of the grass growing over the rim of the cliff. Suddenly, the shape of two figures appeared at that spot. Cacy realized that it was those men and that they were watching her through binoculars. She was afraid, but angry as well. She backed up several feet to where her bat lay. Without taking her eyes off the men high, high above, she slowly knelt down and picked up her bat. The men didn't move, but kept watching the little girl who was staring back. Slowly Cacy stood up straight, lowered her eyebrows in a cold stare, and spun her bat like a sword and sheathed it effortlessly into her backpack. Rook couldn't help but giggle at the sight of such a little tyke thinking that she'd gotten the best of them.

"Aw, crikes! I can't believe they survived that fall!" Rook shouted, slapping down his binoculars.

"Oh yeah, that was more exciting than watching them get sucked out of the lava tube." Bishop smirked, still keeping his eyes on Cacy below.

Rook slapped Bishop's shoulder, which made the binoculars poke his eyes.

"Geez! What'd you do that for?" Bishop squinted his eyes.

"Argh, if we only knew back at the bar that weird kid would be trouble," Rook spat in regret. "The other one, the smart looking one: I haven't seen her before. Anyway, they're both back on foot now. Let's drive down to the valley. There's not a whole lot of trees down there, so it should be easier to track them. I'll round up the dogs."

Bishop lit a cigarette and took three deep puffs before flinging it down the cliff. Back at the bottom, Cacy watched the two men disappear from view. Only one ti leaf had turned into the magic carpet; the others remained the same. She concluded that the other ti leaves had different purposes. It worried her that the leaf that could have helped them easily travel to the other side of Hawai'i Island was destroyed. Suddenly, she remembered that she wasn't in this all alone. She looked around in all directions and began calling out Kiara's name.

"Don't talk to me!" Kiara's distinct voice shot from above. Hanging slumped over a tree branch like a damp bath towel on a rack, Kiara glared at her cousin. When the ti leaf had slammed to a halt at the shore, it catapulted Kiara into a nearby tree.

Cacy tried to hold in a laugh at seeing her ultratidy cousin shimmying down a tree branch to jump off. Kiara eventually held on to the branch with both hands. She hung there, kicking her legs in the air. She was too scared to let go.

"Just jump, Kiara!" Cacy called, placing her arms at her sides. "What? You want me to catch you?"

"You be quiet, Cacy!" Kiara said as she contemplated the distance to the ground. "Falling from a high altitude is different when there's no supernatural assistance involved." She then closed her eyes tightly and let go of the branch. Three feet below, Kiara landed easily on both feet but slipped on the wet ground and fell to her butt. Cacy fell down on her butt as well, laughing hysterically.

Chapter 15

Journey by Foot

After several minutes of arguing about who was at fault for destroying the ti leaf, Kiara took a leadership role. First, she insisted her cousin take off her backpack so she could examine it. Second, she explained that a dart hit the backpack while they were being chased on the ti leaf. The dart was gone but a small hole the size of an ice pick puncture was clearly evident.

"It must have fallen out," Kiara surmised. "I assume they do not want to kill us. Otherwise they would have used bullets."

Bullets or not, Cacy was enraged. She felt violated. "I don't care! What kind of a person shoots at kids?!" Cacy shouted. "I knew I should've taken them out with my bat when we had that chance."

Kiara held up her bloodstained fingers to Cacy's face and stopped her cold.

"Look at this," she reminded her emotional cousin. "We have bigger problems. If we don't get this ki'i to

Puʻuhonua o Hōnaunau by sunrise, bullets won't be the cause of our demise and every living creature in this park will be decimated by Pele. Don't you recall all those videos back at the visitor center showing lava flows burning up forests?"

Cacy looked down at the blood stains on her fingers and silently turned to walk into the woods.

"Our ti leaf is gone so we gotta go by foot. Puʻuhonua o Hōnaunau is on the west side of the island, so I'm heading west." Cacy explained. "My watch says it's three thirty."

"Three thirty-five and thirty-seven seconds," Kiara said, holding up her watch and outpacing her. "You are always behind."

It was warm and muggy. The ground was moist and the dense understory of ferns licked their legs as they maneuvered quickly through the forest. After half an hour they began to feel tired and down in spirit. Cacy took out the two remaining ti leaves and tried shaking both like the first one hoping to see if they would transform into something to ride, but nothing happened.

"Put them away, Cacy." Kiara said dejectedly. "You're just going to damage them."

The girls came to an area of flat grass, which made a welcome walking path. Cacy walked ahead with her eyes peeled while Kiara trudged behind, sulking. Suddenly, something off in the distance caught Cacy's attention. She stopped in her steps.

"Hey!" she called to Kiara. "You smell something?"

Kiara looked at Cacy as if she was going crazy. Suddenly, she caught the whiff of something in the air that made her grab her nose in disdain.

"Ugh! Did you just fart, Cacy?"

"That wasn't me!" Cacy denied. She looked around and heard a dull, low rumbling sound from behind the tall grass and a fallen tree log several feet away. "Shh. There's something over there. Let's check it out."

"No let's hide. What if it's those men again?" Kiara warned. She would not budge.

Cacy didn't listen. She slowly walked to the fallen log and climbed over it. The grass stood about five feet high. Leaning on the top of the log, Cacy slowly and carefully reached out to spread the grass apart. Peering into the distance she saw more of the grass shaking. The ground vibrated with the oncoming sounds of rumbling and branches breaking. She thought that it might be the Hummer coming closer. Instead of fleeing, she stayed fixed to the spot. Her eyes widened in horror and the grass exploded in front of her as a gigantic black shadow charged out and knocked her off the log. She heard a roar and rolled on the wet ground as a huge beast several

feet long leaped over the log, sending forest debris flying in its wake. The black beast was on four hairy legs and swung its long head side to side, sending sprays of hot saliva in the air. It bucked and flexed the massive muscles in its thick neck. Black hairs raised up like spikes and when it roared, its long, sharp fangs looked ready to bite and tear.

Kiara watched her cousin get knocked down by the beast and stood frozen looking at the behemoth as it circled and swung its head. Cacy raised herself and saw it continue to kick dirt and spin.

"Run!! It's a grizzly bear!!" Cacy screamed.

Kiara stared at the monster with both curiosity and disbelief. "Cacy, there are no grizzly bears in Hawai'i. It's a—" She stopped midsentence. Suddenly, the realization of the danger hit her. "Wild boar!!"

Kiara turned around, making a dash for a nearby tree. Adrenaline made her climb up like a squirrel. She made it several feet and crawled onto its lowest branch. The wild boar roared and charged the tree. It smashed into the bark, splitting it into pieces. Kiara screamed and held on to the vibrating branch. Shaking off the impact, the boar snorted hot air and whipped thick sprays of saliva up at Kiara. Some of it hit her right in the face and got on her glasses.

"Go away!! Go Away!!!" she screamed, grabbing small berries and throwing it down at the wild boar.

Suddenly a large rock struck its brawny neck and bounced off. Both Kiara and the boar turned to see where it came from. Cacy stood off back by the log, holding another rock. The boar looked back and snarled at Cacy.

"Oops. I think I just made it more angry," Cacy said to herself.

The boar glared. It flexed its ugly snout, huffed hot breath, and scraped its front leg like a bull about to charge. Kiara shouted to her cousin to run. Cacy kept her eyes locked onto the boar's eyes. It watched as Cacy dropped the other rock from her hand. Instead of easing off, the boar gave what looked like a drooling, sinister smile and aimed its razor-sharp tusks at her. In a blast of flying dirt, the wild boar charged forward. Cacy dropped her mouth open in fear and instinctively reached for her bat. She drew it forward and held a batting position, ready to swing for her life. As the wild boar got within striking zone, it prepared to leap. A loud, sharp whooshing sound sliced through the air, followed by the sound of a hard slap. Suddenly more whooshing sounds filled the air. With each sound of flesh slapping, the wild boar staggered. Inches from reaching Cacy, the beast raised itself on its rear legs and twisted in agony. An awful squeal shook the forest. On one side the beast was pierced by what looked like over a

dozen long arrows. But these arrows had no quivers at the end. They were short, mini-sized wooden spears. The boar fell on its nonpierced side with a hard splat. The white of the boar's eyes slowly faded to a dull lifeless stare as mosquitoes began to settle and roam on its body.

Cacy's heartbeat was still racing as she kept her grip on the bat. Kiara sat on the branch and didn't say a word. Both girls looked to where the spears hailed from. Slowly coming forward from behind the bushes were several little people. They looked human and they had dark Polynesian features. There wore a combination of ancient Hawaiian clothing and modern day adult T-shirts like long robes. One of them, Cacy recognized. It was the strange little man she had seen back at the Volcano House.

Chapter 16

Secrets Revealed

"You!" Cacy yelled, pointing her bat at the familiar little man. "It's you! I saw you in the kitchen at the Volcano House driving away in the nēnē goose. I wasn't seeing things!"

The news startled the rest of the little men. They looked at their singled-out companion with surprise. He gave Cacy and the others a look of embarrassment and disappointment.

"Zeke, what's the human girl talking about?" said one of the little men. He had a long curly beard while the others were clean shaven and youthful looking. A small ancient Hawaiian style helmet on his head seemed to signify that he was the leader of the pack. He continued angrily, "You know we're supposed to be a hidden secret from the public. You're not applying yourself!"

"I'm sorry, Obah," Zeke spoke up. Zeke walked up to Cacy while the others stayed in their positions. "It's true, while I was leaving our shopping list for the kitchen staff, this human girl wandered in. I was so surprised and scared to be seen by a visitor for the first time. I didn't know what to do except flee in the goose."

Cacy took a liking to Zeke now that he had spoken. She introduced herself, shaking his little hand gently while apologizing for startling him. She also explained that the other kids and teachers thought she was crazy for yelling about it outside the Volcano House, and how no one believed her. This set all the little men at ease, and the others came up to her. Each little person introduced himself. Kiara waved to them but remained in the tree watching this whole scene unfold in silent amazement.

"Are you what people call Menehune?" asked Cacy. The little men broke into wide grins.

"Oh, thank goodness you got that right!" one of them exclaimed. His name was Amos. "We hate it when humans refer to us as leprechauns, elves, dwarves, gnomes, or even munchkins! We may be small in size and number, but we are a proud indigenous people." The others nodded in agreement.

"All the workers, scientists, and rangers in the park know about us, and they help to keep our existence a secret from all visitors," Zeke said. "Well, it's not a secret anymore to you two. We were on a hunt when we saw the both of you approaching. We knew a boar was near, but we didn't know how to warn you to stay away without revealing ourselves."

"What? You're actually going to eat that thing?" Cacy said, looking back down at the ugly dead beast. The mosquitoes swarmed around the boar's drool and dripping snout. The sight made Cacy feel sick.

"Oh yeah," said Obah, butting in and licking his lips. "Wild boars and even feral pigs are a danger in the park. They uproot and destroy endangered plants, plus they create breeding grounds for mosquitoes, which can spread diseases to native birds. It's actually okay to kill them, plus they make good eating!"

While he was saying this, the others were busy bringing out and assembling an old stretcher to carry the carcass. One of the Menehune, named Mali, was busily getting ropes secured around its body. It was the largest wild boar they had ever caught.

"Now that you've seen us, you and your companion must come back to the village and be our special guests for the feast this evening." Obah placed one of his little hands on Cacy's heart and the other one over his own. "Just promise that all you see and meet will be kept a secret from others."

Cacy was ready to leap at the once-in-a-lifetime invitation, but quickly remembered that a more important mission was at stake for her—and Kiara, who still remained on the tree branch. But before Cacy could answer, Kiara gave a shout.

"It's still alive!!!" she screamed, pointing at the wild boar.

The boar had wiggled and kicked its leg. Obah, Zeke, and Cacy turned around to see that the wild boar was raising its head and twisting its body to stand back up. Blood sprayed in the air as the beast's body knocked over the Menehune with the ropes. Mali fell on his back and screamed. The ropes tangled in his flailing arms and he couldn't get free. The boar gave a ferocious grunt. Even being wounded, it seemed more dangerous as it staggered to its feet and leaned over the struggling Menehune. Blood and saliva showered over him as the beast opened its jaws and prepared to crush his head. Mali screamed again.

"Spears!!" Shouted Obah. "Give me a spear!"

"We used them all up!" Zeke said, looking down at his empty hands.

All the others dropped the stretcher and watched helplessly. Kiara tried to cover her eyes but still watched the horror from between her fingers. Then a long wooden missile struck the giant beast between the eyes. Everyone heard the awful sound of bone cracking, followed by a horrible squeal. Everyone watched Cacy's bat bounce off the boar's head and

land rattling on the ground. The wild boar staggered two steps backward. Then, with a loud thud, the beast collapsed flat on its belly next to the Menehune. Its eyes were closed and its breathing stopped for good. The others ran up to pull away their rescued friend and unbind him. Zeke picked up Cacy's bat and reverently handed it back to her like a sword of honor and valor. She took it back and began to weep. Kiara refused to jump down from the branch and chose to struggle with climbing down the tree. She cautiously approached the fallen beast, and with a reading of the Digital Data Pad, she confirmed that it was indeed dead. Kiara rejoined her cousin and asked what's wrong.

"I...I never killed an animal before," Cacy said, choking on a tear. "I feel bad."

"Both of you, this is rather nonsense," Obah said, trying to sound comforting. "Both of you saved his life. If Kiara had not warned us up in the tree, the wild boar could've attacked us by surprise as well. And your bat stopped it before our friend Mali was mauled."

After Mali was untangled and cleaned up, he ran up to the girls and gave them each a hug. The girls felt better. In no time, all the spears were pulled out of the boar's body and it was tied on top the stretcher. Its body size out-measured the stretcher's length, and the boar's snout extended past the front while the rear legs stuck out beyond the other end. Arranged like pall bearers, the team lifted the massive carcass with simple ease. The girls were amazed at the strength the little men possessed. It would've taken a mechanical crane to lift and carry such a heavy load. Cacy and Kiara began to explain how and why they were in the forest and about finding the ki'i and their need to complete Hi'iaka's mission. Obah gestured to the girls to come with them instead. Zeke encouraged them to go along as well. The others followed closely behind, carrying the boar on the stretcher.

"We know both Hi'iaka and her sister Pele," Obah said, leading the way back to the village. "And we might be able to help you with your mission long before sunrise tomorrow." This was the first good news Cacy and Kiara had heard all day. "First, you must be our honored guests as we feast on the boar for dinner," he continued.

Looking back at the dead, bloodied boar on the stretcher, the girls thought of it as bad news coming again.

Chapter 17

The Kīpuka

As the group made their way back to the village, Obah and Zeke listened intently to Cacy and Kiara's recount of their experiences throughout the day. It helped the girls to better accept and deal with their situation by finally having others to talk to about it. Cacy mentioned what a fantastic journey they had to share with their schools. This stopped the hunt party in its tracks, and Kiara gave her cousin a shocked and angry look.

"Hey, mango head," Kiara scolded like a teacher, "didn't you hear the Menehune say that their existence is to be kept a secret?"

"I only meant..." Cacy quickly replied but realized she misspoke, "I'm sorry, Obah, I wouldn't tell about you folks."

"Don't worry, Cacy," Obah said reassuringly. "We know what you meant. Tourists come here expecting to see lava flows, not people like us. Come, come! We're almost there."

The group was upbeat again, except for Kiara. She didn't say anything more as she pondered how the Menehune would get them to Puʻuhonua o Hōnaunau in time, and, even worse, eating that wretched wild boar.

In minutes, the trail transformed. They went from walking through a warm forest to an open windy desert. The vast land before them was black dried lava. It was similar to the moonlike terrain they had seen as they entered the volcano park. Far off in the distance were steep slopes surrounding the land like they were in the bottom of a barren crater. There was nothing but the solid overlapping layers of smooth and jagged rocks. Then they saw a tiny forest smack in the middle of the crater. It was like a tropical island in the middle of a black solid sea.

"There it is!" Obah announced, pointing his finger to the distant forest. "There's our kīpuka."

"What's that?" Cacy asked with fascination.

"The magic of isolation," Zeke jumped in. "After a lava flow hardens, sword ferns are one of the first plants to colonize. Then more seeds and plants grow, attracting birds and animals. Over time, an entire forest forms. Sometimes new lava flows will circle around a growing forest and isolate it so it continues to survive on its own and without any predators. Plants and creatures trapped in that forest can adapt over time into new species found nowhere else. These pockets of isolated forests are called..."

"Kīpuka." Kiara butted in proudly with the answer. "An island hole on land."

"Yes, Kiara," Obah said. "For centuries, Menehune families lived in that kīpuka with the safety of secrecy and isolation. When this land became a national park, we arranged to have our kīpuka kept secret from all visitors, but the park rangers and volcanologists know about us. We help them and they help us."

"Wait," Cacy began, "you mean if I asked a park ranger or someone at the visitor center if Menehune existed here, they would deny it?!"

"That would be dishonest," Kiara pointed out.

Zeke felt that he had to answer this one since he had been spotted by Cacy.

"Maybe it's not, Kiara," Zeke explained. "If the public doesn't know about us in the first place, they wouldn't ask about it. Besides, haven't you two ever known someone you'd like to pretend you didn't?" The question pierced both girls' hearts with guilt.

Obah wanted to change the subject and quickly led the group across the ropy and jagged lava rocks to the edge of the kīpuka. Columns of steam vapors rose like ghostly forms from warm spots in the ground. Obah explained that there were steam vents far below the rocks. Drawing closer, the girls realized that the tiny forest was actually rather large and tall. Thick ʻōhiʻa trees and ferns bordered the kīpuka like the fortress walls of a castle. It seemed that there was hardly enough space between the massive trees for the group to enter with the wild boar. Then, Obah took out a small conch shell from under his robe and blew it loudly. The long blast echoed through the crater before subsiding. The group watched several of the trees slowly raise from the ground and begin to overlap themselves. The girls stepped back, fearing that they were about to fall. Obah stood still and smiled and winked slyly at the girls. To their astonishment, the giant trees slowly folded into themselves and parted in the middle like curtains in a grand theater. The kīpuka's secret entrance was wide open.

Before them was an eclectic mixture of campsite, junkyard, ancient Hawaiian village, and theme park. They saw modern tents, lanterns, grass huts, gas torches, an abandoned jeep, tree houses, rock sculptures, tarps, and dozens and dozens of Menehune. There were both males and females, young and old. Some wore large T-shirts while others wore traditional malo or kīhei. And if the adult Menehune were little, the children were tiny.

They played and frolicked like young puppies around their parents. The citizens of the kīpuka noticed that the returning hunters were not alone and, one by one, they stopped their casual activity to look at the human visitors. Cacy and Kiara stared back with equal amazement and nervousness.

The Menehune clustered and began to chatter among themselves about the outsiders. Some smiled out of courtesy, others looked at the girls with suspicion. These certainly were not scientists or park rangers, the Menehune thought. As the group entered the kīpuka, the sound of mechanical cranking and heavy chains startled the girls. They looked behind and watched the faux curtain of trees close together. The entrance was actually an illusion of trees made of flat panels which could vertically fold up. The Menehune carrying the wild boar went off with their catch to a preparation area. Obah and Zeke remained with the girls and announced to the crowd who their guests were, and their selfless acts of bravery. Immediately the girls were welcomed into the 'ohana of the Menehune village.

"Ah," said Obah. "Girls, here comes our great village elder and leader."

Approaching with a waddling gait was an old Menehune in a white T-shirt that fit like a gown. He held a black umbrella with a bamboo handle,

which served as a walking cane and resembled a tall shepherd's staff. A long white beard reached the ground, almost dragging under his bare feet. He had a long, stiff mustache that pointed out farther than his rosy cheeks. Atop his crown of silver hair was a purple wizard hat adorned with white stars and moons. Creases and wrinkles on his face revealed a long lifetime of both joy and sorrow, yet his eyes were wide and twinkled with youth.

All the Menehune stepped back in reverence for the old little man. Both Zeke and Obah bowed their heads in respect. The man stopped in front of the two girls and gave them a silent look-over.

Then, Obah addressed their dear leader. "Hello, Old Futt."

The last guest, what was his name? ...Ah, Mark Twain! Funny fellow, he's the one who gave us this umbrella. He said it wouldn't be much help when an eruption rained down lava." Tapping the tip of the umbrella firmly into the ground, Old Futt started off in a youthful strut, as if leading a marching band on parade.

Old Futt led the girls through the village and introduced them to various Menehune families. Zeke and Obah went to prepare the feast area. The kīpuka was sectioned like a small town. The older Menehune lived in grass huts while the younger generations chose more modern abodes like tree houses or used camping tents. Specific huts were built for community needs such as storing canned foods and camp supplies. Electricity was provided by gas generators donated by volcano park staff. There were game areas where Menehune honed their hunting skills, such as spear throwing and climbing over obstacles. If they were not busy in sports or training, they involved themselves in things like reading, music, craft-making, and construction. In one area, a group of Menehune mechanics wearing lantern helmets worked on large mechanical nēnē geese. One was welding sheet metal and shaping a new body. Another was using tools on an engine. All the mechanics wore little aprons cut from blue jeans.

"Look, Kiara!" Cacy said with excitement, pointing to the geese. "That's what I saw Zeke ride off in from the Volcano House!"

"Okay, okay," Kiara said dryly, "so you were telling the truth." She remembered how silly Cacy had looked running out of the Volcano House like an idiot, rambling about a little man in a nēnē goose. She remembered watching Cacy's teacher scold her in front of everyone. She remembered being embarrassed to be her cousin. It began to bother Kiara that her memory was so good.

As Old Futt spiritedly led the girls along a stone walkway between blossoming fruit trees, strange musical chimes filled the air. The girls looked up at a towering koa tree and saw hundreds of plastic bottles swaying in the thick twisting branches. Smaller bottles hung by their own strings with a tiny stone swinging inside each one to make it ring like a bell. The bottoms were cut open and as the wind blew, the bottles bumped and rang with a harmonious rustling. Larger bottles with holes poked in their sides collected the wind to create dull flute-like sounds. The strange music above was both soothing, like the pattering of soft raindrops, and haunting, like ghostly moans.

"This is our area of relaxation and healing," Old Futt explained. "As we clean up any litter we find in the park, we collect the plastic bottles to make this a musical tree. It was better than leaving them on the ground."

"It sounds so beautiful! There must be hundreds of them hanging up there!" Cacy said, looking above and feeling the enchanting effect of the chimes.

"And it's getting larger!" Old Futt added. "Bottled water!! Nearly everyone who comes into the park drinks bottled water to quench their thirst while hiking and looking at lava flows! Pele gives them a great memory and what do they do? They dump their empty water bottles on the land! Shame!"

"Wait a minute," Kiara said with interest, "how is this kīpuka able to get enough water to keep all these trees and plants alive when it's surrounded by dried lava?"

"Aha! I knew that uniform and fancy gadget on your waist signified something of high aptitude," Old Futt replied cheerfully. Kiara didn't know if that was a compliment, and Cacy didn't know if that meant he thought Kiara was smarter than her. "Come, girls. If you stay too long under the tree, the soothing music will actually lull you to sleep."

The tour passed some other tents. Sounds of giggles could be heard within. As the girls looked back, they saw the tiny heads of Menehune children peeking out. Cacy waved hello and the kids rolled their eyes, giggling before hiding back in their tents. One stood at the entrance giving a hand wave and flirtatious grin. Old Futt walked ahead and stopped at the entrance of a stone cave. The rocks were porous and cool. The echoes of dripping and rushing water could be heard. The girls peered into the cave and saw the dancing reflections of water against the walls. Steps carved from stone led to the bottom.

"It's a swimming pool?" Cacy inquired.

"No, mango head, it's an artesian well!" Kiara corrected her.

"Actually, it's both!" Old Futt answered. "Down there is a grotto. The water flows from the snows of Mauna Loa and is purified through layers of volcanic rock. Somehow an old lava tube passing underneath the kīpuka became a channel for an aqueduct. Even in a drought, all the plants and trees here are well nourished. We installed a pipe system to connect water to locations all around the village and even build fountains. One of Pele's magic lava stones is at the bottom of the grotto. It gives the water healing power and rejuvenates us. At my age, I should have passed on decades ago. I believe the water keeps me alive and strong."

"How old are you?" both girls said in unison.

"Well, I don't remember the exact year I was born," Old Futt said thoughtfully. "But I do remember as a child when the missionaries and whalers were at war on Maui. That's where I'm from originally. Our village is made up of Menehune from different islands who have escaped the outside world over time."

Then, Old Futt's eyes drifted again to a distant memory. "My parents died when I was a youth, but I had a younger brother. One night in Lahaina, the war with the whalers and missionaries got so severe, a vessel at sea fired their cannons at a church. The fires that broke out caused looting by the sailors who were ashore. We lived in the cellar of a missionary's home. My brother hid in a large chest when we heard the rioting above us. I still remember being terrified, hiding behind a table and seeing looters come down and steal the chest. I tried to run up the stairs after them, but the fires..."

Old Futt suddenly stopped and dropped his head down. Cacy placed her hand on Old Futt's shoulder while Kiara tried to remain stoic. He remained silent with his eyes closed for several seconds. The painful memories he had brought back were hard to put away again. Again, he gave a long exhale.

"Well, now!" Old Futt tapped the tip of the umbrella on the stone pavement. "Can't show tears to our guests now, can we?! Tell me, Kiara, I keep noticing the interesting object on your waist. By chance, girl,

do you know anything about electronics? Like how to repair things?"

Kiara raised her eyebrows and widened her eyes. "What do you need me to fix?" she asked with an air of confidence.

Chapter 19

News from the Outside

"I don't believe this!" Kiara exclaimed loudly. "I was already impressed with the construction of the folding trees and the mechanical nēnē geese, but this is rather out of place!"

"But do you think you can fix it?" Old Futt replied eagerly. "We don't know where the problem is."

Cacy just stood silently and stared at the bizarre setup Old Futt had led the girls to. Firmly mounted on the side of a large koa tree trunk was a giant flat-screen television. Audio speakers of different models and sizes were hung from the stretching branches overhead to create surround-sound effects. Electric cords wrapped around the branches and trunk just like street trees decorated with Christmas lights. The grassy patch before the large screen was strewn with pillows, lauhala mats, and makeshift chairs. Kiara was already examining the cords connecting the TV to a gas powered generator and looking up at the satellite dish mounted on a high branch.

Her face displayed deep concentration. Cacy knew her cousin was actually happy because Kiara loved problem-solving and complex critical thinking. This was a challenge to her intellect.

Kiara asked for a team of Menehune to climb the tree and make adjustments to wires and the satellite dish as she stayed on the ground giving directions. She made it clear that she had had enough of tree climbing. With the Digital Data Pad, she was able to identify damaged wires and then reroute connecting cords. Feeling uncomfortable doing nothing, Cacy asked if she could help.

"I doubt it," Kiara replied sweetly but with a touch of sarcasm. "You might know how to set a VCR's clock for your teachers, but this is something far more complex than what they teach in PUBLIC school."

Cacy burned with anger at the snide comment, but out of respect for the Menehune she refrained from saying anything nasty. Silently, she watched Kiara operate her Digital Data Pad and speak fancy technical terms, knowing that it was only to show off how smart she was. Cacy secretly wished the television wouldn't work. With the gas generator turned on, a curious crowd of Menehune gathered around the tree. Some took places on the mats and pillows with great anticipation. The children wrestled and bounced with so much excitement their mothers had to put them on their laps to keep them still. With a press of the remote, the television screen turned on with a blue light and a bright-colored picture. The crowd cheered and applauded wildly for Kiara. Cacy folded her arms and acted unimpressed.

"You did it!" Old Futt shouted, raising his umbrella. "We haven't been able to safely watch the outside world for months."

"Wait." Kiara proudly held up the remote control as if about to do an encore. "I have to reset all the channels."

The channels flickered through sports, infomercials, cooking, movies, Korean dramas, poker matches, and cartoons, and the growing audience of Menehune cheered as each new channel popped up on the giant screen. After about twenty channels, this was becoming annoying to Kiara and amusing to Cacy.

"Old Futt, I can't believe you all gather to watch TV out in the open like this," Cacy said.

"Why?" Old Futt replied. "On O'ahu, don't people set up movie screens on the beach?"

Suddenly, the crowd's reaction turned from happiness to shock when a channel stopped on local news coverage of Hawai'i Volcanoes National Park. It was showing an aerial view of the rain forest where the Thurston Lava Tube was located.

"Turn it up, Kiara!" Cacy yelled to her cousin.

Everyone watched the familiar green volume level bars increase at the bottom of the giant screen, and they leaned forward. The sound of the news boomed throughout the kīpuka for all to hear. The screen showed a montage of tourists, police, park rangers, and worried school students and teachers.

"As the search for the two missing girls continues," the voice-over of the reporter said, "FBI agents have now joined local law enforcement and park rangers. Both girls are in the sixth grade and were on field trips with their schools from Oʻahu. One of the girls is named Cacy Dang from Malulani Elementary School. She is described as wearing a red shirt, blue pants, and carrying a pink backpack. The other girl is Kiara Yoon from Central Academy. She wears glasses, and was wearing a blue and white school uniform. Both of the girls' parents are being flown in from Oʻahu. The girls were last seen with their schools in the Thurston Lava Tube. Police have closed off the entire length of the tube, and have discovered the murdered body of an unidentified adult male." The final news image showed police surrounding other officials as they carried a covered corpse on a stretcher, coming up the rocky steps. A swarm of photographers buzzed around them.

The reporter concluded the story by stating that Hawai'i Volcanoes National Park had been locked down and all vehicles leaving the park were being inspected. Kiara shut off the TV with the remote and all the Menehune stared speechlessly at the girls.

"We didn't do it!" Cacy shouted, raising her arms up.

"Of course you didn't," Old Futt said, calmly tapping the tip of one end of his long mustache. "Well, this is a complex situation. If we take you back to the searchers, they wouldn't believe your mission and you'll never get to Pu'uhonua o Hōnaunau before sunrise to prevent the curse. At the same time, the murderers are looking for you and that ki'i. Either way, your lives are still in danger and so is the secrecy of the kīpuka." He closed his eyes and took a deep breath and long exhale. Cacy and Kiara stood next to each other as members of the Menehune kīpuka gathered around them in support. The little children held on to the girls' hands and some tugged on Kiara's pleated skirt. They all watched Old Futt, who was always known and respected for his wisdom and ability to come up with the answer to any problem. He took his umbrella and began to write on the ground with the pointed tip. Everyone leaned forward, trying to see what he was writing. Then, kicking out his little stubby foot from under his long shirt, Old Futt wiped away the writings.

"Arghh!" he jeered, walking away. "Let's go eat!"

"Eat?!" Cacy whined.

"How can you think of eating at a time like this?" Kiara added.

Old Futt stopped and turned around to face everyone, looking very serious. "My dear children," he began, as if lecturing the girls, "You came here as honored guests for a feast. Let us keep that as planned! Now is the time for dinner, not feeling sorry for ourselves. Let's first celebrate and be thankful for our abundance and blessings. You two might be missing to the outside world, but you are not lost when you have each other. Plus, I can smell that roasted boar is ready!"

He winked at the girls and led the way to the dining area.

The Lū'au

As the sun began to set, a shining full moon illuminated the night sky with a bluish glow. In the kīpuka, recycled Christmas lights hung from the surrounding fruit trees as colorful decorations. Torches were ablaze and lit up the kīpuka's village and lū'au yard. A large area was swept of dirt and covered with straw mats, rolled-out sleeping bags, and beach towels. The girls sat side by side on a purple towel. Next to them was Old Futt, Obah, Zeke, and Mali. Each person had banana leaves as place mats. The Menehune sat forming a large circle so everyone could see each other. Children formed their own circles with an adult Menehune to keep order. Everyone was happily sharing stories with those on their left and right and even across the circle. A small band of Menehune played joyful music on instruments they had created. Then, Old Futt picked up his umbrella and planted the tip into the ground and pulled himself up. All became silent.

"Tonight, we celebrate more than just the goodness we have by being here together," Old Futt began solemnly. "Much of what we have to live well here comes from the goodness and generosity of the scientists and staff at the volcano park. They help to keep our existence a secret from the outside world. Here now, we have Cacy and Kiara. They are no longer outsiders, but our welcome guests. They have shown bravery, helpfulness, and trustworthiness."

The Menehune applauded. Mali gave the loudest cheer. Old Futt waited for silence and then continued.

"What makes us strong is not isolation from the outside, but that we can rely on each other. We survived over time because we learned to work and live together despite all our differences and hardships. We choose to conquer pride and selfishness within ourselves and have chosen to do what is right. Tonight, our guests must travel to the other side of the Big Island and set things right so everything in this park can survive. But first, we feast and celebrate being together here."

Old Futt removed his wizard hat and gave an invocation thanking Ke Akua above for the food. When he was done, he placed his hat back on, dropped back down, and called for the feast to be served. The band continued to play and like a well-practiced team of waiters, a crew of Menehune appeared from behind a large tent. Some carried paper plates, others carried large covered aluminum trays of food above their heads. Steam and delicious aromas filled the air as covers were removed. The younger Menehune served the elders and heaps of different foods were plated and served to everyone. Cacy and Kiara looked at their piled plates and couldn't believe their stomachs would be able to fit all the food they had. Old Futt explained that the chefs used special lava stones to cook on. They magically heated up quickly to boil, fry, or even roast food. What would take many hours to cook in a traditional imu now took minutes.

"Do all of you feast like this every day?" Kiara asked while scrubbing her wooden chopsticks together.

"Oh, no! Tonight is special with you and Cacy," Old Futt said, throwing his long beard over his shoulder and giving them another deep and overly emphasized wink. "Once in a while some of us go out in disguise as little children with volcanologists to eat at the pancake house in Hilo." The girls laughed at the thought.

Everyone feasted on thick, juicy slices of meat, steamed vegetables, Menehune-style stew, fresh exotic fruits grown only in the kīpuka, poi and fish from the Volcano House kitchen, wild hen, noodles, pastries, and fruit punch made with pure kīpuka

water. As they all ate, everyone chatted and laughed heartily with one another. When plates were empty, it was a race of hospitality to serve extra helpings.

Cacy shoveled her dinner with a fork and her cheeks ballooned as she tried to chew. The Menehune giggled and Kiara looked over at her cousin, thinking she was making a pig out of herself. With her chopsticks, Kiara took her food in moderation, but found herself delighted with each tasty dish. Soon she found herself stuffing food into her mouth and gleefully disregarding the proper table manners she was raised on. The food and fruit punch were delicious, but Kiara began to think that perhaps it wasn't so much the menu she was enjoying, but rather the company she was eating with. Then, without a thought, Kiara reached for another serving of roast meat for herself and placed some slices on Cacy's plate when she had finished her serving. Cacy didn't notice this because she was busy talking to Old Futt. But he noticed and knew that something significant had occurred between the two girls.

Then, as everyone was about to push away their plates and take a long nap, Old Futt announced the special treat for Kiara and Cacy. A Menehune chef carrying a silver dome-covered tray approached. Everyone sat straight in anticipation with their eyes following the tray.

"This is prepared and served only to honored guests like visiting scientists," Old Futt explained as the Menehune presented the tray to the girls and lifted the cover. A billowing cloud of steam and the sizzling tray underneath made the crowd light up with excitement. The thick, round slice of meat on the platter was dark brown and charred with perfect grill marks. The chef served each girl an equal share. The outer skin was crispy, and the meat inside was succulent and juicy with a generous portion of tasty fat. Even though they were full, the girls' appetites returned as they tasted the crunchy skin, which crackled with flavor. They savored the juicy texture and tenderness of the meat.

"This is so delicious!" Cacy wiped the grease running down the side of her mouth. "It's better than the roast pork our grandmother buys in Chinatown markets."

Kiara mumbled in agreement as she was busy chewing with delight.

"I'm so happy, girls." Old Futt beamed. "The snout is always the tastiest part of the wild boar."

Kiara's mouth dropped open wider than her eyes and spilled all the chewed contents onto her lap. Cacy ate another fatty piece and looked over at Kiara, going, "Mmmmmmmmmmmm!"

Chapter 21

Going on Alone

"**I**s she going to be all right?" asked Zeke as some of the Menehune carried Kiara into the guest tent to lie down on a sleeping bag. "We have medical supplies here, even though we haven't had any injuries in the kīpuka for several decades."

"No, I think she just needs to rest a little after eating too much." Cacy dumped her backpack in the tent corner next to Kiara's head. She didn't want to admit that the special treat of wild boar snout grossed out her cousin. "I'll stay with her while they get the jeep ready."

Kiara was awake, but groaned from both a bellyache and the thought of eating the snout. It had made her even more sick seeing Cacy egging her on by eating more of it. When the girls were alone, Cacy jumped onto a cot and lay down on her stomach. Even she was wishing she hadn't eaten so much.

"That was so disgusting," Kiara said, rolling her eyes over to her cousin. "When Old Futt said what it was, I pictured that wild boar dead with all the mucus and blood running out of its nostrils. Can you imagine how many parasites were living in—"

"Stop! You're gonna make ME sick!" Cacy interrupted, raising herself up on her side. "I didn't mind. I'd rather eat something that could eat me than the other way around."

"That doesn't make any sense." Kiara snickered.

"Listen, I still got my musubi from lunch this afternoon. Maybe that'll get the oily taste out of your mouth."

Kiara sat upright. "You got a musubi? Let me have it."

Cacy reached down for her backpack and opened it. She pulled out her sweater and felt the ki'i wrapped inside it. Knowing that they must soon deal with it brought on a feeling of anxiety. Underneath the sweater was her crushed box lunch. She opened it and handed Kiara the musubi, which was still wrapped in plastic.

Kiara took it and even though she was full, she relished the familiar smell of the nori wrapping and took a bite. Ah, rice. She loved to eat rice. The bland flavor eliminated the greasy aftertaste of roasted snout and cleansed her palate. As she chewed, she noticed an odd sweet flavor. In less than a minute, the musubi was gone. Kiara handed the plastic wrapper back to Cacy and immediately began to look drowsy.

"You okay?" Cacy said, taking the wrapper.

"I...I feel a little sleepy," Kiara whispered. Her eyes fluttered and she leaned back on the sleeping bag. In a few seconds, Kiara was passed out.

"Hey, you can't sleep now," Cacy scolded. "They're about to drive us to Puʻuhonua o Hōnaunau pretty soon. Wake up!"

Cacy reached out and pushed her cousin's shoulder. Kiara didn't flinch. Not wanting to leave any rubbish, Cacy started to place the plastic wrapper in her box lunch. She noticed a puncture in the box and wondered how that got there. Then, a thought of fear and horror made her look closer at the hole. It was the same size as the puncture hole in her backpack where Kiara said the men had shot a dart. She sat upright on the cot and raced through her memories. The men shot a dart and not a bullet. A wet spot inside her backpack. The puncture holes being the same size. Cacy flattened out the crumpled plastic wrapper. Holding it up to a light, she saw a puncture mark the same size as the other two. It soon became clear what had happened, and Kiara was paying the price for it. It comforted Cacy to know that Kiara was just asleep and not dead. But how long would she be asleep and how much of the knockout liquid got into the musubi?

Cacy ran out of the tent to tell the others. She headed to the banyan tree where the old jeep was parked. When she got there, she saw a group of Menehune standing by the vehicle with grim looks on their faces. She could already hear one of them saying, "How will we help them now with the jeep broken?"

"Broken?!" Cacy repeated loudly. They all turned to look at her.

Zeke was with them and walked up to Cacy. He took her by the hand and led her back to the guest tent.

"It's not good, Cacy," Zeke said sadly. "The jeep won't run and our best mechanic doesn't have replacement parts. Can Kiara take a look at it?"

"Kiara is knocked out by some poison dart," Cacy began as she recounted the chase and the events that led to Kiara's condition. "Zeke, even if she could fix the jeep, she might be asleep beyond sunrise tomorrow. By then it'll be too late! Unless..."

"Unless what?"

"I can go on by myself." Cacy tried to convince herself of what she was saying. "I'll go by foot if I have to! As long as the ki'i is returned before sunrise, everything should be okay. I'll ask the kahuna to pardon Kiara while I'm there. It's fair, isn't it?"

"I don't know, Cacy," Zeke warned. "Maybe Old Futt can help."

"Old Futt can watch over Kiara," Cacy answered and looked down at her watch. "It's already past eight o'clock. Get me a map and a flashlight, and I'll find my way. If I meet people searching for us, I'll make them believe that I have to get to Pu'uhonua o Hōnaunau before sunrise. The longer we wait, the less time I have. I have to leave now!"

"We'll go with you!"

"No!" Cacy insisted. "You folks have to keep your secrecy and you've been so good to us already. I don't have time to say good-bye to everyone, but please explain to Old Futt and everyone else that I'll come right back somehow. Please promise!"

Zeke worried. "All right. I'll open the gate just a little so you can get through. I'll meet you there with the map and flashlight."

Cacy darted off to the guest tent. Kiara was still fast asleep. With a pad and a pen she found in the tent, Cacy wrote a message and left it for Kiara to read whenever she woke up:

Kiara—
You were knocked out by the dart that hit my backpack. It must have got into the musubi you ate. The jeep was broken. I went to Pu'uhonua o Hōnaunau to return the ki'i on my own. I will have the kahuna pardon you as well so don't worry about

the blood stain and the curse. Stay here with Old
Futt. I will come back.

—Cacy

Cacy left the note next to Kiara's hand and took
her backpack with all her belongings. She reached
behind her and felt the handle of her bat to give
her confidence. Cacy stepped outside the tent and
looked up at the bright full moon. It gave enough
light to see well. She met Zeke at the gate and stood
nervously as he pulled a lever that opened a faux
tree panel just wide enough for one person to walk
through. Zeke ran up to Cacy and gave her a big
hug.

"Ke Akua go with you, Cacy," Zeke said with
moist eyes.

Cacy took a deep breath and stepped boldly
out of the kīpuka into the dark field of lava rocks.
Using the new flashlight, Cacy maneuvered across
the cold desolate landscape under a clear night sky.
Zeke followed the beam of the flashlight as it moved
farther into the forest ahead. Then, guilt and worry
came upon him. He ran to grab a flashlight and
spear and raced out to join Cacy. With Menehune
speed and agility, he covered the distance with ease.

When he reached the end of the lava field and
headed up the pathway leading into the forest, Zeke

thought he heard Cacy far ahead in the darkness. It sounded like her, but there were voices of two men as well coming from another direction. Making his way to the top of the rocks, he ran into the forest. Cacy's flashlight beam was seen in the distance, but it wavered and shook like a spinning spotlight pointing to the sky. Zeke's keen senses picked up the strange odor of human cigarettes and followed the scent. A loud bang, like a rifle shot, startled him and he dove to the ground. The frightening noise and echoes were followed by a scream and the sound of scuffling. Zeke stood up and ran. Far ahead, two red lights flashed on. The revving of a loud engine shook the quiet forest, and Zeke watched in horror as an adult male dragged Cacy out of a large net and threw her into his vehicle. The man then jumped into the vehicle, which sped off, smashing down small trees.

"Cacy!!" Zeke cried out as he tried to catch up with the vehicle. He leaped up into a tall tree above and sprinted through branches to get a good look. It was a big yellow vehicle and Cacy was in the backseat between two dogs. As he chased the vehicle, running and jumping from one tree to another, Zeke took aim with his spear for one of the tires. Leaping from a thick branch with a loud shout, he hurled the weapon, but it struck the driver's side door and only scraped it.

The Menehune found her sitting and crying under a nearby fern tree with her head in her hands. They stood at a distance and some of the children began to cry as well. Old Futt walked up to Kiara and placed his hands on her shoulders. She looked up with red watery eyes at the old leader. Hot tears flowed down her cheeks. Old Futt gave her a tender and caring expression as he presented the Digital Data Pad.

"Technology is good," he began, but it cannot be the answer for all our problems and needs. Cacy knew that and that's why she went on with the faith that she would still make it."

"But even if she hadn't been captured," Kiara said, taking off her glasses to wipe her face, "I doubt she would have reached Pu'uhonua o Hōnaunau on her own before sunrise."

"Perhaps. Perhaps not, Kiara," Old Futt said firmly. "But, she had faith and hope. Those who only put their trust in technology will often be disappointed. A person with faith and hope will never give up even when things don't go well."

"Old Futt, this is the first time I've ever felt helpless," Kiara admitted. "I always had the right answers to tests and exams. I don't know what to do now!"

"When you met Hi'iaka, what did you learn about yourself?" Old Futt inquired.

"Well, I was surprised when she mentioned that since Cacy and I are part Hawaiian, it saved us from instant death when we touched the ki'i," Kiara reflected. "I believe it also allowed us to receive the Language of the Land and speak Hawaiian."

"Just looking at you two, I'd never have thought that you are both part Hawaiian. It's said that the ancient Hawaiians received help in times of trouble from 'aumākua," Old Futt said. "They are guardian family spirits. Perhaps you have access to that as well."

"You mean like a guardian angel?" Kiara said with curiosity.

"In a way, yes," he said. "But, either way, you'll need to take a leap of faith and believe they actually exist. If not, you're just talking to air." Old Futt gave Kiara an encouraging look.

Kiara looked at her Digital Data Pad: It wasn't damaged at all. She clipped it back to her waist and knelt as if to pray. Folding her hands and bowing her head, she allowed her thoughts to clear and her heart to open up. Everyone got down on their knees as well and remained silent. Old Futt looked up at the hundreds of bright stars sparkling like diamonds in the sky. It brought back memories of old Lahaina nights. He then caught sight of a large shooting star. The star glowed with great luminosity and had a long tail. Beautiful, he thought.

The light fell closer to the horizon and grew in size. His eyes widened as he watched it change course and head directly toward the kīpuka. Others looked up and panicked, thinking that a meteor was about to strike the village. Just as the great glowing sphere reached the treetops, its form stretched out, taking the shape of wings. A powerful wind blew through the kīpuka, shaking trees and knocking off lanterns. Everyone covered their faces from the wind and blinding light above. The musical tree with the plastic bottles was playing wildly. Old Futt reached to grab Kiara away, but she remained in place with her head bowed in concentration.

The giant form of light began to peel away like an onion layer, revealing two round menacing eyes that burned like yellow beacons around black pupils. Some of the Menehune cowered in fear as the light touched the ground and slowly morphed into an immense solid form. They recognized it as a pueo, the native Hawaiian owl. Beams of light fanned out from the edges of her wingspan, which was as long as a school bus. Kiara opened her eyes and stood up as if awakened from a trance. The pueo's wings folded in and the glow faded. The bird of prey stood majestically at a height of nearly twenty feet. The owl's piercing eyes met Kiara's and looked deep into her changed heart and soul.

Kiara approached slowly without fear or trepidation and reached up to touch the brown and white plumage. The Menehune marveled in awe at the sight of the 'aumakua towering over the little girl. Old Futt nodded with an expression of proud satisfaction.

"'Aumakua," Kiara said, stretching out her arms and pressing her cheek against the warm feathers, "I BELIEVED that you would come to help me!"

Chapter 23

Kidnapped

"So tell us," Bishop said, lighting up a cigarette and blowing the smoke in Cacy's face, "where's the smart-looking girl? Did she fly off on another leaf and leave you behind?"

"I'm not telling!" Cacy yelled after coughing away the thick cloud. "You better let me go, or else!"

"Ooooooo!" Rook teased, looking over to his partner. "Sounds like she's a tough one!"

"Yeah, even you couldn't get her back in the tunnel," Bishop shot back.

Cacy tried to lean forward and make a move to open her door and jump out. But Bishop reached back and pressed his hand on Cacy's face, shoving her hard back into her seat. The backpack crushed into her back. The dogs clamped their teeth into the padded shoulder straps to restrain her. Using duct tape, Bishop bound Cacy's hands at the wrists. When the dogs released their hold and the men weren't looking, she continued to struggle but soon gave up trying to break free from the binding.

"Where are you taking me, and why do you want the ki'i so bad?" she asked.

The men didn't answer.

"The police and park rangers are looking for us," Cacy added as if to make them scared. "So you're trapped here in volcano park."

"We figured that out a long time ago, Cacy Dang," Rook replied as he took the Hummer over the uneven surface of lava rocks. The bumps jolted the dogs and made Cacy bounce in the seat like a bad carnival ride. The nighttime view out the windows revealed a vast wasteland of old lava flows and petrified trees. Off in the distance, Cacy could see the moonlit shine of the ocean miles away. They were heading toward the uninhabited coastline of the volcano park.

"How do you know my name?" she demanded.

"News is all over the radio about you and your friend Kiara," Bishop said as he pointed out facts and details that had also been mentioned in the TV report she'd seen back at the kīpuka. "You see, with missing children and a murder, we can't exit the park back at the entrance. We have to make other arrangements with our boss so we can leave here. She's the one who wants to see the ki'i and how you and Kiara control its power. Since we only got you, it'll have to do."

"But..." She stopped short of spilling the details of the cursed kiʻi and the mission to take it to Puʻuhonua o Hōnaunau. She thought of her cousin still asleep in the kīpuka and about how she'd never awake and would probably be dead by morning now that Cacy was kidnapped. Cacy did her best to avoid crying and began to look around for anything in the Hummer she could use to try to cut apart the duct tape around her wrists. Nothing. The cigarette smoke was filling the back of the Hummer, and Cacy politely asked if they would open the windows, thinking that she could make a dive out of the car. Back in school, Cacy learned that asking for things politely, especially with teachers, really helped. (At least it worked whenever she needed to go use the bathroom during class.) Bishop ignored her request at first, but since she sounded less aggressive now, he rolled the front windows down and allowed her windows to open just a small crack. It wasn't what Cacy had been hoping for, but the fresh night air blowing in felt good.

"Thank you," Cacy said, adding to the polite routine. She remained alert for any opportunity to escape.

The view outside the Hummer showed coconut palms. It was a sign that they were now close to the coastline. Does their boss live on the beach?

Cacy wondered. Then, a most bizarre sight caught her attention. Bishop noticed it and told Rook to check outside his window. Rook slowed down to take a better look and even he was amazed at the sight.

"Crikey!" He exclaimed. "This is like a modern day city of Pompeii."

Several yards outside the Hummer was a traffic stop sign. Instead of being high on top of a pole, the red octagonal sign was only half exposed above the surface of the lava flow. As they looked beyond the park, they saw the charred rooftops of homes that had been drowned by a flood of rushing lava. Rook spotted an old burnt car half submerged in the rocks. Cacy's heart broke as she reflected on the videos she had seen earlier of homes bursting in flames as molten lava wrapped around them. She thought of Pele destroying every living thing in the park tomorrow. Just as in the old tale of the greedy King Midas who turned everything into gold just by touching it, lava ignited and destroyed anything in its grasp.

"The lava flow must have been at least ten feet high in some spots," Bishop said, peering at the exposed remains of the old town. The Hummer hit the charred skeletal frame of a house, and it collapsed into black powder and sticks.

"It's gonna happen again tomorrow!" Cacy blurted out. "Pele is going to destroy the whole volcano park because the ki'i was taken!"

The men turned around to look at Cacy. Even the dogs gave a quizzical expression. Both Rook and Bishop began giggling and guffawing in her face.

Rook turned back to driving over the rugged terrain with a teasing chuckle. "Aw, there, there, no worries, child. Tomorrow we'll all be long gone from this island."

Chapter 24

The Lava Flows of the Fire Goddess

None of the Menehune felt brave enough to come up and touch the giant pueo 'aumakua. The hard stare of her large golden eyes was too intense and penetrating.

"Dearest Kiara, my time here is short." The owl spoke with a gentle but direct voice. "If we are to find your cousin, we must leave now. Say your good-byes and let us be on our way."

Kiara was looking at a large foldout map of Hawai'i Volcanoes National Park and the Island of Hawai'i. Old Futt pointed out the secret location of the kīpuka so they had a starting point.

"Yes, I'm ready to go, 'Aumakua Pueo!" Kiara answered as she folded the map back up. "Old Futt, I didn't think we were always that close to Thurston Lava Tube! It seemed like Cacy and I traveled much farther to come here."

"Well, now you know the secret location and you can also see the shortcuts we use to go anywhere in the park." Old Futt winked. "You'd better go now. Remember what I shared. There's always hope. Ke Akua be with you."

Old Futt reached up and Kiara bent down to hug him. Zeke, Mali, Obah, and many of the other Menehune lined up to embrace Kiara as well. They were all used to adult scientists and park rangers as guests in the kīpuka. Cacy and Kiara were now special friends. Plus, they all knew that the future of the park depended on the two girls finding each other and making it to the Place of Refuge, Puʻuhonua o Hōnaunau, before sunrise.

The Menehune watched and waved to Kiara as she climbed upon the back of her ʻaumakua. Clinging to the shoulders of the pueo, Kiara straightened herself up and looked over to everyone.

"Thank you for everything!" She smiled. "I'll always remember you!"

The mighty pueo lifted her chest and expanded her wings, heading toward the stars. With a mighty flap, strong gusts of wind blew down on the Menehune. They quickly moved back as the winds kicked up and the pueo lifted into the air and spiraled upward. Kiara held on tightly but managed to turn and wave down to everyone below, who were waving and cheering back. Old Futt and the rest of the Menehune watched their friend and the pueo zoom high above the treetops and silhouette the full moon. In seconds, the pueo 'aumakua and Kiara were out of view.

Soaring over the forest was exhilarating to Kiara, and the wind whipped through her hair. She looked down without fear at the moonlit land below. Together, they glided over rugged craters, sleeping rain forests, and smoking vents of underground lava flows. They circled the common areas of the park, like the Volcano House and the Thurston Lava Tube. Blue lights of police cars and flashlights from search parties moved about far below. It disappointed her that she couldn't land and ask for help. This was a task that had to be done on her own, and she wasn't going to give up.

The owl's night vision was sharp and she scanned the land for the yellow vehicle Kiara described. Flying high over the length of the Chain of Craters Road, Kiara could see the distant orange glow from the fires of lava flows. It was the first time she had seen real lava, and she thought of all the scientific readings she had looked forward to doing on the field trip. The flows oozed like hot blood pumping from cuts in the solid body of the land.

The pueo ʻaumakua spoke loudly over the roaring winds. "Kiara, I don't see the vehicle down there! Shall we try searching another area?"

It was disappointing news to her since they had covered most of what she had studied on the map of the volcano park. Her worst fear was that the Hummer managed to leave the park. If so, they could be anywhere on Hawaiʻi Island. She remembered what Old Futt had said and it gave her the will to keep searching within the volcano park.

"Yes!" she called back out over the blowing winds. "We have to keep trying!"

Miles away they saw the eerie but beautiful smoke rising from Puʻu ʻŌʻō, a vent on Kīlauea's east rift zone. Tonight, the famous cinder-and-spatter cone was erupting wildly, sending bright rushing lava flows all the way down to the ocean miles away. Its fountains of fire gushed over a thousand feet high. The collapse in the west flank of the cinder cone allowed lava to run its steady course. Kiara wanted to take a closer look, but the thought of Pele burning the whole volcano park tomorrow made her too afraid to even go near the vent. Then, Kiara had an idea. At first she quickly dismissed it as foolhardy, but she realized that time was running out and that she had little choice. She decided to seek Pele and told the owl to fly to the volcano.

"Pele?! You really want to go see Pele?!" asked her 'aumakua with sound of apprehension.

"Maybe I can ask her not to destroy the park or give us more time," Kiara said speculatively. "And if she's really as powerful as they say, maybe she can help us find Cacy."

The owl made a sweeping turn and headed toward the active volcano vent. Even at night, the glowing lava and the billowing gas clouds of sulfur dioxide created a bright orange and violet glow like the sky at sunset. The molten lava against the black surface of land was both beautiful and frightening at the same time. As they flew closer to Pu'u 'Ō'ō, the frigid night air quickly turned hot and thick. The crackling sound of the raging rivers of lava below grew louder as they headed upstream. Slower flows cooled into black skin and ripped apart as they moved along. Bright, viscous channels of yellow and orange lava intertwined and branched apart like arteries carrying the hot lifeblood of the Fire Goddess. The rising heat began penetrating Kiara's uniform and toasting her skin. The owl veered away from the scorching torrents of lava below and took a course over solid land. They came to the blazing mouth of the vent and circled the spewing cauldron from a safe distance. The lake of rising magma within exploded and splashed violently, looking like the center of an endless fireworks show.

Not knowing how to meet the Fire Goddess, Kiara braced herself upon the back of the owl and with a loud but respectful shout, she called out, "Hello, Goddess Pele! Hello! May we please talk to you? I need your help!!" Kiara felt a little embarrassed addressing someone she could not see, but she wouldn't dare land without asking the Fire Goddess's permission first.

As they continued to circle the vent, the eruption reached a high point, sending a gusher of molten lava that looked like it could reach the stars. The rumble of the fires rose to the level of cannon explosions, sending shock waves through the air. Kiara hid her face and covered her ears as the owl broke off and veered farther back to avoid burning her feathers from the flying spatter. Kiara peered over the head of the owl and squinted, trying to look into the bright orange eruption. Two huge eyes appeared in the inferno and smoke. They were blazing red and stared hard at Kiara and the 'aumakua. Even as they circled the vent, the eyes followed them without blinking. Out of sheer fright of the staring eyes, Kiara buried her face in the owl's back. A loud female voice boomed from within the fire.

"Do not look away!" the voice commanded. "I will reveal my face to you. If you are of pure heart and

intentions, you will live. If not, the flames will burn you up!"

I'm more terrified than pure of heart! Kiara thought as she wrapped her arms tighter around the owl's neck. She dared not look away, and she fearfully looked back at the red eyes within the eruption. Slowly a face appeared in the flames. It was beautiful, young, strong, and Hawaiian in appearance. For a moment, the face looked like Hi'iaka, but the Fire Goddess appeared slightly older and far less expressive.

"Welcome," Pele said with satisfaction but no hint of a smile. "Land on the other side of where the collapse is. I will meet you there."

A sigh of relief left both the owl and Kiara. They flew to the side they were directed to and landed safely. The air was still warm, but they were far away from the flows and the night breeze was a welcome relief. Standing high at the top of the cone's rim, with her back to the violent eruption, was Pele. Splashing lava showered over her silhouette but the flaring droplets harmlessly slid down her deep brown skin and clothing. She looked down at the two and did not take her eyes of them as she descended the jagged slope barefoot. Beneath her feet were the orange glows of fire that singed and branded the rocks with her footprints. Kiara remembered feeling

indignant when she had first met Hi'iaka in the rain forest. This time, however, she immediately felt Pele's power. Standing in her realm and in her presence compelled a feeling of fear and respect. Kiara felt her legs getting weak. The 'aumakua pressed her body against Kiara's arm to give her courage. Despite the heat, her palms were cold from nervousness as Pele approached.

Up close, the Fire Goddess still looked a lot like her younger sister, Hi'iaka, but the differences were more obvious. Pele, too, wore a head lei, but the leaves fanned out and curled like flames. Her hair had the shine and texture of strands of curling pāhoehoe. Orange and yellow light eerily flashed and glowed between her long black coils of hair. A bright red tapa cloth wrapped her body and an orange kihei was draped around her shoulder and waist. Around her wrists and ankles she wore fresh green maile leaves that did not burn. But her eyes, they were the most beautiful and startling feature. Pele had light brown eyes but they twinkled with a red gleam. She stood taller and stronger than her younger sister and exuded the prowess of a lion.

Both Kiara and her 'aumakua bowed like they were in the presence of royalty. This greatly impressed Pele, and she nodded her head in approval. Upon rising, Kiara wanted to start telling Pele all about the events of the day in order to explain her request for help. Yet she realized that this would be too long, and perhaps disrespectful. She recalled stories about Pele and how many people made offerings, such as food, to appease her. Kiara didn't have any big or significant offering, and the silence was unnerving. Pele kept waiting, her unblinking stare on Kiara.

With a slight feeling of embarrassment, Kiara reached into her vest pocket and pulled out a package of candy she remembered buying from the gift shop in the Volcano House. It was a small bag of her favorite snack, rock candy. Throughout all the excitement of the day, she never even opened the bag. Sheepishly, she offered it to the great Fire Goddess, who looked at the bag and took it. Any moment, Kiara worried, Pele would snap her fingers and a ball of flame would fall down and destroy her and the ‘aumakua for such an inferior offering. Instead, Pele opened the bag and poured candy into her hand. To Kiara's surprise, the Fire Goddess broke into a huge smile and hearty laugh.

"Rock candy?!" she said with a glow. "I love to eat this!!!"

Chapter 25

Digital Upgrade

Pele crunched down on a mouthful of the sugary rock candy and chewed it easily. Kiara gritted her teeth with a squirmy feeling seeing Pele munching it down instead of just letting it dissolve slowly. The Fire Goddess poured another handful out and then gave the rest of the bag back to Kiara.

"Here. I'll feel guilty if I eat a whole bag," Pele said with a slight laugh.

Kiara took the bag and stuffed it back into her vest pocket. She wasn't feeling afraid anymore, and the Fire Goddess now seemed more real as a person, sort of like a health-conscious deity.

"I remember when Old George at the Volcano House used to toss gin and 'ōhelo berries to me in Halemaumau Crater," Pele remarked as she ground the second handful of rock candy between her teeth.

"Who?" Kiara asked.

"It's a long story," Pele replied after gulping. "You came here to tell me yours."

A soft nudge by the owl 'aumakua prodded Kiara to get back to the matter at hand. She folded her hands and slowly stepped closer with a humble and beseeching pose. Kiara began by introducing herself and sharing about being on a school field trip joined by her cousin's school. As Kiara recounted the events of the day, Pele continued to listen intently. Her eyes still did not blink but they showed much emotion whenever Kiara brought up Hi'iaka. When finished, Kiara exhaled a deep, tired breath as if she had completed giving a first-place-level history speech.

Pele looked down at Kiara's Digital Data Pad. "So, is that what you used to stun the dogs chasing you and your cousin on the ti leaf?"

The nonchalant and unrelated question took Kiara off guard. Isn't Pele going to offer to help find Cacy or hold back the destruction of the volcano park? she thought. Does she even care? Then she realized that Pele was showing the same unemotional and stoic attitude that she herself showed others, especially Cacy. Kiara lowered her face in disappointment, catching a glimpse of her Digital Data Pad. Again, useless.

"Let me see that, Kiara," Pele said, pointing to Kiara's invention.

Kiara unhooked it from her waist and gave it to Pele. Both Kiara and her 'aumakua looked at each other but said nothing.

"Crude, but very, very impressive," Pele said, examining the device and switching it on as if she knew exactly how to operate it. "Ahh, you should have seen all the expensive geo-electrical equipment I've burned up through the years since volcanologists began researching my home." Pele typed through all the data files and noticed that there was hardly anything collected.

"I was looking forward to collecting my own scientific data on lava, gases, and geological conditions," Kiara admitted. There was no longer any enthusiasm in her voice.

"Yes, it's a shame you never got to really use it...until now," the Fire Goddess said with a red glow in her eyes.

Kiara stepped back in fear but watched in awe as Pele held up the Digital Data Pad with her left hand and waved her right hand across it. The eruption of Pu'u 'Ō'ō rose to a crescendo, causing the ground to shake. The 'aumakua and Kiara lost their balance and almost fell down. Pele's eyes glowed brighter and orange flames fanned out between her locks of hair. Kiara was ready to leap on her 'aumakua's back so they could fly off to safety, but she stayed with eyes affixed on Pele as electrical blasts shot from her right hand and into the Digital Data Pad. All the lights on the device flashed into changing colors, and it beeped and buzzed wildly. Electrical currents continued to surge into the device and just as Kiara thought it was about to explode, Pele stopped her action and the ground ceased its shaking.

"Here you go," Pele said calmly as she handed the Digital Data Pad back to Kiara. "Now you have all the readings and data you could ever want. Some scientists spend years just to get even half the information in this."

"Th-th-thank you," Kiara replied nervously as she tapped the device with her fingertips before taking it back, for fear of getting electrocuted. Pele gave a loud laugh.

"You are more than welcome." She smiled. "I've given it a digital upgrade and installed a few extras, which you'll need to fight those two men."

"What?!" Kiara said with surprise, looking down at the device.

"Key in 5-6-0 on the number pad, then press the red button," Pele instructed.

Kiara did and, with a loud whip-crack, a huge arc of yellow and orange electric currents shot out from the antenna of the device. The kickback felt like a garden hose at full blast when the trigger nozzle is squeezed. She watched the wild stream of electricity hit a large nearby boulder and wrap it in a static web of lightning streaks. The boulder flew back and rolled several feet before coming to a stop.

"Incredible!" Kiara declared, taking her finger off the red button.

"Remember," Pele said sternly, "use that only for an emergency. Now, I suppose you want me to help locate your cousin."

"Yes! Can you?" Kiara replied with renewed determination.

Pele knelt down, placing her palm on the ground and motioning for Kiara to do the same. Kiara felt the warm layer of lava rocks and the pulsating flow of magma.

"Pele...I mean Goddess Pele, what are we doing?" Kiara asked.

"Shh," Pele whispered. "Listen to the land with your heart. I can feel what goes on in this park and the theft of the ki'i put me in my angry mood tonight. Close your eyes and you'll see with your heart."

Kiara closed her eyes and continued to feel just the warmth of the rocks. Soon the image of the Hummer flashed in her mind. She then saw Cacy sitting in the back seat with her wrists taped up. The Hummer traveled passed remains of burnt houses and dried lava flows over a ghost town.

"I see it, too, Kiara," Pele said as she locked in on the vision. "Kalapana!"

"Kalapana?!" shouted Kiara as she opened her eyes and stood up, straightening out her skirt.

"It's a village my lava flow destroyed in 1990." Pele explained. "Don't worry. No one was killed or hurt. It was a slow flow that filled a bay and consumed a black sand beach. The whole area is now off-limits to everyone. Those men must be taking that route to avoid capture leaving the park. Now go! Once they reach the ocean it will be too late. Even I can't do anything once they are off land."

Kiara shot off like a sheriff about to leap on his horse and ride off to the rescue. But the ʻaumakua refused to lower herself to allow Kiara to mount.

"Child!" The owl spoke sternly. "Haven't you forgotten something?"

"Oh, you're right, ʻAumakua Pueo!" she admitted and turned back to speak to Pele. Again she folded her hands and took a pleading tone.

"Goddess Pele," she began, "thank you. If I may please ask, spare the park and don't destroy it even if we can't get the kiʻi to Puʻuhonua o Hōnaunau by sunrise."

Pele was moved by the selfless request. For a moment, even the surging lava flows nearby slowed abruptly. Then, Pele walked closer to Kiara until they stood face-to-face, and for the first time, Pele blinked her eyes.

"I would never destroy the entire park as that sister of mine claimed!"

"You mean…"

"Yes," Pele interrupted, "she made that up. She's always been making me look like the bad girl or even getting jealous of me. Once, she even stole from me someone I was in love with. It's a long-ago legend, and it's been a while since I've talked to her. I still love her, though, and I continue to give her new land to build her forests on."

The news was amazing, and a relief to Kiara. "My cousin is so worried about the park being destroyed," she shared. "I can't understand why Hiʻiaka would tell us you would do that as part of the curse."

"Maybe my sister really does believe I'll destroy the park, since she thinks I'm sore at her," Pele wondered. "I did smolder one of her rain forests recently when Puʻu ʻŌʻō stopped after I sent a series of small earthquakes through the park and a new channel of lava opened up…Anyway, the park is safe, but the curse of the kiʻi is still on you and your cousin. The two of you must still take it to Puʻuhonua o Hōnaunau before the sunrise in order to live!"

"Goddess Pele," Kiara said, placing one hand on her upgraded Digital Data Pad and extending her other one. "Thank you. I wish I could repay you for your help."

Pele shook Kiara's hand warmly, admiring her bravery and respect. Most humans she appeared to in the park were too afraid to touch her because they thought they would catch on fire.

"There is one small favor to ask," the Fire Goddess said, arching an eyebrow.

"What?" Kiara inquired.

"I know you don't have them on you, but I'd like to have one of my sister's magic ti leaves as gift," Pele said. "Will you leave one for me?"

Kiara didn't know why Pele wanted a ti leaf, but she promised to do so. If she were to keep that promise, Kiara knew that it first meant finding her cousin. Kiara mounted her 'aumakua and waved farewell to Pele. The Fire Goddess watched the giant owl and the little girl zoom up into the air and circle the eruption one last time. With a tip of the wing, they flew off toward the old village of Kalapana. Pele headed back to the rim of the eruption. Reaching the top, about to step back into the gusher of lava, she paused.

"I think she might need my help," Pele said to herself.

The Fire Goddess walked along the flaming rim to the mouth of the flow and picked up a long, thick sheet of rock. She rubbed the edges and melted it down smooth to form the sheet into a long board. Taking it into the flowing lava, Pele dove atop her magic long board and surfed down the molten rapids toward the coastline.

Chapter 26

The Hitchhiker

"Is that brat done yet?" Rook yelled out of the driver's side window. He honked the Hummer's horn loudly to emphasize his annoyance and impatience.

"Quiet!" Bishop yelled, standing by an old brick wall of a burned-down house. "Someone might hear us!"

"Mate, we're the only ones out here for miles!" hollered back his partner.

"Are you finished yet?" Bishop called over the wall.

"Yeah," Cacy said as she buckled her belt. "It's hard to pee with your two dogs watching me. Are you gonna tape my hands again now?"

"Just sit quietly in the back for the rest of the time and you'll be fine." Bishop flicked away the end of his cigarette. The dogs continued to guard their little prisoner as she walked back to the Hummer. Bishop followed behind and was the last to get back in. Rook looked over to Cacy and noticed that her wrists were not taped up again. Bishop gave his partner a reassuring look that it was okay.

Cacy remained silent along the ride but kept looking at her watch. It was almost midnight. She felt disgusted that she couldn't use the bathroom excuse to make an escape anymore. As she stared outside her window, she tried to brainstorm other distractions to cause.

"What the...?!" Rook yelled as he hit the brakes. Both men were thrust forward and Cacy nearly fell on top of the coffee holders between the front seats before slumping back into the rear.

The three of them looked out the window and saw the phantom figure standing before the headlights of the Hummer. Rook was ready to step on the gas pedal and swerve around the figure, but it held out its long bony hands, signaling the vehicle to halt. Bishop reached behind and grabbed Cacy by the collar, then threw her down to the floor.

"Get down and don't say anything," he ordered, "or you'll never get back up!"

The mysterious figure on the road floated toward the passenger window. It was dressed in a flowing white robe that reflected the moonlight. Long white matted hair covered the figure's face and shoulders. Bishop reached for the pistol in the glove compartment and rolled down his window. Already the figure was standing on the other side.

"Oh, boys," spoke the figure in an old, raspy, female voice. "Can you please give tūtū a ride?" The old crone's wrinkled and bony fingers stroked Bishop's door. He cringed back in his seat with a sudden chill up his spine. The pistol dropped to the floor.

"Old lady," barked Rook, "what are you doing out here all by yourself at night?"

The old hitchhiker peeled away the dried hair blocking her face, which was still hidden in shadow. Her exposed features were covered in deep creases and wrinkles. She had no lips, just cracked leathery skin pulled over her gums. Her mouth line stretched from ear to ear over hollow cheeks in a freakish smile.

"Oh, tūtū went walking and tūtū got lost. Can you take tūtū home?" cackled the old hitchhiker. She gave a disturbing giggle and reached inside the vehicle, attempting to unlock the rear door. As her hair moved out of the way and exposed her profile, both men caught a glance of the hitchhiker's face. She had no nose and empty eye sockets like a bare skull.

"Sorry, lady!!" Rook yelled out as he stomped on the gas pedal and left the old woman twirling in a

cloud of dust. Bishop gave a nervous sigh of relief and lit another cigarette.

"What the hell was all that back there?" Bishop said letting out a puff of relaxation.

"How do I know?!" Rook said, wiping sweat off his brow. "She even gave me the spooks."

Cacy was still hunched over on the floor of the Hummer when both men suddenly let out a horrible scream. She covered her ears and chose not to get up as she listened to the two men yelling.

"Put your window back up!!!"

"Oh my God!"

"Hold on!"

"Faster!!"

"Oh my God! She's still outside your window!"

"No way!"

"She's still outside the window!"

"Go! Go! Don't stop! Keep Driving!"

"Don't look at her!!"

"Faster! She's holding the door handle!!"

Cacy heard the sound of banging and scraping outside the windows. The Hummer swerved and accelerated several times before it finally decreased speed. She couldn't take being bounced around anymore and slowly rose back to her seat. Rook continued to drive and Bishop stared forward blankly.

"What happened?" Cacy asked quietly.

Bishop turned around slowly. His skin was white and his eyes wide with both fear and terror. For a moment, Cacy worried that he was about to hurt her for speaking up, but he turned back in his seat and said nothing.

"I can't wait to get off this island," Rook murmured as his fingers trembled while steering.

Cacy looked out of the left window. The men were oblivious to it, but she noticed a large rock wall about four feet high. In the moonlight it appeared that the wall was part of a rectangular structure nearly the size of a basketball court. It was an ancient heiau site dedicated to Pele. Decades ago, her lava flows consumed the surrounding homes but left her temple untouched. The barren landscape was full of high slopes made from old lava flows as well as earth cracks and crevices formed over time.

"Look!" Bishop yelled, pointing. "There's a girl up ahead!"

Far off in the distance stood a little girl dressed in blue and white.

"Kiara!" Cacy screamed from her seat.

Chapter 27

Standing in the Headlights

"**B**limey!" Rook cheered with a grin. "She's all by herself! Looks like we'll get the second girl after all." Instead of driving up to her, Rook stopped the Hummer just short of twenty yards away, in case there were law enforcement officials hiding behind nearby boulders.

Bishop turned on the interior light so that Kiara could see clearly inside the Hummer and that they had her cousin. Cacy made a quick slide to the door to get out, but the dogs bit right into her backpack and held her firmly in place. Hot breath and saliva brushed her ears.

"One more stupid move like that and I'll have them snap your head off!" Bishop yelled in Cacy's face. He got out of the Hummer and hid his tranquilizer-dart pistol at his side. Rook reached under his seat for his handgun in case any police officers showed themselves.

Kiara remained motionless, standing directly in

the high beams of the headlights. She didn't even unhook her Digital Data Pad.

"Release my cousin along with the ki'i." she called out. "You can go on your own way afterward!"

"Bishop," Rook whispered, "You're too far for a good shot with the darts. Stall her."

As Bishop called out threats to Kiara to give up, Rook turned off the interior light and stepped out of the Hummer. Leaving his door open, he unlocked the rear door and reached for Gladius, who was on the left of Cacy. The dog silently jumped over the rear seat and out of the vehicle. Falchion bit harder into his piece of shoulder strap and growled as if to warn Cacy not to scream out to Kiara. Her heart pounded with anger and worry.

"Last chance, little girl!" Bishop sang sarcastically. "Come on over and give yourself up. You can't run away!"

"No!" Kiara shouted defiantly.

Is Kiara crazy, Cacy wondered. How did she get here all by herself and find the Hummer? It was too hard for Cacy to figure out an answer. Bishop gave an evil grin to his partner. Rook returned the same look. With that, he let go of Gladius, who took off at top speed toward Kiara, barking loudly. Cacy let out a scream, calling her cousin to run. Kiara did not run but stood in place. The two men watched as the dog broke his sprint and leaped into the air to bring down his target with his powerful jaws. Kiara did not even blink but raised her arm in front of her chest to block the attack. Gladius snapped his razor-sharp teeth into Kiara's skinny forearm with the force to knock her backward. For a moment, it seemed like the dog had frozen in midair as Kiara kept her footing. Instead, Rook, Bishop, Cacy, and Falchion watched in shock as Gladius burst into flames with his teeth still locked on Kiara's forearm. She shook the burning dog with her forearm as it screamed in horrific pain. The smell of burning flesh and the dreadful shrieks pushed the men back in fear. Then, Kiara gave one last shake of her arm and the charred, smoldering carcass of Gladius plopped to the ground. His eyes and muzzle were burnt off. Black smoke pumped out from inside the exposed bones of his jaws and eye sockets. Kiara's bite wounds were deep and bright orange in the headlights.

"What in the bloody world...?" Rook quaked, trying to stay calm. Bishop and Cacy remained speechless and just stared blankly at the gruesome sight. Falchion gave off a loud whine and leaped over Cacy's seat and out of the Hummer. Before anyone could stop the him, Falchion ran off into the night, whimpering in fear. Anger quickly consumed Rook.

He raised up a shiny .500 model Smith & Wesson magnum. It was known as the most powerful handgun in the world and had enough power to stop and kill a grizzly bear. Cacy screamed again as she watched Rook position his arms on the door of the Hummer. Bishop dove into the Hummer to restrain Cacy and prevent her escape. With a boom that nearly made Cacy's ears pop, Rook fired the magnum, striking Kiara in the belly. She clutched her stomach and bent over bleeding, but in a few seconds, stood back up. Her unblinking eyes glowed bright red.

"What are you?!!" Rook demanded, trying to hold the magnum in his shaking hands. "You're not that girl! You're not even human!"

"I'm a goddess," Kiara answered back proudly. "You're trespassing."

Kiara's face and body changed before their eyes. In a burst of flames, the image of Kiara morphed into Pele the Fire Goddess. Cacy cheered now, knowing that it wasn't actually Kiara, but quickly grew fearful that Pele herself was here and about to destroy everything earlier than believed. Rook wasted no time trying to comprehend this supernatural encounter and quickly fired off the remaining four bullets in the magnum. Each shot echoed loudly in the night air. Three bullets struck Pele. Each time,

she hunched over in pain and spat on the ground. Her saliva sizzled a hole in the lava rock. She rose up straight and snarled in a rage. Her locks of hair waved out with a burst of orange flames between them.

Both Rook and Bishop dropped their guns and staggered toward the back of the Hummer. Pele's eyes were glowing hot as she stared down the two men. She raised her right hand with her palm up. Sparks formed and danced from the center of her hand. They collected and grew into a glowing ball covered by blue flames. The fireball, about six inches in diameter, changed to yellow and orange and floated above her hand. The flames reached several feet into the air with embers blowing in the wind. The Fire Goddess whipped her fireball directly at the Hummer. Cacy watched it zoom straight at the Hummer as the men dashed to the ground for cover. The fireball smashed into the front engine, sending the Hummer skidding several feet backward and causing it to rise on its rear wheels. Cacy was thrown back hard and nearly went into the rear cabin where the dogs had stayed. The bat handle protruding from her backpack hit her on the head and she fell to the floor, dizzy.

"Let's get out of here!" Rook shouted over to his partner.

"Get the girl, we need the ki'i!" shouted Bishop as he braved the flames engulfing the front of the Hummer to retrieve his cigarettes and the satellite phone to call the Queen.

Rook dove into the backseat to grab Cacy, but she kept kicking at his hands. She was stuck on the floor with her backpack wedged between the front and rear seats. She kicked and screamed till she saw Rook turn upside down and fall out of sight. A second fireball had struck the Hummer and made it flip over and land on its rooftop. Bishop and Rook would've gotten thrown with the vehicle if they still had their arms inside it. On impact, all the doors slammed shut and the locks broke. Cacy was now sprawled on the ceiling and felt the crunching of the metal body of the car as it began to collapse down on its own weight. For now, the glass still remained intact on all four sides of the Hummer, and Cacy saw clumps of burning lava falling outside the vehicle as the disgusting smell of burning tires filled the air. The fireballs turned into pure molten lava upon impact. Both Bishop and Rook ran off downhill toward the coastline. As Pele in her blind rage threw more and more fireballs, she forgot that Cacy was still in the Hummer.

Pele watched the men running away. Her rage escalated and the ground began to shake.

Surrounding rocks began to split open and the ground began to rise like a bubble. Smoke rose from under Pele and a ring of fire ignited around her.

Thinking they were at a safe distance, Rook and Bishop stopped to catch their breath and look back at Pele. They saw the Hummer on fire and upside down. Any second it would explode from a combination of fuel mixed with the ammunition left inside. They saw Cacy still trapped, and she still had that cursed ki'i! Molten lava was breaking through the hard crusts of the black rocks and creeping down a high slope toward the Hummer at the bottom. Already pockets of bubbling lava were spewing up from underground wherever fireballs landed.

"Whoa! Look out!!" Bishop suddenly yelled.

Looking straight up, they saw a fireball coming down at them. They dove in separate directions, both landing on jagged rocks and cutting their hands and foreheads. The fireball slammed the ground with a shake and burst into sprays of lava. A small drop of the molten shrapnel hit Rook on the back of his thigh and it burned through his pants and seared his skin like a branding iron on cattle.

"Ugghhhhh!!" he shouted as he jumped up and patted his burn to try and cool it off. Far off in the distance they heard the dreadful laugh of the Fire Goddess.

As the men hurried away into the night, the Fire Goddess began to form another fireball until she heard the voice of a little girl screaming for help. Pele's eyes stopped glowing and she waved away the flames in her hand. Again, the voice cried for help. Her blind rage stopped.

"Oh, no!" Pele said to herself. "I forgot about the girl!!"

Cacy wiggled around and managed to draw out her bat. Like a battering ram, she banged it on the window until it cracked into a web and then shattered. Smoke filled the interior of the vehicle and she continued to cough even when she managed to get her head out. She placed her arms on the upside down door and pulled her way out on her back to avoid the broken glass on the ground. Looking up, she saw the flames blanketing the vehicle and quickly crawled away. When she stood up, she saw no escape. She was surrounded by walls of flames and pockets of spreading lava flows. It's real lava, Cacy thought, and this is not the way I wanted to see it.

Pele watched from a distance but was helpless to make the fires and lava flows stop; they now had to run their natural course. She placed her hands over her mouth and felt awful that in her rage against the men she forgot the very person she had wanted to help.

"Run to the other side of the vehicle!" Pele called out. Already, thick, viscous lava had spread between her and Cacy. Even if Pele could've stopped the flows and let it cool to a hard skin, the heat was still hot enough to burn Cacy alive. "Run to the other side!" she called again.

Cacy heard it over the roaring flames and the crackling of the lava. The fumes and heat made her dizzy again and penetrated her clothing. She staggered around the burning Hummer and saw a row of tall boulders that stood high above the wide flow of the lava oozing downhill toward her. She climbed up the closest boulder. Small chunks of rocks that looked like burning coals were rolling steadily down the slope. When they struck the boulder, sparks and glowing embers rose up to Cacy. The lava flow on the slope was moving closer, like a thick slow-moving flood. It's only cake batter, it's only cake batter, Cacy told herself to stay calm.

"It's like baking in an oven here!" she yelled in disgust.

As she prepared to jump to the next boulder, the Hummer blew up in a large mushroom cloud several feet behind her. The force threw her over the burning rocks below and onto the next highest boulder. She covered her face down on the warm boulder at the sounds of bullets exploding and whizzing over her head like fireworks. Pele clenched her fists in joy seeing that the girl had landed safely. Cacy gave a short sigh of relief and slowly stood up, careful not to lose her balance. She was six feet above the ground and the boulder was about ten feet wide across. Lava slowly wrapped the boulder and the rising heat was making it hard to breath. For a moment, a thin black crust formed over the passing flow. The skin expanded like a balloon and popped apart, spilling more fresh lava higher around the boulder. The rubber bottom of her shoes began to get hot and soften. The burning wreckage of the Hummer was slowly being eaten up by the lava flow that had already gone through the inside. Metal body parts twisted and vaporized as easily as a Styrofoam cup dropped on a campfire. It's hot, but at least I'm safe on this boulder, she thought.

Cacy looked over to the Fire Goddess and saw that she had a sorrowful look. She recalled what a park ranger had said earlier: "Pele's lava destroys, but creates new land at the same time." Cacy believed that Pele's expression and appearance to help meant that she had not wanted things to happen this way. Perhaps, Cacy hoped, Pele would spare the park now because of this. The Fire Goddess's expression changed to shock and fear when she glanced at the top of the slope.

The overlapping flows of lava had loosened other large boulders higher up on the slope. They began to tumble downward, splashing into the orange flow and covering themselves with molten layers. Cacy followed Pele's eyes and saw two lava-coated boulders slowly coming straight at her. She looked all around her and saw nowhere safe left to jump to. She hoped that the boulders might change course and miss the one she was standing on, but closer and closer they came, sometimes pausing, and sometimes skimming the surface of the lava flow. It was a slow wait for death. Pele attempted to wade through all the lava to get to Cacy, but she only made it burn and run even hotter. All she could do was watch Cacy suffering from the heat of the lava surrounding her as the two boulders tumbled down the slope. They were now glowing red-hot and bubbling on the surface.

Pele looked down in despair and placed her hands over her face. She remembered all the humans and deities she had innocently hurt throughout the ages because of her anger. Though she was still well revered and worshipped, she knew that her vengeful wrath was oftentimes more powerful than her fires themselves. She looked back up, and through her fiery tears, she saw the real Kiara circling high above on a giant pueo.

Chapter 28

Never Alone

"Look! It's another eruption!" Kiara said, looking down at the area of erratic lava flows. The sight below looked like the aftermath of a fierce battle. "I see someone in that ring of fire! Is it Cacy?"

"It's Pele!" The owl 'aumakua could see better with her sharp eyesight. "She's pointing to the flows coming down that slope."

The pueo took a sharp turn downward, and Kiara spotted her cousin standing on a boulder surrounded by molten lava. Cacy was too busy watching the two boulders coming closer to see her cousin above her.

"CACY!!!!" Kiara cried out.

Cacy was squatting down and gasping for air when she thought she heard Kiara's voice.

"CACY!!!" Kiara called again. This time, Cacy looked up and saw a giant owl high overhead.

"I must be seeing things," Cacy said to herself. As she followed the sight of the owl circling above, her balance gave out and she slumped over on her side.

The sudden slip made her reflexes awaken, and she stopped herself from sliding into the lava below her. Shaking away her dizziness, she saw Kiara on top of the owl waving to her.

"Kiara!! Kiara!!" Cacy called back as she stood up and waved her arms like a swimmer calling for help.

"We can't land, Kiara!" the 'aumakua said, turning her head toward the girl.

"Can you scoop her up in your claws?" Kiara asked.

"My talons are too big and sharp. They'll kill her if I try to grab her," the 'aumakua said with regret.

Pele watched as the owl made a low, sweeping circle and extended her claws, then zoomed back up away from the heat. She knew what Kiara and the owl were hoping to do, and it was useless.

"Yes, it might work," Pele said to herself with renewed hope. "Cacy!! Hold out your wooden stick over your head!!"

Cacy heard the Fire Goddess over the raging flames and drew out her bat. She grasped the center with her hands and raised it high. Kiara saw her cousin position herself, and she and the 'aumakua knew that it meant a one-shot attempt in a deep swoop.

"Hold on!" The 'aumakua said as she soared higher to get into her bird-of-prey mode of attack. "We have only one try!"

Kiara held on tight as the owl gained altitude. The air was thin and freezing. The two boulders moving toward Cacy were about to hit. Pele watched the owl stop and silhouette the full moon before turning down. The 'aumakua accelerated and Kiara screamed like someone on the drop of a roller coaster. Wind blew wildly through her hair as the 'aumakua headed for Cacy. Nervously, Cacy watched the giant owl approach and open its razor-sharp claws like it was about to kill a rodent.

Pele covered her hands over her mouth in anticipation. Everyone's heart was pounding. The two boulders smashed into each other, causing a high fiery splash. Cacy's eyes widened and her grip froze on the bat as she felt her boulder shake from the sudden impact of the other two. She shut her eyes just before the open claws seized upon her. The 'aumakua snatched the ends of the bat and shot back into the air just before the boulder shattered from the collision. A wave of molten lava splashed over where Cacy had just stood. Pele watched the 'aumakua soar upward with Cacy holding on, her feet kicking in the air.

"They did it!!!!" the Fire Goddess cheered. Her flames rose in excitement and she raised her fists in the air with joy. A gusher of lava shot behind her, sending exploding bursts into the air like a fireworks show. She watched the two girls and the 'aumakua fly off over the distant hills and disappear.

"Cacy!" Kiara called over the shoulder of the 'aumakua.

"I'm here!" her cousin called back. The cool winds were a welcome relief after the raging fires below. Cacy looked up and was greeted by the hard staring eyes of the owl glancing down at her and then looking ahead for place to land. They were still over a hundred feet in the air.

"Cacy, hold on!" Kiara shouted.

"Don't worry!" she yelled back from under the owl. "That's the only thing on my mind right now!"

Soon the owl found a large clearing and made her descent.

"Get ready," the 'aumakua said to Cacy. "I have to let you go before I land."

They glided in and when the 'aumakua was several feet above the ground, she released the bat. Cacy did her ninja roll on the ground to break the fall. Up ahead, the 'aumakua touched the cool, grassy earth and folded in her wings. Kiara slid off her 'aumakua's back and raced to Cacy, who was still wobbling as she stood up.

Together again, and face-to-face, they were speechless. A million questions raced in their heads, and they had many apologies to make. Instead of

arguing and blaming each other for their actions, they just looked at each other. Kiara's hair was a mess and Cacy's face and arms looked sunburned and her clothes were dirtied with black ash and the smell of sulfur. The silence broke as the two girls embraced, both laughing and crying. From that point on, they knew that they would never be alone.

Chapter 29

A Walk to the Shore

"Cacy, this is my family's 'aumakua," Kiara said after wiping tears of joy from under her glasses. "Old Futt told me about family spirit guardians when I had lost hope after learning that your were kidnapped."

Cacy looked at her feathered savior, still in disbelief about the gigantic size of the pueo. The pueo closed her eyes and bowed her head. Cacy went to give her a big hug.

"Thank you," Cacy said, pressing her cheeks against the warm soft feathers as if they were a giant pillow. "Thank you both. I thought I was going to burn up from the lava flow back there."

"Kiara," the 'aumakua said, "Now that you are both together and safe, I must leave you."

"What?!" both girls said in surprise. Both of them had expected that together they would fly off to Pu'uhonua o Hōnaunau without anymore setbacks.

"We need you to fly us to the other side of the Big Island to return the ki'i!" Kiara said loudly, almost demanding in tone.

"My dear child," the 'aumakua began, "I was only sent to help you to find your cousin, and my time in this world is limited. Already I must return to the realm of the ancestor spirits. Do not worry. Both you and Cacy can make the rest of the journey on your own if you stay together and believe in yourselves."

The thought of being so far from Pu'uhonua o Hōnaunau and so near to sunrise overwhelmed Kiara, who felt no control over the situation. She looked down at her feet and began to cry, but Cacy picked up her bat off the ground and twirled it like a sword before sheathing it behind her into her backpack. She took a deep breath and walked back to place her hand on Kiara's shoulder.

"The big owl is right," Cacy whispered to her cousin. "We're even farther away from the Place of Refuge now, but the worst is over. We can do it!"

Kiara looked at her cousin with renewed hope. The 'aumakua stretched out her wings to wrap the girls in an embrace. As the girls held the 'aumakua tightly, they felt her warm form slowly replaced by the night breeze. They opened their eyes to see that she was gone. High above, a bright star sparkled and rose to join the heavenly clusters filling the dark blue sky.

They looked at their watches. It was well past midnight, giving them just about six more hours before sunrise. The salty air and the distant sounds of the nearby ocean was invigorating. Not knowing how to return to the public areas of the volcano park, they decided to head to the coastline and follow it to reach Pu'uhonua o Hōnaunau. It was an incredibly long walk, but by following the coast they would eventually reach its bay.

They raced down the hillside, using the trek to catch up on each other's stories since leaving the kīpuka. The time walking to the coast was shortened by the tales they each excitedly shared about being caught in a net and thrown in the Hummer, flying to Pu'u 'Ō'ō to meet Pele, and fond memories of their Menehune friends back at the secret kīpuka.

"So Pele said she's not going to destroy the volcano park after all?!" Cacy said with elation.

"No!" Kiara smiled. "She said it might have been a misunderstanding with Hi'iaka."

Cacy shared about how Pele appeared as Kiara before breaking into a fiery rage after being attacked by the dog and shot at.

"I really thought it was you on the road!" Cacy laughed.

"Well, it shows she knows who to emulate." Kiara winked.

Throughout their downhill trek over ancient lava flows and patches of grassy lands with high palm trees, they gave no care or worries about the time. They were together and happy to be with one another. Soon, Cacy and Kiara reached the shoreline. The sand was black and shiny. It gave a crunching sound as they walked unevenly along the beach, looking at the moonlit waves crashing along the shore and tumbling the tiny black grains. Pieces of charred lumber lay along the shore. Cacy kicked one of them and it crumbled into ashes. Over a mile away, lava from Puʻu ʻŌʻō was spilling into the ocean.

"Look!" Cacy said, pointing to a distant sea cliff. "Lava is pouring into the sea."

Plumes of purple and green acidic smoke rose from where the cascading lava flow spilled from an outlet in the side of the cliff and into the pounding waves. Even far away, they heard the hiss and sizzle of the ocean as it boiled and rumbled under the molten fall. Kiara marveled at the raging war of fire and water as she unhooked her Digital Data Pad to take a reading. Even though it was now full of volcanic data, she aimed her device toward the spill and keyed in "temperature" and "speed."

"Incredible!" Kiara said with excitement. "I would have had to stand right next to a flow to get a reading, but now it can receive data even this far away!"

"Ho, you don't want to be standing next to lava, trust me," Cacy said, looking at the blinking lights on the device. "What's it saying?"

"That flow is 2,100 degrees Fahrenheit and 20.5 miles an hour," Kiara answered with giddiness. She saved her reading and placed her Digital Data Pad back on her waist.

"You could've just asked me," Cacy joked, referring to her recent experience. "Lava is hot as he—"

"A boat!!" Kiara interrupted. "Look, that's a boat over there!" She pointed to the far-off silhouette of an old fishing dock extending seventy-five feet from the shore. A sleek twenty-foot-long rigid-hulled inflatable boat with an outboard motor was tied below the end of the pier.

"It must be part of the old village that used to be here," Cacy deducted. "If that boat still has gas, we can take it to Puʻuhonua o Hōnaunau! Come on!"

The girls sprinted on the uneven black sand. Kiara had to stop several times to shake the black pebbles out of her shoes. Cacy stopped ahead and dove to the ground to hide in the darkness. She waved to her cousin to do the same. As Kiara crawled over

to Cacy, they both saw the figure of a man walking out of the shadows on the pier. Their hearts began to race.

"Is that one of the men?" Kiara whispered, trying to lay as flat on the sand as she could.

Cacy spat black sand off her lips. "I see only one person and he doesn't look like either of them. Besides, Pele must have gotten them with her fireballs."

"It looks like he's got some sort of uniform on," Kiara said, crawling closer to her cousin. "Maybe it's a police officer or he's part of a search team looking for us."

They waited in the dark for a minute. Kiara felt a sharp scraping on her ankle. She kicked her feet out and a painful pinch made her shout.

"Ow!!" She rolled over, shaking her leg. With her other leg, she kicked away a sand crab.

The figure on the pier turned to the girls' direction and exposed them with a powerful flashlight beam. The light both blinded and scared the girls. Cacy raised herself up, waving her arms in the air.

"Don't shoot!" she yelled. "We're the missing girls everyone is looking for!"

Kiara rubbed her ankle and stared at her cousin with disbelief.

"What are you doing?!" she panicked.

"C'mon, Kiara," Cacy said as she stood up and brushed the black sand off her clothes. "He's not Rook or Bishop."

Reluctantly, Kiara followed her cousin as she walked to the dock to meet the man. He turned off the flashlight as the girls stepped onto the wooden planks and walked up to him. Kiara kept her eyes on the boat moored at the end of the dock.

The man wore a black uniform and a small badge. Cacy surmised that he must be a security guard or a park officer. He sheathed his long flashlight into his belt hook.

"Didn't mean to scare you. Are you girls okay?" he asked.

"We are!" they said with relief. Cacy explained that they were being chased by two men who murdered someone in Thurston Lava Tube. She was careful not to mention the ki'i, flying ti leafs, Menehune, and Pele.

"Officer, this may sound preposterous," Kiara added, "but we are in dire need to get to Pu'uhonua o Hōnaunau, also known as the Place of Refuge, before sunrise. Can you take us there first on your boat before we rejoin our schools?"

He looked at the two girls with surprise and scratched his forehead.

"Uh, sure," he said. "Why don't you get in the boat already." Together they walked down the edge of the pier. The winds kicked up and the girls folded their arms, shivering. The man in the uniform climbed down a short metal ladder and into the boat. He led Cacy by the hand as she carefully stepped down to join him. She sat excitedly on the rear seat as he helped Kiara board. The two girls looked at each other, expressing the joy of their good fortune.

"Just relax, girls," the man said as he stood up to look at the other end of the pier. "We got more... officers coming to join us. Ah, here they come."

As the man waved his flashlight beam to his approaching passengers, Cacy caught a good look at the man's badge shining in the moonlight. It was like no other badge she'd seen before. Kiara noticed it, too. She told Cacy that it was chess symbol of a pawn piece.

"What did Hi'iaka warn us about when she disappeared?" Cacy asked uneasily.

Kiara thought for a long moment. "She just said avoid her sister Pele." Then Kiara's eyes widened with fear. "And to avoid seeking the help of other humans."

"Crikes!!" a voice yelled from the top of the pier over the boat. "Look who we got here, mate!"

The sound of the voice startled Cacy. She looked up and saw Rook and Bishop standing on the dock above them. They were haggard and disheveled but glowed with insidious delight as they looked down at the two girls. Before the girls could move, the man in black grabbed them and handcuffed them together. Rook and Bishop boarded the long inflatable craft, causing it to sink several inches. The man in the uniform untied the boat from the pier, then he pushed Cacy over so he could get to the stern and turn on the outboard motor. He stayed seated in the back, steering the boat as Rook and Bishop sat in the bow keeping evil grins on the girls. Cacy and Kiara trembled and said nothing but held each other's hands under the metal cuff. They turned their heads to avoid looking at Rook and Bishop. It was even worse seeing the island of Hawai'i getting smaller in the distance.

Aboard the Chaturanga

The inflatable boat streaked and bobbed across the turbulent waves, causing the girls to suddenly break apart their hands and hold on to the seating. As one leaned quickly in one direction, the other was yanked as well. This gave Rook a sense of enjoyment as he watched the two girls struggle through the bouncing and the icy sprays of water stinging their cold bodies. Bishop sat cramped in the front of the inflatable but managed to wiggle a pack of cigarettes from his back pocket. The pack was crushed flat but with a look as if he had found a gold nugget, he pulled out a cigarette still straight and unbroken. Bishop held it steadily in his fingers and close to his body to avoid getting it wet, or worse, losing it overboard with the bouncing of the inflatable. He nudged his partner.

"Sorry, mate," Rook said loudly over the wind and waves, almost yelling into his partner's ears. "I don't have a light."

Bishop crushed the cigarette packet and tossed it over the side of the inflatable, still holding on to his cigarette.

"Hey!" Cacy shouted from her seat.

Both men and Kiara looked straight at her in surprise. With her free hand, Cacy slowly reached into her side pocket and pulled out a box of matches. She held it up clearly for the men to see. Bishop salivated and licked his lips like a dog seeing a big juicy bone.

"Where did you get that?!!" Kiara scolded. "You know you're not allowed to have contraband like that!"

"I got it from the restaurant in their hotel," Cacy replied. "It said it was free 'take one.' In fact, that's where I first saw these two men drinking beer in the bar."

"Bat-girl has a good memory, mate," Rook said, watching if the girl was about to make a deal for the matches.

"Let me guess," Bishop shouted over the howl of the ocean wind, "you want to us to let you both go in exchange for the matches!"

Cacy kept her eyes locked on Bishop. Everyone else had their eyes locked on the box of matches as Cacy slowly held it out. Kiara couldn't believe her cousin was actually going to trust the men. Just as Bishop moved forward, Cacy swung her arm out and tossed the matchbox into the waves. Were it not for his partner holding him back, Bishop would have fallen over as well. Cacy broke into a fit of laughter.

Bishop glared at the girls and moved in close with his hands aimed at Cacy's neck. Kiara yanked on the handcuff to pull her cousin—who was furiously kicking up her legs—away from him. Rook tried to grab his partner again to keep him from falling over. For a moment, it seemed as if a fight was about to break out on the inflatable. Everyone was screaming with every movement someone made. The mayhem was broken by a giant bright light from above that covered the entire craft. Everyone looked up with their hands over their faces to shield them from the glaring beam.

"Ho!" Cacy shouted, almost falling back in her seat and taking Kiara with her. "It's a UFO!!!"

Kiara stared around the glow to see a giant form cutting through the waves and approaching the side of the inflatable.

"It's a spotlight, mango head!" For a brief moment, Kiara felt good actually calling her that again.

"The *Chaturanga!*" the officer called out. He immediately got on his communicator to give instructions to the crew aboard the ship.

"Relax, mate, there'll be smokes back on board," Rook said, taking his partner by the shoulder to ease him. "We got the girls and the ki'i. Let the Queen have at them."

The spotlight continued to hover over the inflatable as the massive ship came to a stop alongside it. The girls were amazed at its size and height. It was like a building lying flat on its side. High up on the top deck they could see the silhouettes of uniformed men working a large crane and lowering a special stepladder that extended like a telescope down to the inflatable. The crane slowly dropped several steel cables, which the officer began to hook onto his craft so it could be towed and raised back on to ship later. When the stepladder touched down, the officer removed the girls' handcuffs and motioned them to climb it. The winds were too strong to lift everyone in the inflatable with the crane.

"You first," Cacy said, pointing her thumb to the stepladder.

"What?!" Kiara turned in shock. "Wh-why me?!"

"You're older."

"Both of you, knock it off and get up there!" Rook and Bishop roared in unison.

Kiara nervously took hold of the brass handles of the stepladder and slowly made her way up. After she climbed several feet, Cacy followed. It wasn't the height of the climb nor the fear of slipping and falling into the ocean that Kiara was dreading. She feared what would happen to her and her cousin once they were on board. The higher they climbed, the harder the winds blew, making them shiver. Cacy paused to look down, only to see Bishop coming up quickly behind her. Rook assisted the officer connecting cables to the inflatable.

As she approached the top of the railing, crew officers extended their arms to lift Kiara onto the deck. She stopped and looked down at Cacy.

"C'mon, child!" an officer on board called. "Hurry, it's getting windy here!"

Reluctantly, Kiara made the final steps and took the hand of one of the officers. Watching her cousin get whisked over the railing, Cacy raced up the stepladder to join her. Together they stood surrounded by several adult male crew members wearing immaculate black and white tunic uniforms. Cacy had expected to see the deck of a pirate ship and a motley crew of bloodthirsty cutthroats with shaggy beards and swords. Instead the girls looked with amazement across the ship and saw the lower decks. There was a swimming pool with its own slide, hanging gardens complete with waterfalls, marble statues from ancient cities, and fine outdoor furniture. Cacy pointed over to a large section housing a line of luxury exotic cars and a platform with a giant letter "H" in a circle.

"That's for helicopters to land," Kiara answered. "Look, on the lower deck! It's a chessboard!"

"It's the biggest I've ever seen!" Cacy exclaimed. At the end of both sides of the board were chess figures standing up to three feet high. A tall seat for calling moves stood on both ends behind the rows of figures.

"Did I tell you I was..." Kiara began.

"...state student chess champion last year, yeah," Cacy finished with dry tone.

As they looked at the grandeur of the ship, they had nearly forgotten about being there against their will. Hands suddenly touched the two on their shoulders from behind.

"Don't touch us!" Cacy whirled around, extending her left hand to block and ready with her right hand to draw out her baseball bat. Kiara jumped back from being startled and placed her hand nervously on her Digital Data Pad. Cacy looked over at her cousin.

"What are you gonna do, take their temperature?" Cacy said, glancing to her.

"Easy, easy," said the Captain with his hands raised and a gentle smile on his weathered face. He motioned to the officers and crew to keep their distance and return to duties.

Cacy felt rather embarrassed to be so rude and for threatening to hurt such an old man. The

Captain introduced himself and welcomed the two to the *Chaturanga.*

The girls kept their suspicions but attempted to carefully explain that they needed to get back to Hawai'i Island before sunrise. As he lit his pipe and blew out a thick plume of deep, rich smoke, the Captain listened to their hastened pleas.

"Cheer up," the old Captain said, "I'll see what I can do. This is the first time having children on board. In fact, I was hoping Rook and Bishop returned empty-handed."

"Captain!" Rook shouted, standing a deck above them at the door to one of the cabins, holding a bottle of beer. "The Queen wants you to bring the girls to the trophy room. Need any help with the brats?"

"Mr. Rook." The captain turned with a glare and a puff of smoke, "I shall have no problems escorting these charming young LADIES!" With that, the Captain took the two girls by the hands and walked past under Rook as he leaned over the railing, keeping an eye on the girls. Cacy turned around and stuck her tongue out at Rook, making him choke and spit out his beer just as he took a drink. Before he could do anything after that, the Captain and the girls rounded a corner and were out of sight.

Stopping at the door of the Queen's trophy room, the Captain took a deep breath. He was a man of honor and loyalty and yet he knew what it would mean and cost if he dared to cross the Queen. He looked at the girls and knew that once they entered, they might not come out alive. Memories of other guests who had met dreadful fates in the Queen's lair played over the Captain's mind. He could recall hearing their loud pleas and awful screams of pain and torture as the Queen laughed and later ordered their lifeless bodies to be tossed overboard for the sharks. Nearly all of those guests were relic-hunting competitors who led lives of greed, dishonesty, theft, and murder, not innocent children caught in the middle of a botched artifact theft. The girls wondered why the Captain was just standing at the door. Cacy looked at her watch and grew frustrated at the time passing. In just a few hours, the sun would be rising over Hawaiʻi Island.

"C'mon, Kiara!" Cacy said. "We've been chased all day and taken here just to see this so-called Queen. I'm fed up with all this!"

Cacy went up to the door and banged her fist on it several times, as if it were a classroom that had been closed during recess or lunch, and she wanted to get back in.

The door slowly opened to a bright large room. A male servant wearing an ornate blue tunic and white silk sash stood behind the door and welcomed

the three in. Cacy walked in first, followed by Kiara then the captain. The girls stood speechless seeing this room, which resembled a museum. Shiny white marble floor tiles stretched across the wide hall, surrounded by display cases full of jewels, treasures, tapestries, paintings, sculptures, suits of armor, and weapons from around the world and throughout time. The large glass windows reflected the light and images in the room with a mirror effect. From behind a large marble column a strikingly beautiful woman with light brown skin and shiny black hair appeared. She was dressed in a red and gold silk gown and was adorned with precious jewelry in her hair and on her ears, neck, and arms. The jangling of her many golden bracelets echoed in the room as she motioned with her hand for the girls to approach.

"Welcome," the woman gently said in a deep accent. "I've been expecting you."

Chapter 31

Hospitality and Revenge

I t took awhile to visually absorb all the treasures of the room and the mysterious, exotic host who bade them to come forward. With a turn of his hand, the servant closed the steel door on the Captain, slid the bolt in place, and locked it. Taking his key, he silently bowed to each person and exited down a spiral staircase behind the Queen. The three females were alone and had not taken their eyes off each other.

"Please forgive my two assistants if they have shown any rudeness or aggression in bringing you here," the Queen spoke as she guided the girls to a large table and seats that had been hand-carved in the Orient.

"If?!" To both girls, "rudeness or aggression" was an understatement. Cacy bursted out in an angry huff and marched right up to the Queen.

"Miss!!" she shouted, looking up at her. "Your stupid guys kept harassing us all day and threatened to kill us so they could get back the—"

"Ki'i," the Queen finished, showing no emotion. Both the girls were taken aback at the correct response. "Please, sit down. I will explain the whole situation and perhaps I can give you some compensation for all your troubles."

Cacy remained indifferent; she was too concerned about the time being wasted. On the other hand, Kiara was silently fixated on a large, handcrafted table several feet away. Atop was a large chessboard and exquisitely sculptured chess pieces. Her eyes lusted after such a magnificent set and her brain hungered for the intellectual challenge of a game. In no time she was seated at the table admiring and touching the large shiny figurines. The Queen sensed that Kiara wanted to play a game and seized the opportunity to make a deal.

"Beautiful isn't it?" The Queen smiled as she took a chair across from Kiara. Cacy sat down next to her cousin. "Each piece is handmade from precious stones from my home country. Right now you two have a different type of piece and if you hand it over, you can have the entire chess set. It's worth over one million American dollars."

"Why do you want that old ki'i so bad?" Kiara asked.

"Why does one want to control the chessboard and is willing to sacrifice her pieces in the process?" she replied, leaning forward. "Power."

"But there's no power in the ki'i," Cacy insisted.

"Not from what my men saw and reported to me," said the Queen with a wave of her finger, creating a rattle from her bracelets. "The power to control weather, the power to defy gravity, the power to create pure energy? If I could learn all its secrets to destroy my enemies, I could easily return to my home country again to rule it."

"What do you mean return home?" Kiara questioned. "Look at all the stuff you've already got right here."

"Yeah, it's like you have your very own museum here," Cacy added.

"These are just treasures, ancient weapons, and religious relics I've amassed since leaving my home country of Shaktisaali, where I was part of the royal family."

Kiara perked up. "Yes, I've heard of Shaktisaali." She now recognized the cultural attire of the Queen. "It's in the Himalayas between China and India."

"Uh, yeah." Cacy nodded in agreement even though she was lost in the conversation. "Uh, I knew that."

Kiara's eyes rolled over to her cousin, giving her a doubtful look. "Yeah, right," she murmured.

The Queen continued to explain. "Many years ago, the military leaders led by my brother, the crown prince, secretly turned against our royal family and assassinated our parents as well as the man who I had planned to marry one day. I was still studying abroad at a university at the time and warned never to return to my homeland. Since then I've been living at sea on this vessel as a rightful queen without a country. With my family's wealth I've managed to create a secret business collecting and selling artifacts worldwide. My brother is now dead and the military leaders there are weak. The time is right to return as the rightful ruler of Shaktisaali and take revenge on all of them. It's just like playing chess isn't it? Revenge and power. The ki'i was part of a business deal, and I want it."

"You can't have it," Cacy insisted firmly. "It was stolen from its resting place and it has to be taken back to Hawai'i."

For a moment there was utter silence in the room as all three stared at each other. Just then, the servant returned up the staircase with a silver tray of tea and pastries to serve the Queen and the girls. Both Rook and Bishop followed him. They were showered and cleaned up and wearing new clothing similar to what they'd had on before. Bishop's hair was still damp with gel and hair cream to make his hairdo. A freshly lit cigarette hung from his lip. Rook held a dark pint of cold beer and took large gulps, wiping his mouth with his sleeve.

"Ah, please, forgive my lack of hospitality earlier," the Queen said as sweet yak butter tea was served and small dishes were placed at the table. The servant bowed to show the girls an assortment of pastries on the platter while holding out silver tongs to serve whatever they chose. Each selection looked too sweet and scrumptious to pass up.

"No, thank you, we ate a big dinner," Kiara said, looking back at the Queen and trying to avoid the stares of Rook and Bishop. Cacy reached out and grabbed several large pastries off the tray and began eating hastily. The servant took the tray and left the room shaking his head. Kiara watched Cacy stuffing her mouth and tried to forget that they were related.

"Thanks, but we can't give it up no matter what," Cacy mumbled while chewing and dropping crumbs on the floor. She secretly swept them with her shoes under the table to try to hide the mess.

Rook moved closer to Cacy, who was ready to jump from her chair. Before things could escalate, Kiara held her cousin's shoulder.

"Wait! What if we play for the ki'i?" Kiara said loudly.

"What do you mean?" asked the Queen. Rook and Bishop held their places.

"I'll play you a game of chess," Kiara answered in nervous voice. "If I win, you let both of us leave this vessel with the ki'i. If you win, you can have the ki'i. We still go, but promise to say nothing to anyone about you. Fair?"

The Queen sat back in her chair and examined the girls. "Agreed," she said, leaning forward again.

"And you can still keep your chessboard," Cacy butted in, trying to sound helpful.

The Queen looked over to her assistants and told them to take a seat elsewhere. Then, she took two pieces off the chessboard and hid one in each hand. Kiara pointed to the Queen's left hand. She opened it and revealed a white piece. The sides were chosen and the game was on. For the first time, Cacy was in total support of her cousin. Forget all that stuff I always tease her about for being too intellectual, she thought. She'd better be super brainy! The Queen pulled her time clocks closer to the board.

"No time clocks, please." Kiara took a deep breath and adjusted her glasses. "We play speed."

Kiara picked up her first chosen piece, a pawn. Just the sheer weight and beauty of the piece was something to behold, but did not distract from her concentration. With slow care, she moved it two spaces forward. The Queen took her own pawn and placed it in front of Kiara's piece. The next move involved a knight. Again, Kiara found herself studying the intricate design of the horse piece before

placing it on her chosen spot. As the Queen finished each move, Kiara quickly began a counterattack, calculating all possible moves the Queen could take. Soon, Rook and Bishop got off their seats and moved in closer to the board. Cacy watched in amazement as chessmen swiftly moved to and fro and were taken off the board. She began wringing her shirt, watching as more of Kiara's pieces were being captured by the Queen. With all her rooks, bishops, knights, and even the queen lost, Kiara calmly adjusted her glasses with her right hand before making one last move.

"Checkmate," Kiara said calmly with a smile.

"What?!!" Everyone including the Queen shouted, looking at the remaining scattered pieces on the board. It was evident. While too occupied hunting around the board capturing Kiara's chessmen, the Queen's king was slowly cornered and trapped by Kiara's two remaining pawns.

"You got pawned," Kiara said, giggling at her own pun.

"You did it!" Cacy screamed with delight, wrapping her arms around Kiara and squeezing her tightly. "Okay, let's go! We gotta hurry before the sun rises."

The Queen sat back in her chair and stared blankly at the board. It was the first time she had ever lost a game. Even while growing up as the

princess of Shaktisaali, her countrymen knew her as the top chess player. She was silent, but the rattling of her jewelry was evidence of her body quivering in discomfort and venomous anger. As she sipped her yak butter tea it went down sour.

"Yes, I promised to let you both leave the vessel if you won," the Queen said slowly, placing her cup down. Then she began to laugh and clapped her hands loudly. She stood up, looked at Rook, and pointed directly at Kiara. "Take her! And toss her off the ship!"

Chapter 32

Breaking a Deal

With his huge bearlike grip, Rook clamped on to Kiara's shoulder and yanked her high over his head. She kicked, twisted, and screamed, making it hard to handle her. At the same time, Cacy was held tightly in both arms by Bishop. She struggled to stand up and help Kiara, but she couldn't break free to reach her bat. The thick smell of cigarette puffs brushed the side of her face as Bishop giggled at the sight of his partner, who looked like a fisherman losing control of a fresh catch.

"She's got a lot of fight for such a scrawny thing," the Queen remarked while resetting the board with her pieces. "Oh, and gentlemen, don't forget to remove the ki'i." With regal callousness, the Queen rose and dismissed the two men to the disposal of the girls.

"If you kill us, you'll never learn how to use the ki'i!" screamed Cacy, whose face was burning red with fear and anger.

For a moment, everyone stopped and thought about what Cacy said. Both Rook and Bishop looked at the Queen for a response. Her majesty herself didn't know whether to call Cacy's bluff and have the girls tossed over without ever knowing how to activate the power within the ki'i, or to see if the little girl would divulge its secrets. The offer is too amusing to pass up, the Queen thought. She motioned Rook to drop Kiara, and he gladly let her land like a crumpled rag doll on the carpet.

"Your majesty," inquired Bishop, "You're not actually going to let this tyke allow the ki'i to do what me and Rook saw in the lava tube? That ki'i power sucked them away from us!"

Rook nodded in firm agreement with his partner. "It's a pork-pie trick to escape."

"Your concern is noted and appreciated," the Queen said, walking around the table, helping Kiara stand up, and pulling out her guest's chair for her to sit. The Queen then approached Cacy face-to-face. "Take out the ki'i and place it on the table."

As the Queen returned to her seat across the table, Kiara kept looking and mouthing words to her cousin. She tried to speak Hawaiian, hoping it would not be understood by the others in the room, but the power had either worn off or could not work while they were off the island. Instead, using strange squints and murmurs she tried to tell Cacy, "What, are you nuts?! You don't know anything about making the ki'i work!" Cacy knew what her cousin was trying to say and tried to calm her down with a subtle wink of the eye. Kiara saw this and rolled her eyes back.

Digging through her backpack, Cacy moved her bat to the side and pulled out her red sweater. She unrolled it and slowly revealed the ki'i. Under the bright lights of the room, the statuette looked dirtier and more sinister. Rook, Bishop, and the Queen gazed upon its rustic beauty with awe and avarice. Cacy then quietly rolled her sweater back up, placed it in her backpack, and zipped it up with enough space for her bat to move around loosely. Instead of putting it back on, she carefully leaned the backpack on the floor against her chair with the bat handle standing straight up between her knees.

The Queen took out a gold-and-pearl-handled magnifying glass to examine the ki'i. Unafraid, she held the relic and studied the detailed carvings on its face and its reddish brown surface, which also had mysterious tinges of magenta. The gaping expression of its mouth looked like both a horrific shriek and an evil laugh. Strangely, though it was carved from wood, its weight made it seem as if it were made of five pounds of solid rock. The Queen gently shook it, thinking that it might be hollow with heavy objects hidden inside. There were no signs of it being so.

"Now," said the Queen, laying the relic carefully on the table next to the chessboard, "I desire to know how the power is contained and called out from this."

"We learned all this from Hiʻiaka, the Goddess of the Forest," replied Cacy.

"You can't talk about this!" Kiara bursted out at Cacy. Rook quickly held her back in her seat.

Cacy faced the Queen and ignored her cousin. "The power has to be called with the secret words. You know, like 'Open Sesame,' but it's in Hawaiian."

"Ah, of course, ancient words!" the Queen agreed. "The same goes with the legend of all relics."

"We need to set the room just like the lava tube and turn off the lights," Cacy added. "That's how the magic lights appeared."

"Your Majesty..." Rook began.

"Bishop," the Queen interrupted, "turn off the lights in this room...and Rook, keep your hands on the girls. Do not let go of them."

Bishop squashed out his cigarette and lit another one to make sure there was enough light as he switched off all the lamps in the room. Looking outside the windows, the night sky was clear and bright enough to see the stars and the ocean. It took awhile for their eyes to adjust, but everyone was able to make out each other's shape in the darkness. The light of the full moon coming in cast a ghostly blue haze with the cigarette smoke. Bishop took Cacy from Rook's grip but instead of sitting down, Cacy felt around the edge of the table and went up to the Queen. With Bishop holding her shoulders, Cacy leaned toward the Queen and whispered the magic words to make the ki'i come alive with power. Kiara sat wondering what her cousin was trying to do.

Reaching her seat, Cacy sat down and asked the Queen if she was ready to reveal and shout the secret magic words. Bishop kept both hands on Cacy's shoulders.

"I admit," said the voice of the Queen in the dark, "I feel rather silly having to shout it, but let us begin." The Queen straightened herself up, making her bracelets jangle like soft chimes. She cleared her throat and placed her hands over the ki'i. There was a sense of nervousness among all of them and the grips on the girls' shoulders grew cold and sweaty.

"Ho'omākaukau!" shouted the Queen. "E komo mai!!! E komo mai!!!"

Just then, a ray of moonlight passed through the room. It quickly lit the Queen's shaking hands, the ki'i, and Cacy's face. Kiara saw that her cousin's eyes were closed, but she was grinning. Suddenly, the Queen's language switched back to English.

The Queen raised her hands in the air and shouted, "I...CALL...YOU...KIKI! KIKI! Hey, KI-I-I-K-I-I-I-I-I!!!!!!"

There were no flashing lights coming from the ki'i. Not even a glint. Cacy couldn't hold it in anymore and bursted out laughing. Kiara began to shake in her chair, boiling with anger at Cacy's laugh and hearing that, that NAME that she hated!

"AAAAAAAAAARRRRRRRGGGGGHHHHHH!!!!!!" Kiara suddenly screamed at an ear-piercing level, frightening everyone except Cacy. The high-pitched wail made them all cover their ears just as the windows shattered from the vibrations, sending in a rain of broken glass and rushing cold winds. Kiara's long scream reached bow, stern, port, starboard, and all levels of the ship. In the ship's bridge the old Captain heard the cry and thought the poor girls were being tortured. Enough of the Queen's business, he thought. He went to his desk drawer and took out his revolver and placed it into his outside coat pocket.

Kiara's scream was the diversion Cacy waited for, as both men let go of the girls to cover their ears. The Queen fell back in her chair as Cacy swiped the ki'i and jammed it quickly into her backpack and

drew out her bat. In a smooth swift motion, Cacy zipped her backpack, slung it back on, and reached out for her cousin. Grabbing Kiara by her bow tie, she told her get down and pulled her to the carpet. All the while the three adults were distracted and disoriented in the darkness. With a loud shout, Cacy jumped in the air with her bat high above her head and swung it down like a sledge hammer with all her might. The million-dollar chessboard and all its pieces exploded into worthless bits.

"Stop them!!" shouted the Queen, trying to hide behind her chair. "Don't let them out of this room!!"

Rook and Bishop made haste trying to find the girls in the dark and made their way to the turn the lights on. The sound of glass popping and shattering above was a sign that Cacy was breaking the lamps with her bat. Both the Queen and Kiara kneeled on the carpet to avoid the flying debris and shuffling of feet and furniture. Cacy's eyes had gotten accustomed to the darkness earlier, and she made her way to all the glass display cases around the room. She smashed every glass and whacked every relic she could, including knocking down a row of standing suits of armor, which fell like clanging dominoes. Rook kept tripping on broken artifacts trying to catch Cacy who was making her way to her cousin.

"Kiara!" Cacy called, swinging her bat to create more chaos. "Where are you?!"

Amid the calamity, Kiara had calmed down. She realized that all this talk about secret magic words had been to create a diversion for escape. The Queen would have killed them no matter what happened. In fact, Kiara felt rather proud that she actually shattered the glass. She slowly rose to signal to Cacy to head to the door.

"I'm here!" Kiara called out, picking up broken chess pieces and throwing them around hoping to hit Rook, Bishop, or the Queen. Suddenly, Bishop lunged out from the darkness and grabbed Kiara by the legs. She screamed in terror and tried to kick out.

"I'm coming, cousin!" Cacy shouted. She felt a large presence behind her and she tumbled forward out of blind instinct. Again, she missed the lethal swing of Rook's kukri blade. In the tumble, she lost hold of her bat and lay flat. She looked up at the dark form of Rook standing above her, about to strike down with this blade. In finger's reach, she felt what she thought was her bat. She rolled to her side and lifted her weapon. It seemed bigger and heavier, but with all her might she swung it directly at Rook and made hard contact between his crotch and inner thigh. The giant staggered in pain and fell

back to the carpet. Catching the moonlight, Cacy looked at the bat and noticed that it was actually an authentic medieval mace, with iron spikes at the end of a metal ball.

"Cool!!!" she said. She noticed her bat lying on the carpet and again looked at the mace. For a moment, there was a tough decision to make. She tossed the mace aside and picked up her trusty bat. Another ray of moonlight illuminated the room and Cacy saw the Queen kneeling on the carpet behind her chair. Their eyes locked. The Queen had a cold, icy stare of hatred. It was deeper than what she felt about those who had taken over her throne and country. As the moonlight disappeared again, so did the Queen, into the darkness. Cacy would never forget that look. She had to find Kiara before the crew members showed up.

"Kiara?" Cacy called.

Kiara's mouth was covered by Bishop and his other hand gripped her left arm behind her back. Fear made Kiara see flashbacks of all the events of the entire day. Like changing channels on a television, she saw quick images of Ms. Fitzgerald, park rangers, ferns, Hi'iaka, waterfalls, dogs, giant boars, Old Futt, her owl 'aumakua, Pele, and the Digital Data Pad. Her mind's eye locked onto the Digital Data Pad. Kiara could hear Cacy approaching closer. Bishop was holding her as a trap and she couldn't warn Cacy. Slowly, with her free hand, she unhooked her Digital Data Pad and clicked the numbers 5-6-0 and then the red button.

A soft hum came from the Digital Data Pad and a thunderous blast of electricity shot from the antenna, arced in midair, and zapped into Bishop. In a flash of sparks, he flew off Kiara and landed several feet away, shaking and smoking. His hair stood straight up. Cacy watched the whole spectacle and looked at her bat with slight disappointment.

"You all right?" Kiara said, standing up and adjusting her uniform before clipping back her Digital Data Pad. Cacy just shrugged her shoulders.

"Well," Cacy mumbled, "I kinda thought YOU needed help...Hey, can your digital thingy open that door?"

"Stand back," Kiara said, and again she unclipped her Digital Data Pad, pressing 5-6-0 and the red button. The Queen and her two sore henchmen watched the bright dancing rays of electricity silhouette the two girls as the heavy door before them blasted off its hinges and landed flat on the deck with a loud boom. A rush of night wind came in as the girls rushed out.

The girls raced down the deck and found a place to hide behind a row of wooden crates. Their hearts pounded with adrenaline as they squatted low.

"We're free!" Cacy whispered semi-loudly, wrapping her arms around Kiara's shoulders. "We're free!!"

"Cacy," Kiara said, turning seriously to her excited cousin, "we're still trapped on a ship in the middle of the Pacific Ocean with people who want to kill us."

"Yeah, but...we're together."

Just then, the ship's siren went off and the entire crew was alerted to find the girls.

A flashlight beam showered over the girls and they panicked. They looked up and saw the Captain standing on a deck ledge over them. He turned off the flashlight and motioned them with his finger over his lips to be quiet.

"Captain!" the voice of the Queen called out from somewhere above the girls. "Do you see anything?"

"Nothing, your majesty," the Captain called back. "All clear over here."

After a few tense seconds, the Captain motioned for the girls to stay where they were. The echoes of footsteps and shouting could be heard coming from various parts of the ship. The Captain quietly came down to the girls and stood next to the crates. He acted like he was looking around and talked through the side of this lips.

"I'm glad you girls are all right," he murmured while shining his flashlight around the decks above them. "Follow me. I'll take you to the inflatable boat."

Chapter 33

A Long Swim to Hawai'i

The girls carefully followed the Captain in the darkness as he led the way, still acting as if he were part of the search team. Sometimes they duckwalked or crawled quickly to keep up and remain in the shadows. Kiara was in front of Cacy and with each sudden pause, Cacy would bump into her, causing both girls to get mad at each other.

"Shhh!" the Captain scolded, getting flustered and shaking his pipe at them. "You two want to get caught?! I'm risking my own life helping you two. Now, when we reach the inflatable, I'll help you down the ladder. Undo the line, drift silently behind the ship, and when we're far enough away, turn on the motor and head north by northwest back to the island."

"Question," asked Cacy, raising her hand. "Which way is that and how do you turn on a motor?"

"I can do it, mango head." Kiara turned to her cousin. "Remember, my dad has a fishing boat. I know how to operate it." She then pointed up to the stars and said, "See, that's Ursa Minor and there, the little 'bob' is the North Star. If you head—"

"All right! All right!" Cacy interrupted. "Let's go before the sun rises and the stars disappear."

As they passed each porthole and door, they waited for the Captain to signal it was safe to proceed. Suddenly, the Captain stopped at the railing overlooking the main deck. He called to the crew members below to go search the cabin areas. The girls listened to the sound of footsteps run under them and disappear.

"The coast is clear," the Captain said with approval. "Come, but stay in the dark as much as possible."

Slowly and quietly, they walked down the stairwell leading to the ladder above the inflatable raft. The girls' hearts pounded with excitement and they tasted freedom in the salty fresh breeze.

"Good!" the Captain exclaimed with a hand clap. "The inflatable is still there. They didn't raise it back on the ship." Teary eyed, he shook hands with the girls and wished them a safe journey. The girls hugged the Captain and thanked him.

The Captain gingerly helped both girls take hold of the ladder, and they began their descent. As the inflatable dragged alongside the ship, it bobbed and

bounced on the choppy waters wrapping its hull. Kiara hesitated on the ladder, worried about missing the inflatable and hitting the water. The Captain shined his flashlight directly onto the inflatable so the girls could see the craft for easy footing. Halfway down the ladder, the light beam jerked and disappeared. The flashlight dropped past the girls, almost hitting Cacy on the head. They watched it hit the water: The beam was quickly consumed under the black depths. Both looked up and saw the Captain standing wide-eyed looking down at them. In slow-motion, the Captain attempted to draw the revolver from his coat pocket but quickly slumped on the railing with his arms dangling overboard. His eyes remained opened but lifeless.

"What happened to him?!" yelled Kiara. Cacy didn't know what to say.

The Queen appeared over the railing next to the Captain. Rook and Bishop soon stood over as well as, and a handful of other crew members shined lights in the girls' faces.

With a cold smirk, Rook grabbed the shoulder of the limp Captain and yanked on his back, pulling his bloody kukri high in the air for both girls to see.

"No!" the girls cried.

"This is what happens to those who disobey me!" shouted the Queen as her robe blew in the winds like a giant flame. "Come back up! It's no use trying to escape."

"I'll toss the ki'i in the ocean!" Cacy threatened. Kiara knew it wasn't the right thing to say.

"Go ahead," the Queen challenged. "It'll float and be found, but you won't!"

Cacy looked down at Kiara for a comeback. Instead, she confirmed what the Queen said.

"C'mon!" Kiara tapped Cacy's foot. "Let's go."

Cacy gave the Queen and all her crew a silent but bitter look of resolve and continued down the ladder with Kiara. A few feet above the rocking inflatable, they knew they would have to time it perfectly to land in the craft safely. Kiara watched the movement of the inflatable moving with each wave crest and closed her eyes as she tumbled into it. With the dragging of the ship, it was hard to stand up and help Cacy, but Kiara tried her best. On the last few rungs, Cacy slipped under the whipping sprays of water and plunged into the ocean. The Queen and all those around her cheered. Immediately, she ordered the ship to halt. A crew member turned on a spotlight and scanned the surface for Cacy's body.

"Cacy!! Cacy!!" Kiara called out for her cousin.

The rushing waves around the ship began to subside and Kiara saw crew members coming down the ladder to get her. She had no ki'i, and worse, she thought, she had no cousin. Again, she called out frantically for Cacy. As the crew members were about to board the inflatable, Kiara moved to the rear, ready to use her Digital Data Pad to blast them.

Down in the dark depths, sinking under the weight of her clothing and backpack, Cacy struggled to save her breath. She thought of leaving Kiara and dying with the ki'i, both never to be seen again. The silence and the darkness underwater held a peaceful sense the less she struggled, and she allowed her body to float in the undercurrents. She thought of the happiest moment of the day: seeing Kiara on her owl 'aumakua and being reunited. As bubbles leaked though her lips, Cacy felt a connection of heart and mind and envisioned herself with her own guardian animal spirit. The connection felt deep and real as she felt a bump on her side.

Cacy opened her eyes, thinking it was a shark about to attack. In a panic, she expelled her remaining air and began to feel the tight squeezing of her throat and ribs. A push from a solid form below her legs quickly raised her to the surface. She gasped and choked, taking in fresh air again. The form below her was hard and smooth. Her hands and legs both swam and crawled in the ocean water as the round gigantic form slowly rose above the

surface. The water flowed off the dark shiny surface that looked like a mound. Cacy tapped on the hard surface, thinking it was some small submarine. As she examined the intricate textures and geometric patterns on the dome, its large head bobbed up and turned to look at her.

"'Aumakua...Honu." Cacy stammered, standing on the peak of the shell. The giant sea turtle gave Cacy a wink with its shiny black eye and submerged its head, keeping focus on the ship far ahead of them. "Kiara!" she called out in a loud voice. The 'aumakua's two front flippers rose with great splendor high above Cacy's head and thrust forward like a swimmer in the butterfly stroke. Cacy dropped down on the shell and held on to the edges above its neck as the 'aumakua sped toward the ship.

As they approached, they saw bright arcs of electricity striking the ship. It was Kiara keeping the crew members from boarding the inflatable.

"Kiara! Kiara!" called Cacy.

Kiara and all those on the vessel watched in disbelief as Cacy glided up, riding on a giant sea turtle over fifteen feet in length.

"Cacy! You're alive!" Kiara screamed and jumped.

"Forget the inflatable!" Cacy called, moving closer and standing up on the shell to help her cousin on. "I found a ride. Meet MY 'aumakua!" She beamed with pride as Kiara took her hand and stepped carefully onto the shell.

The Queen was speechless. Burning with anger she ordered her crew members on the ladder to board the inflatable and follow the girls. The 'aumakua scooped up water with its flipper, sending a giant splash at the Queen. She screamed at the icy feel of being doused with ocean water. Swiftly the 'aumakua turned away from the ship and the girls rode off at top speed, out of range of the spotlight and into the cover of night. The ocean was silent. The Queen called the crew members in the inflatable to come back onto the vessel.

"That ki'i must be returned to me no matter what," the Queen said, glaring at Bishop.

He puffed his cigarette nervously as the Queen passed by to return to her relic room. The first officer of the ship gave orders to put the Captain's body on ice. Back in the relic room, the lights had been replaced and several crew members and servants were busy silently sweeping and picking up the shattered pieces of formerly priceless treasures. Rook was there making certain the cleanup was organized. Even he was afraid to say something that would make the Queen even more upset at the losses. He noticed a small folded note lying among the shattered glass and chess pieces.

"They kept saying they need to get back to return the ki'i." The Queen spoke out loud, sitting in her chair and ignoring the water running down her hair and cheeks. "We need to catch them back in the lava tube at the volcano park."

"Your majesty," Rook spoke as Bishop walked over the fallen door and into the room, "they're not heading back to the volcano park."

"How do you know this?!" the Queen demanded. Rook handed the Queen the note he found on the floor. She read:

Kiara—

You were knocked out by the dart that hit my backpack. It must have got into the musubi you ate. The jeep was broken. I went to Pu'uhonua o Hōnaunau to return the ki'i on my own. I will have the kahuna pardon you as well so don't worry about the blood stain and the curse. Stay here with Old Futt. I will come back.

—Cacy

A bright smile appeared on the Queen's face. She leaped out of her chair and skipped over mini piles of shattered relic pieces to a drawer and pulled out an empty black jewelry box. Rook picked the note off the table and handed it to Bishop. He read it and gave a deep laugh as he expelled a smoke puff. The Queen held the jewelry box with both hands and walked up to Rook and Bishop. The two men instinctively moved in closer to her for orders.

"You two," began the Queen, "go to Pu'uhonua o Hōnaunau in the inflatable. We'll first take the ship closer there." She handed the jewelry box to them.

Rook looked at the box and opened it.

"I think this is too small for the ki'i, your majesty," he said.

She laughed as she headed down the spiral staircase to her bedchamber.

"Don't be silly," she said. "That's for bringing me the hearts of those two girls."

Chapter 34

The Place of Refuge

The surface of the rich blue ocean shimmered under the light of the moon and a cool breeze whisked against Cacy and Kiara. For a moment, Kiara felt like trying to stand on the peak of the shell and act like she was surfing on an endless wave. Cacy was busy riding on the front of the shell above her 'aumakua's neck, with her legs in the water as she searched for Hawai'i Island. Slowly, Kiara stood up and turned sideways with her feet firmly placed against the grooves of the shell pattern. With a sheepish grin she extended her arms like a board surfer and bent her knees. Waves rushed around the sides of the shell and she felt like she was riding them. Cacy suddenly turned around.

"What are you doing?!" she asked.

Kiara pounced back on the shell on her hands and knees. "I-I-I'm just stretching!" she insisted. "I was getting tired sitting down."

Cacy shuffled herself up to the peak to join her. "I'm thinking," she whispered, "sea turtles swim faster under the water. We need all the time possible to beat the sunrise. I can't even see the Big Island yet."

"You may be right," Kiara said and then had a twinkle in her eye. "Here, let me put my glasses and Digital Data Pad in your backpack."

When Kiara was done doing so, she told Cacy to move on her stomach down to the front of the shell. Both girls laid flat side by side on the shell with their bodies sloping downward to the 'aumakua's neck. With their firm grips under the rim of the shell, Cacy called out to her 'aumakua and explained Kiara's plan. The 'aumakua nodded several times and waited for the signal.

"Ready?" Kiara said.

"Ready," Cacy replied. "Go!" she shouted ahead. Both girls took a deep breath.

The 'aumakua submerged several feet. The rush of the ocean almost made the girls lose their grip, but they held on as their bodies lifted off the shell. The rushing undercurrents wrapped them as they torpedoed at incredible speed. After less than ten seconds their knees felt the 'aumakua's shell lifting them back to the surface. They exhaled and took another breath. Again, the 'aumakua dove downward and sliced through the water with ease as its flippers propelled them faster. The pattern to rise for air and then speed underwater continued several more times. On the last rising to the surface, the girls saw a wonderful view far ahead of them. The familiar sight of the orange fountains of lava pouring into the ocean from the coast of Hawai'i Island was like coming home.

Too excited to take in a breath of air, the girls gagged when the 'aumakua submerged and veered to the left. On the next rising, the girls gasped and coughed. Cacy called out to the 'aumakua and said it was okay now to stop the pattern.

"Where are we?" Kiara asked while blowing water out of her nose. The black coastline far ahead seemed so close. The lava flows were nowhere to be found and only a few speckles of light could be seen on the island's silhouette.

"We must be moving up along the coast to where Pu'uhonua o Hōnaunau is," Cacy surmised.

The girls moved back to sit at the top of the shell and looked at the silent island. Lights from cars and houses would appear and vanish behind the lush coastline of trees and farmland. The air was warm and breezy, allowing their clothing to dry. Cacy unzipped her backpack and handed Kiara her glasses and the Digital Data Pad.

"Oh my gosh!" Cacy exclaimed, shaking water off the device. "I forgot about it getting all wet!"

"Don't worry," Kiara said, wiping her glasses with a dry spot on her skirt before putting them on. "It's built to be water resistant to one hundred meters." She gave it a click and the device rebooted.

The 'aumakua began to change direction. The girls looked down into the waters and noticed dark shapes of all sizes and forms around them. They were reaching shallow waters and reefs made of coral and trails of lava rock. Because of its massive size, the 'aumakua had to maneuver around and above the submerged rocks to avoid hitting them with its flippers and underbelly. Soon the waters became clear enough to see the bottom and the lava rocks jutting the surface looked like tiny black islands. The girls saw yellow and red fishes moving below them as the bottom turned to a dark emerald teeming with seaweed clusters. The 'aumakua made a right turn around a bend of smooth flat lava rock extending from the island. The palm trees rose majestically in the distance, and just below it was the shape of a large Hawaiian hut and a wooden tower. The girls looked at it and couldn't say a word. Thick posts surrounded the hut and the tower like a fort. Fearsome wooden images of the Hawaiian god Lono stood high behind the posts like a coven of giant monsters. Standing outside its perimeter, above the rocks sloping to the ocean, were two guardian images that stared viciously back at the girls. In the dark, they seemed almost alive. Cacy thought back to the postcard she had purchased in the visitor center. The scene was just like the photograph, but it looked less scary in daylight. Silently, the 'aumakua passed around the eerie structures and paddled to the mouth of a small cove nearby. Several feet away and rising above the water like a misplaced telephone pole was another wooden image. It was much lighter, having been bleached over the years by the sun.

The 'aumakua stopped over two hundred feet from the shore. The girls looked around to see that the water was too shallow and cluttered with lava rocks for the 'aumakua to move any farther.

"We're here," Cacy said with both joy and welling sadness. "We're here. That hut area is called...Hale 'o Keawe. The temple was used to house the bones of twenty-three chiefs. That's where we go to return the ki'i and get rid of the curse!"

Kiara looked at the distance of water separating them from their salvation. They seemed so close, yet so far from it.

"We came this far," she said "I guess we can swim it."

The 'aumakua rose its head high out of the water and got the girls' attention.

"What is it?" asked Cacy.

The 'aumakua nodded its head and snapped its mouth loudly before lowering it back into the water.

The girls watched before them as some of the lava rocks in the water began to move. Some rose up and drifted along the surface.

"What's going on?" Kiara said out loud.

"Watch!" yelled Cacy as the remaining light of the moon showed the moving rocks to be sea turtles. They gathered in groups and then used their shells to form a long line of stepping stones leading directly from the girls to the shore.

The girls couldn't contain their laughter and joy. Kiara carefully stepped off the 'aumakua's shell and onto the closest sea turtle. All the sea turtles were full grown, but they looked so tiny next to the 'aumakua.

"Thank you!" Kiara called and smiled to the 'aumakua. Cacy stepped off the 'aumakua's shell and onto a sea turtle. She knelt down and pressed her hands on the 'aumakua's shiny cheeks. She kissed her 'aumakua on its head and whispered her gratitude. Both Cacy's and the 'aumakua's eyes were wet with seawater and tears.

With each step onto a sea turtle's shell, the girls felt their weight pushing it down. Some of the sea turtles struggled to keep floating in place.

The girls worried about it being uncomfortable to support them, so they quickly skipped across each shell, offering a fast apology and thanks to each turtle. Midway, Cacy briefly turned around to look at her 'aumakua again. Just as Kiara's 'aumakua had disappeared after doing its task, a bright light glowed under the water where it stopped and then sped off into the horizon.

"Hurry!" Kiara called to her cousin.

"Okay!" Cacy turned back to her and quickly skipped over the remaining sea turtles.

Once hitting the sandy shore, Kiara dove down and lay on her back. "Land!" she yelled. "It's so good to be on land again."

Cacy jumped onto the sand and waved to all the sea turtles. They immediately swam off or submerged to their former locations in the cove. Cacy looked around at the Place of Refuge. She saw both ancient and modern structures for both natives and tourists to visit during the day as another national historical park. A faraway hut housed a long canoe. Scattered all along the beach were giant palm trees. Just a short walk away, up a sandy hill to the right, was the Hale 'o Keawe. Looking at it, she felt a profound sense of what it meant to be part Hawaiian. Kiara looked toward the ancient sanctuary and felt the same way. Situated on the sand next to Kiara was a sign.

"Hey, Kiara, you better read this," Cacy said dryly.

Kiara got up and dusted her clothes. She stood next to Cacy and looked at the sign:

BASKING HAWAIIAN SEA TURTLES

Green turtles (honu) are native to Hawai'i and can be found in the shallow coastal waters of our islands. The turtles commonly come to shore to feed on seaweed (limu) growing on the bottom.

Green turtles crawl out on the sand and rocks to bask and rest. This basking is a natural behavior special to Hawaiian green turtles. It is a criminal offense to ride or touch the turtles.

State and Federal law requires a distance of twenty feet from basking turtles.

"Uh-oh," Kiara said, shrugging her shoulders, "I guess we have to be forgiven for this also at the Hale 'o Keawe."

Chapter 35

Ceremony

The girls silently approached the wooden fence of Hale ʻo Keawe. Each thick post was made from palm tree trunks sliced to about five feet in height and sharpened at the tip. Connected to the fence was the Great Wall at Hōnaunau, built from stones stacking twelve feet high and stretching seventeen feet thick. The one-thousand-foot-long wall separated the royal grounds from the sanctuary on the other side. Cacy paused where the rock wall and the posts met. In the corner was a short carved image of Lono i ka Makahiki, or Lono of the annual festival. Ironically, it stood sullen on a plain base, looking like a lonely child given time-out in a corner.

"Uh, excuse me?" Cacy said, looking eye to eye with the image. "We're here to meet the priests and return a kiʻi."

"Why are you talking to a statue?" Kiara chided. "C'mon, let's see if there's a door for the wooden fence."

They walked along the wooden posts surrounding the Hale 'o Keawe. Towering on the other side were the grouping of image carvings they had first seen from the ocean. The gaping mouths and frightening eyes of each Lono image was just like the ki'i. Each had its own elaborate headdress ascending several feet high. Away from the other corner of the wooden fence were the two guardian images facing the ocean. They were believed to be part of the order of Kāne, the creator. The girls stood next to them and guessed they were at least six feet high. Kiara remarked that the one with the braids had a resemblance to Cacy.

"Actually, this one with the flat head matches you." Cacy returned the compliment.

In the corner of their eyes, they both saw something big moving in front of the fence. They jumped in front of the two images to hide and slowly peeked around their chests. Standing at the front of the Hale 'o Keawe was the transparent apparition of a kahuna, or priest, dressed in a glowing white kīhei that billowed in the breeze. He stood taller than the average adult and his bare muscular arms and lower legs showed brown human skin. His face and identity was concealed within a gourd helmet. Strips of tapa cloth hung below the front rim of the helmet and dried foliage adorned its round top. A lei of shredded ti leaves draped his shoulders. The girls knew that the kahuna was looking directly at them even though the large round eye opening of the helmet was pitch-black. He seemed fearsome yet holy to behold. The religious specter's form fluctuated as the girls watched. At one moment his whole body would be visible and in another, his head would vanish. Then, his whole top half would be seen but his legs dissolved. Both Cacy and Kiara remained frozen behind the guardian images, chilled with fear until the kahuna raised his right arm out and waved them to come forward.

"You go first," Kiara whispered. "You have the ki'i."

Cacy took a deep breath and stepped out from behind the guardian image. Kiara slowly joined her. Together they walked the several steps forward to meet the kahuna, and they began to hear deep voices performing an oli, chant, in Hawaiian. The ability to understand the Language of the Land again worked for the girls, and they knew what they were hearing. It was a call to worship and address the gods. They saw that behind the kahuna were other priest spirits that appeared from within the Hale 'o Keawe and floated through the solid fence to join them. Each one wore a gourd helmet that hid his face. One of the spirits held a tapa cloth in his hands and another carried a large koa bowl. The

chanting grew louder, faster, and more powerful as if it would wake the whole island. The girls covered their ears and trembled, stepping back.

Suddenly, the kahuna raised his hands high in the air and the chanting ceased. All the priests, including the kahuna, extended their arms out to welcome the girls. A force of mana, spiritual power, fell upon the entire beach as the kahuna read into the eyes of the girls and saw their entire journey since yesterday morning when they had entered the volcano park. There was no need for any spoken explanation. The priest with the tapa cloth approached the girls and held it out to Cacy. She knelt down and took off her backpack and brought out the ki'i. After putting her backpack on again, she reverently handed the ki'i to the priest, who carried it on the tapa cloth. In unison, all the priests offered a prayer chant of purification. The priest with the koa bowl held it over the ki'i and poured sacred water on it to wash away all that defiled it. A hissing sizzle and foul-smelling yellow smoke rose from the ki'i. After enough water was poured out, the priest with the ki'i wrapped it in a new tapa cloth. A deep sigh of relief came over the girls knowing that the ki'i was finally delivered and off their hands.

Their hands! Both girls looked at each other and remembered all about the blood stains on their

fingers. Kiara and Cacy held their open palms for the kahuna to see. He stepped behind the girls and placed his hands on their shoulders as the priest with the bowl approached them.

"Oh no!" Kiara whimpered. "Our hands are going to get burned."

The priest began to slowly tilt the koa bowl over their hands.

Cacy dreaded the pain and winced, saying, "It's better than being dead at sunrise! Ewww! Close your eyes!"

They both gave a loud shriek of fear as the sacred water poured generously over their entire hands, running through their fingers. It was cold and refreshing like the ocean. The girls saw the blood stains painlessly bubble up like blisters and then wash away.

"Look!" the girls said to each other almost simultaneously. "The blood stains are gone!"

The curse was over and their hearts leapt with joy. The kahuna and his fellow priests performed another chant of purification and a final blessing declaring the girls clean and free to leave the Place of Refuge. Each priest approached the girls one by one to place their hands on them and gently touch their foreheads with the front of their helmets. It was awkward being so close to them and not seeing any trace of a human face within the helmets. As slowly as they had first appeared, the priests chanted and walked through the fence, gradually vanishing on the grounds of the Hale ʻo Keawe. The girls watched the priest with the wrapped kiʻi, and as his form dematerialized so did the kiʻi.

"Where did the kiʻi go?" asked Cacy.

"I think it went to the spirit world so it could never be stolen again," Kiara said with a slight shiver thinking what that world would be like.

The kahuna stood on the stone steps at the front of the wooden fence and explained to the girls that it was known as hoʻoponopono, or to make things right. He then told the girls that at sunrise they could rejoin the human world in safety, but until then, they were to remain on the grounds of the Puʻuhonua o Hōnaunau. By this time the moon was nearing the horizon with just about another hour till sunrise. The kahuna bowed to the girls and stepped back, passing through the wooden fence. His form then drifted toward the middle of the tall Lono images and faded away. Silently, the girls went to the stone steps to peek over the fence and into the Hale ʻo Keawe grounds.

"Let's go sit down by our two friends," Kiara said, motioning to the two guardian images.

The girls sat on the sand, leaning their heads on the butts of the images. Their heads rested comfortably between the cheeks. To help pass the time, they tossed small stones and reminisced about the scares and fun they had riding a giant ti leaf down a waterfall, killing a giant boar, almost getting burned up in molten lava, and riding their 'aumākua. Out of nowhere, Kiara pinched Cacy hard on the shoulder.

"Ow!" Cacy screamed. "What's that for?!"

Kiara laughed out loud; she loved feeling free to be so open with emotion.

"Ha! Ha! Ha!" she guffawed, trying to talk. "That's...that's for using that nickname I hate to get me to yell on that ship! Ha! Ha! Ha!"

Cacy rubbed her shoulder and startled to giggle as well. "Yeah, that was pretty funny!" she replied.

"Ha! Ha!!" A loud voice boomed above them, sounding almost like it came from the image itself. The girls were so startled by this that they nearly leapt off the ground.

A strong hand suddenly grabbed Kiara and held her against the guardian image. She screamed in terror at seeing Rook again. With his other hand he reached in his vest for his kukri. Cacy managed to slip away from Bishop just as he jumped from the other side of the guardian image. She fell a few feet forward into the sand, taking in a mouthful. Bishop repeated his loud sarcastic laugh.

"Hello!" Bishop grinned. "The Queen so misses the two of you. Good thing somebody dropped this note for us to find you." He held out Cacy's note to Kiara and let it fly away in the wind.

Cacy turned over and spat out sand. The men could only laugh at such a sight, as sad as a turtle struggling on its back. Kiara reached down for her Digital Data Pad but Bishop grabbed it off her waist and tossed it down to the rocks leading to the water. She quaked with fear, feeling helpless without it.

"Now," Bishop began while lighting a cigarette, "we've been chasing you two around all day yesterday and tonight. It ends here! Give us the ki'i and oh, I promise, you're gonna feel a whole lot better."

"We don't have it anymore!" Cacy yelled. "It's gone to a place where humans can't steal it anymore!"

The two men looked at the Hale 'o Keawe and thought the girls must have hidden it in there. Bishop motioned for him to bring Kiara to the fence. As both of them passed, Cacy threw a handful of sand at Bishop's eyes. The blast of sand caught him off guard. He backed away, cursing and rubbing his eyes. The tiny grits stung and burned intensely. The only way to wash it all out was to stagger down the rocks to reach the water. Cacy quickly rolled on her side and with one swift swing, she drew out her bat and struck Rook hard in the back of his knee. The painful impact caused him to release his hold on Kiara as he dropped to the sand.

"Run and hide!" Cacy yelled to her cousin. As Kiara raced off, Cacy sprinted to the wooden fence, trying to shake the sturdy posts. "Help us!" she shouted, hoping the kahuna and the other priests would return. The Hale 'o Keawe remained empty and silent.

Chapter 36

Duel

Cacy looked frantically around, shouting at the tower, the hut, and the tall Lono images. All she heard were the faraway sounds of the waves hitting the rocks. She turned around and saw Rook staggering back to his feet, growling in pain and full of rage. The glint of the kukri's blade reflected in the moonlight as he raised it high in his fist.

"That's the problem with Bishop," he said, spitting out sand. "Too many speeches instead of just killing you."

Cacy knew that there was nothing to bargain or bluff with now that the ki'i was forever gone. She mustered all her bravery and reached down to pick up her bat. Coming off the stone steps, she kept her eyes locked on Rook's. Somehow a flashback to an old action movie reminded her to never take her eyes off her opponent's and not look at any weapon he had. The eyes signaled their intended moves. Despite his hatred toward Cacy, he couldn't help but be amused watching this little girl perform dramatic swings with her bat as if it were a sword. She stopped exchanging it between her hands and held it straight before her in both hands like a warrior prepared to duel. Keeping her eyes straight at Rook, Cacy slowly moved clockwise, making her opponent limp in the same direction. After matching each other's moves for several more steps in an arc, Rook grew weary.

"C'mon!" he taunted. "Are we gonna dance till morning or can I cut your heart out now?"

Cacy took the bait of the insult and charged forward with a shout. Rook flashed a lean and hungry look of delight, eager to strike her down. But he suddenly lost sight of Cacy when Kiara jumped on his back and covered his eyes with her hands. Cacy stopped in her tracks and couldn't believe what she was seeing.

"Kiara!" Cacy screamed. "Get off! It's too dangerous!"

Rook twisted and shook like a Brahma bull trying to kick off its rider. Kiara yelled and kicked her legs around Rook's back, swinging like a rag doll and trying as hard as she could to hold on. With a swift twist of his torso and a swing of his arm, he whipped Kiara off, almost cutting her in midair with the kukri. With a horrible scream, she flew

several feet over the sand past Cacy and struck the wooden posts. A loud crack was heard as the back of her head smashed against the solid beams. She landed crumpled on the stone steps. For a moment, Cacy stood in shock. She saw that Kiara's eyes were shut and her head was slumped on her shoulder. Streams of blood flowed down the post where her head had struck.

"Kiara!!" Cacy called out as she raced to her cousin.

She knelt down and carefully raised Kiara's head. Tears began to flow uncontrollably as Cacy felt the warm blood soaking up Kiara's hair. Again, Cacy yelled out her cousin's name, but there was no response except for a faint exhale. After that, Kiara stopped breathing and her body slowly sank back against the post. It would have been an easy kill for Rook to come up behind Cacy and finish her off. Instead, he stood back, enjoying seeing Cacy suffer.

"One down, one more to go," Rook said out loud. Bishop was climbing back up the rocks after washing out his eyes. His hair was a damp wet mess and he was furious. When he saw the scene before him, he slowly cheered up.

Gently and with tender care, Cacy straightened Kiara's body against the post and readjusted her glasses. Through her hot tears, she looked at her cousin who seemed both angelic and at peace. Frustration mixed with Cacy's grief. She thought about how unfair it was to come this far and achieve their mission only for it to end like this. She felt painfully alone now.

"Kiara," Cacy whimpered, holding her cousin's hand, "I'm going to finish this for the both of us. I promise."

She stood up and gripped her bat as hard as possible. Her heart was pounding with hate and she coughed, breathing and crying at the same time. Both Rook and Bishop stood waiting for her to move. With a loud shout, Cacy raced forward only a few steps before she felt a strong hand restrain her by the shoulder. She couldn't move another step under the pressure of the grip. She turned her head around, and inches from her face was a gourd helmet. The kahuna had returned.

"What the...!" Bishop said in utter shock. "Where'd he come from?!!" Both he and Rook looked at each other, then back at Cacy and the mysterious being who had appeared in thin air.

Hearing them, Cacy whipped her head back toward them. "YOU CAN SEE HIM?!" she shouted in amazement.

Again she looked back at the kahuna, hoping that he would help her defeat the two men. Instead, the kahuna kept his grip on Cacy's shoulder for several more seconds, giving her time to calm her emotions. Firmly and gently, he moved Cacy out of the way and faced Rook and Bishop, signaling that her involvement was not needed. He raised his fists in the air and gigantic winds began to howl through Puʻuhonua o Hōnaunau like demonic moans. He called out to the gods and pointed directly at the men, speaking in a language only Cacy could understand.

"You have broken the kapu of the gods!" he declared. "Those who seek refuge are free from all pursuers and the shedding of blood is forbidden within these sacred grounds!!"

The cries of many bodiless voices carried and echoed through the winds. Each one repeated together in a ghostly chorus what the kahuna had said.

"I have a bad feeling about this," Bishop remarked, holding his blowing hair down. "Let's get outta here!"

"We can't go back empty-handed!" Rook said firmly to his partner, squinting his eyes to avoid the stinging sand being whipped up around them.

"C'mon, we'll figure out some excuse later!" Bishop shouted.

Both men began to back off, not wanting to relive their experience with the Fire Goddess. Keeping their eyes on the kahuna, they began to head back to the inflatable anchored down by the rocks. Earlier they had paddled the final stretch to shore to avoid being heard with the outboard motor and they were well ready to use it again to get away as quick as possible. A horrible growl like nothing a human could ever identify came from behind them. The men turned around and watched the two guardian statues moving. At first they thought it was a trick on their eyes, but the guardians slowly turned from the ocean and looked directly at Rook and Bishop. The eyes of the wooden images glowed like lava. For the first time, the men screamed in fear. The bodies of the guardians began to flex and ripple as the solid wood came to life. The gaping jaws snapped and curled open, letting off a deep guttural sound from within.

Cacy watched in astonishment as the two guardians thumped their huge fists on their chests with the sound of solid wood being pounded together. They jumped off their short bases and flexed their muscles, enjoying the surge of movement after centuries of paralysis. Slowly they stomped toward the men, showing greater ease and movement with each new step. Rook refused to stand as a target and he rushed the guardians with his kukri. He swung his blade hard into the neck of one of the guardians.

The powerful whack would have lopped off the head of any human, but it merely scratched the hard surface of the guardian. The guardian flung his fist into Rook's forearm, almost breaking it and causing the kukri to fly away and bounce down to the rocks below.

"Good lord!" Bishop murmured, watching Rook curled on the sand and moaning in pain. He dared not move closer to the guardians.

The guardian who hadn't been struck shaped his mouth into a sinister smile. Bishop's eyes widened as the guardian charged forward, ramming his massive head into him. The impact sent Bishop flying back several feet. He landed on his neck and shoulders and rolled over, landing flat on his front side. The other guardian dragged Rook by the ankle to where Bishop lay.

The two guardians were joined by smaller images who came to life. Curious, Cacy turned to look at the tall Lono images in the Hale 'o Keawe. Each image swayed and moved their cylindrical bodies to the chanting of the other priests, who had reappeared and joined the kahuna. Cacy looked sadly at Kiara and wished she could see all this incredible magic. When Cacy turned back to look at Rook and Bishop, they were both laid on their backs. Their heads rested on a large flat stone. The smaller images held their

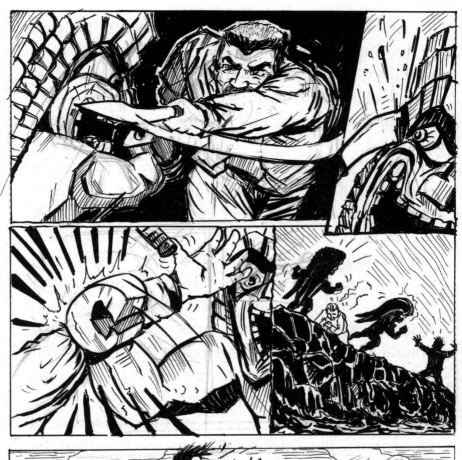

bodies down, and standing over each man's head was guardian. In their hands they carried a large wooden club about three feet long and as large as a bowling ball at its end. She looked down at her own bat, thinking how small it looked in comparison.

The kahuna raised his hand again. All the winds, chanting, and moaning stopped. The silence was chilling.

"It is the judgement of the gods to have you put to death," he solemnly said, and lowered his arm hard, signaling the guardians to proceed with the ceremony.

Both Rook and Bishop were awake and terrified as they looked at all the grinning images around them and the huge clubs about to crush their skulls. Slowly the clubs raised, building momentum like a roller coaster inching over a peak before it rushes down at top speed. Cacy's emotions were mixed. She relished the thought of seeing Rook and Bishop finally suffer for all they did to her, and for taking Kiara's life. Yet, she felt the tugging in her heart and mind that their death was not right. As the clubs reached their farthest distance before swinging, Cacy stepped forward.

"Stop!" she yelled.

All the images, including the kahuna and the other priests, suddenly looked at her. The kahuna raised his hand to signal the guardians to wait. Perhaps the girl had final words of judgement herself, he thought. Instead, Cacy spoke to all.

"Don't kill them," she said.

The kahuna and all the images gasped and looked at each other with gestures of surprise.

"I don't know why," she began. "But doing this won't change anything. My cousin will still be dead. Let them live to be judged by those of my world. They will end up paying for what they did and in doing so, that will be like ho'oponopono, too, won't it?"

The kahuna thought silently and kept his focus on Cacy. Rook and Bishop only stared at the clubs with their mouths quivering silently. The kahuna nodded his head to Cacy. He then called for one of the priests to bring olonā cords from within the Hale 'o Keawe. When the priest returned, the kahuna ordered the images to let go of the men. With relief, Rook and Bishop watched the guardians step back and lower the clubs. Just when they thought they were free, the images picked up the men and dropped them down on their bellies with a hard slam. The images yanked Rook's and Bishop's arms and legs, bringing each man's wrists and ankles together. The pain was awful and Rook was still hurting from the heavy blow in the forearm by the guardian. The men grunted and cursed as the thin but rough olonā cords were wound tightly around their limbs. In the end, they lay on the sand hog-tied, with their arms and legs behind them.

"Those cords have been blessed and no human can break out of them," the kahuna explained to Cacy. She slowly found her sense of humor seeing them tied up like that and ready to be brought to justice. The men struggled in pain and tried to rock on their bellies. With each tug they made with either their wrists or ankles, the olonā grew tighter.

"Argh!" Bishop whined to Rook. "Why'd you have to lose your kukri?!"

"Ah, shut up!" Rook said, sneering at his partner before turning his head away from him.

Cacy turned to the kahuna. Gently she touched his garment to get his attention.

"Is there..." she quietly began, "...is there anything you can do for Kiara?"

"You have shown mercy for these men," the kahuna said. "When I first looked at you two and visioned all the events you went through, I saw that Hi'iaka gave you three ti leaves. Save the third one for later." After he said this, the kahuna walked away from Cacy.

"Huh?" Cacy said, wondering if the answer was "yes" or "no."

She took off her backpack and dug for the two remaining ti leaves. They were both still fresh and green, with a little bruising on the edges. Cacy straightened one out and placed the other one carefully in her pack again before putting it back on. She then knelt at Kiara's body. Tears began to well up again and drops fell upon the ti leaf, causing it to tingle. At first she thought it might grow into a giant form like the first one, but it remained its actual size. Carefully Cacy placed the ti leaf on Kiara's forehead, hoping for a miracle. She recalled a school lesson about how Native Hawaiians used to place ti leaves on their heads to treat headaches. A minute passed and nothing happened. Then, she gently raised the back of Kiara's head, which was still soaked with blood. Cacy felt a little sick at the feel of the soft spongy areas between the fractures. This time she placed the ti leaf behind Kiara's head and held it in place. Again, the tingling feeling returned and grew stronger and warmer in her hand.

The priests and images quietly gathered and stood behind Cacy to watch. All of them, including the kahuna, began calling upon their mana to send into the ti leaf and it began glowing and blinking with the rhythm of a pulse rate. Cacy felt energy emanating from it and flowing into Kiara as the wound closed up. Slowly, Kiara's chest began to move as she began to breathe again. Her eyes opened and she looked directly at Cacy. The suddenness of

it made Cacy scream and jolt. The tingling in the ti leaf stopped and all the blood on the back of Kiara's head disappeared. The ti leaf turned completely red and then quickly shriveled to dust.

"Cacy," Kiara quietly spoke, looking at her cousin who was gushing with tears. "I have a terrible headache."

Chapter 37

The Man in the Blue Suit

Cacy couldn't contain her tears and happiness at seeing Kiara alive again, and hugged her. The kahuna and the priests looked at each other, nodding their heads in approval. Kiara slowly sat up and looked at them.

"Why are they all back?" Kiara asked her cousin. "What happened to Rook and Bishop?"

Cacy helped her cousin stand up and the priests moved aside to show Kiara that both Rook and Bishop weren't going to bother them anymore. The men looked up at Kiara and saw that she was all right. The sight of the two men hog-tied on their stomachs made her giggle. Together both Rook and Bishop groaned and turned away.

"It's all over now," Cacy said, smiling to Kiara.

For a long pause, Kiara thought about what her cousin had just said. It was the best thing she had heard in the past nearly twenty-four hours. She felt more exhausted and overjoyed than at the end of an exam in school. When she turned around she noticed the blood on the posts and pointed it out.

The kahuna knew that it had to be removed quickly and he requested one of the priests to bring another bowl of sacred water. Again, a ritual of cleansing was performed and the water washed away the blood. It flowed down the posts and onto the sand, fading away. Another priest gave two small bowls of water for the girls to drink. It was blessed to give them strength and energy for the new day since they hadn't had any rest. It tasted bitter but the girls felt invigorated. As the sky began to grow lighter and the warm glow of sunrise was stretching over the horizon, the kahuna gave final words to the girls.

"Sit by the guardians, Ki'ei and Hālō, till sunrise to keep watch over the men," he instructed. "When the park rangers show up, let them know you are okay but do not talk of seeing all of us."

"Don't worry," Kiara replied, "there are others who we promised to keep secret from the outside world." Cacy nodded over to Kiara, fondly remembering their Menehune friends at the kīpuka.

"Aloha," the kahuna said as he and the priests gave their farewell blessings again. "A hui hou."

"Wait!" Cacy called out as they passed through the wooden posts. "What about the men? What if they speak about you?"

As the priests vanished on the other side of the fence, the kahuna merely waved his arm in the air and faded away.

"I don't think anyone would even believe them," Kiara said to reassure her.

Together the girls took their old places sitting against the guardian images and facing Rook and Bishop. As the minutes passed, Cacy explained to Kiara what had happened to her after she jumped on Rook. Kiara was amazed at hearing everything about her being dead, the statues coming to life and bringing down the men, and how they were spared execution.

"So what was it like?" Cacy asked when she was done.

"What do you mean?" Kiara replied.

"What's it like being dead?"

Kiara thought silently for a few seconds. "I don't remember. And I really don't want to."

Park Ranger DeAguiar pulled in the parking lot of Puʻuhonua o Hōnaunau just when the sun came up in its full blaze. He sipped his hot cup of fresh-brewed Kona coffee as he started his early morning check of the visitor center and the royal grounds. As he walked through the corridor of murals and wall frescoes depicting the arrival of the Hawaiians to the islands, the kapu system, and the role of the Place of Refuge, he pressed each button, playing an audio lesson for each topic. He'd heard each recording hundreds of times, but never tired of it. Down the steps and past the small amphitheater, he walked along the sand between the tall mounds of lava rocks and headed toward the cove. It was a tradition to come to work this early and enjoy the peace and quiet of having the national park to himself long before the crowds of tourists would arrive. The sky was bright blue without any hint of clouds. He took another delicious gulp of his coffee as he turned toward the Hale 'o Keawe, and spat it out in surprise at the sight of two girls sitting there waving at him, with two men hog-tied on the ground nearby.

Two hours later the entire grounds of the national historical park was inundated with not just tourists, but police officers, reporters, and locals who had just gotten news that the two missing girls from the volcano park were found on the other side of Hawai'i Island at Pu'uhonua o Hōnaunau. Already, buses of Cacy's and Kiara's classmates and teachers were heading there, as well as their parents, who had flown in the night before from O'ahu. High above, helicopters were filming aerial views of the park to show on the mainland news channels. Ranger DeAguiar helped his fellow workers keep the tourists and onlookers at a distance from the Hale 'o Keawe as police officers stood around the girls and over Rook and Bishop. Reporters from the four local television stations crammed close to the police line, talking into their cameras and getting shots of the girls. Some reporters from the newspapers tried shouting out questions to the girls, who just stood together nervously at all the attention. They knew their disappearance was news, but they didn't expect such a huge entrance on returning to the regular world. Both girls weren't sure of what to say and to whom. The police kept asking them why the two men were tied up, and even that was something the girls couldn't figure out how to explain.

Finally, the lead officer appeared and took control of the situation. Cacy looked at him and knew that this Man was the one to talk to. The Man didn't wear a police uniform like the officers, but they all knew him and treated him with complete respect. He was tall, lean, and ruggedly handsome in his blue suit and red necktie. His black hair was combed high like a wave. The Man walked up to the girls and asked if they needed any medical treatment.

Both Cacy and Kiara said that they felt fine and the Man introduced himself, explaining his role as head of Hawai'i's special law enforcement unit. He had three assistants with him and they too wore suits. They all stood out dressed like that on the hot sunny sands. One was younger and Caucasian, wearing a dark brown suit. The second was an older, stocky Chinese man, and the third was a tall, young Hawaiian. Both of their suits were black. They oversaw the officers standing over Rook and Bishop.

"We found a ki'i in the Thurston Lava Tube and those men chased us throughout the volcano park," Cacy revealed to the Man, trying her best to speak as simply as possible.

"And they kidnapped us and took us to a giant ship to meet this woman called the Queen," Kiara added. When the Man heard that name, his reaction was one of deep concern.

The Man called his assistant in the brown suit and gave him orders to contact the Coast Guard, the Navy, and Interpol to begin an ocean search around Hawai'i Island.

"You've heard of her?" Cacy asked.

"Children," the Man began, "this Queen is an international criminal who steals and sells priceless artifacts from other countries. Those two men on the ground are wanted for crimes in several countries. We've had word the Queen might be nearing the Hawaiian islands and we were trying to identify a university professor who might be selling ancient relics to her. A local professor was found murdered where you girls were last seen in the Thurston Lava Tube."

"Was he killed with a big bent knife?" Cacy asked excitedly. "Rook over there tried to kill us with one, but it got lost in the rocks below."

The Man ordered officers to search the rocks and call in for divers. As he turned to speak to the girls more, the assistant with the brown suit came back with word that the parents of the two girls had arrived, as well as the classes from their schools. Kiara and Cacy looked to the crowds excitedly. Police escorted their parents through the crowds and reporters and past the police line. The girls screamed with joy and ran to their parents. They were showered with kisses and hugs. Cameras and cell phones clicked wildly to capture the reunion. Kiara's dad yelled at his wife.

"We cannot have her picture taken looking like this!" he complained.

"Why your hair so messy!" Kiara's mom scolded, taking out a handkerchief to wipe her daughter's face and hair. "Look you! Your uniform all dirty!! Ay-yah!"

"I'm fine, mother!" Kiara whined, struggling as her mom kept dusting all around her uniform. "For the first time I actually got to get dirty and it was fun."

As Cacy's parents embraced her, she looked over and felt sorry that Kiara was always expected to be a high achiever and a perfectionist. Their adventure together brought out the best and the worst in them, and Kiara seemed the better for it. Eventually, Kiara's mom finished combing and spritzing her daughter with hair spray from her purse to make her look proper and respectable. Kiara was relieved when the Man approached again to continue his questions with the girls in private.

When it came to being asked how they got off the boat and ended here with the men tied up, the girls looked at each other, hoping for an excuse without lying.

"We tricked them to bring us here," Cacy began and quickly looked at Kiara as if she would continue.

Kiara glared at Cacy for putting her on the spot and added, "Yes, they wanted to retrieve something in the Hale 'o Keawe relating to the ki'i. And in the dark, we managed to get away from them." Deep inside, both girls struggled with not being able to tell the full story while trying to be as honest as possible. A quick gush of wind blew past everyone. Instead of coming from the ocean, the girls felt it blow from the Hale 'o Keawe itself.

"Ah," the Man began to deduce, looking at Cacy. "And in the dark, you snuck back, knocked them out with your baseball bat, and both of you found the ropes nearby to tie them up. Brilliant, girls!"

The girls looked to each other, both relieved and happy. "Yeah, brilliant!"

"Well it's too bad the Queen still has the ki'i," the Man said, clenching his square jaw.

"Sir!" an officer called out to the Man and approached the three. "We found this kukri in the water as well as this. It looks like some sort of toy."

"It's my Digital Data Pad!" Kiara shouted with joy. She took her device and checked to see if it was damaged. With a click of the button, it rebooted and the screen lit up like normal. She became giddy and jumpy, holding her device like a favorite teddy bear. "There now, let's put you back where you belong, okay?" she said, attaching it back to her waist. Cacy wondered if her cousin hit her head too hard on the posts.

The Man told the officer to bag the kukri as evidence. His Chinese and Hawaiian assistants came up, telling the Man that they couldn't untie the cords to put handcuffs on Rook and Bishop. Already, they were yelling at the pain and stiffness in their limbs.

"Apparently those cords are handmade from olonā, boss," the Hawaiian assistant said with a pidgin tone. "That's too rare and precious to just cut. Plenny hard work fo' make 'um."

The Man thought for a second and then told them to go ask the park rangers for two long wooden poles to slide under the men's wrists and feet to carry them out. In moments, they returned and officers carefully slid the poles in place. It was a struggle for officers on both ends of the poles to lift Rook and then Bishop and place them on their shoulders. The hog-tied men screamed as their body weight pulled on their bound wrists and feet. The poles began to bend downward, almost touching the sand. A roar of laughter came from the crowds, and a barrage of camera flashes caught images of the two men, with Cacy and Kiara standing next to them looking like hunters and their giant trophies.

Cacy and Kiara looked at all the faces in the huge crowd. They saw their parents, classmates, and teachers all happy to see them. Even Momi, Tiana, and Shaun were pleased to see Cacy again, and especially Ms. Windbagg. Ms. Fitzgerald wept joyfully just like when she had been crowned Miss Hawai'i years ago. As they neared the police tape separating them from the crowds, classmates, tourists, and reporters waved and shouted questions. The Man took the girls to his side and raised his hand to make a statement. People from the press stood anxiously, ready to write in their notebooks or holding out tape recorders.

"First of all," the Man said, taking Cacy and Kiara by the hand, "both Cacy Dang and Kiara Yoon of Oʻahu are safe. Their disappearance yesterday from a school field trip at Hawaiʻi Volcanoes National Park was an alleged kidnapping by two suspects sought for the murder of a local citizen in the Thurston Lava Tube. The girls cleverly got the suspects to come to Puʻuhonua o Hōnaunau and bravely subdued them to be turned in to police custody. That's all we can say at this time. Ladies and gentlemen, I present you these two young heroes!"

The Man raised his arms, bringing up Cacy's and Kiara's like champions. Everyone burst into cheers and applause. Parents, classmates, and teachers beamed with pride. The girls looked at each other with surprised and sheepish looks but couldn't help feeling the fun of the moment.

The news report was being shown live across the state. Far away in the kīpuka, the Menehune watched the broadcast on the television Kiara had fixed. Along with those at the puʻuhonua, all the Menehune jumped and cheered seeing their two friends. They did cartwheels, flips, and spins in joy while others hugged shouting, "They made it! They made it!" Old Futt leaned on his umbrella with a deep sigh of relief and expelled a long rich, oily fart of contentment that rippled through the air before dancing with the other Menehune.

"Mali!" he cried. "Get the fellas to bring TWO wild boars tonight to celebrate!"

Back on the news, they watched as Rook and Bishop were being led past the crowd. Extra police and park rangers had to hold back the cheering crowd, which quickly turned to an angry mob. People booed and jeered Rook and Bishop. One local guy in a T-shirt threw a can of soda at the men while some of the students kicked sand at their lowered heads. Despite the pain, Rook shook his body, almost making the men carrying him lose control.

"You think this is over?!" he shouted at Cacy and Kiara. "You're gonna wish you didn't spare us."

"You can't hide from the Queen!" Bishop added with wicked laughter. "No matter where you go, she'll hunt you down and cut out your hearts! She's got loyal servants around the world!"

The crowd grew silent. The girls' parents held each other in fear. Kiara pondered what Bishop said and remembered that there are even other *rook* and *bishop* pieces on a chess board! The Man stepped forward to lead his two suspects out and away as soon as possible. But he was stopped by Cacy, who tugged on his suit.

"Hold on," Cacy said to him as both of the girls slowly approached their adversaries. The girls and the men looked at each other straight in the eyes with disgust. Cacy reached behind her and drew out her bat. Holding it like a battering ram, she jammed it hard into both Rook's and Bishop's sides. The crowd all winced at the feeling of pain in their ribs. Kiara unhooked her Digital Data Pad and pressed 5-6-0 then the red button. The men's eyes widened with terror as Kiara held the device out toward them. A crack of electrical currents flashed through the air and arced into both men, covering their shaking bodies in a static net of blue currents. When she was done, the men hung limp on the poles, groaning. Bishop's hair was a frizzled mess. The surprised crowd looked at the girls as Cacy and Kiara placed their arms over each other's shoulders.

"Don't worry—" Kiara said to the men.

"—we'll be ready." Cacy finished.

The crowd cheered once more for the girls, and the reporters were thrilled to catch the action on video. The Man placed his hands on the girls in admiration and to reassure them that both men would be dealt with. The three assistants came up to show the girls their support as well. The Man then raised his finger, pointing directly at Rook and Bishop.

"Book 'em!" the Man said to his assistant in the brown suit. "Murder one, kidnapping, grave robbing, theft, assault, terroristic threatening, and loitering at a heiau." The three assistants led the officers carrying Rook and Bishop out of the royal grounds and to a waiting police van. The last words the girls heard from the two was Bishop whining about his hair and Rook telling him to shut up.

"We have a special van for both of you and your parents," the Man said to the girls. "You will be taken back to Hilo to your hotel. After you have some rest, I'd like to finish taking down your statements. Come!"

With that he waved to the parents, teachers, chaperones, and students. Everyone rushed to hug the girls. Some asked for autographs and many clicked away pictures posing with them. Even Ms. Windbagg posed for a fun picture with Cacy, getting to hold the baseball bat.

"I hope you're not mad, Ms. Fitzgerald," Kiara said to her teacher. "It's not your fault."

"Thank you, Kiara," she said, giving her star student a big hug. "I'm just glad you and your cousin are fine, and I'm so sad you never got to see any lava."

"Oh, but I did!" she said eagerly. She was about to show Ms. Fitzgerald her Digital Data Pad and all the readings she collected thanks to Pele.

"Yes, yes, I'm sure you'll do a fine report on it, but right now you'd better go with your cousin," Ms.

Fitzgerald assured her. In reality, she was afraid Kiara's device might accidentally shock her.

With the Man leading, the girls and their parents waved good-bye to their schoolmates and the crowd. Park Ranger DeAguiar shook the girls' hands and gave them free bottled water as well as books and postcards of Pu'uhonua o Hōnaunau. As the group passed along the visitor center, Cacy pressed all the buttons to play the audio recordings about the visual displays. DeAguiar laughed and waved farewell.

Cameramen and reporters followed the group to the parking lot, but the girls refused to answer any questions, as suggested by the Man. A luxurious large white van with the Hawai'i state seal was waiting for them. The driver was a uniformed officer who saluted the Man. The girls' parents got into the posh spacious seats, enjoying the special treatment. Cacy and Kiara decided to sit together in the back row. Just as they were about to climb in, the assistant in the brown suit rushed up to the Man to hand him a large satellite phone. On the other line was the coast guard. The news made the Man look down in disappointment.

"What's wrong?" Cacy asked.

The Man paused and looked at Kiara and Cacy. He pulled them aside from the van and knelt down placing his hands gently on their shoulders. "I just received news that an inflatable raft has been discovered adrift several miles at sea with a dead body inside but the Queen's ship has disappeared from Hawaiian waters. She got away from us."

Chapter 38

Keiki o ka ʻĀina

The news crushed all the joy and elation the girls had felt since dawn. The Man assured the girls that his department would discuss their future safety later at the hotel and that they should get some rest immediately. As they boarded the van, the girls moved quietly to the back row and sank down. Their parents thought the girls might be falling fast asleep, so they decided not to disturb them during the 107-mile ride back to Hilo. As the van pulled out of the parking lot and back onto the road leading to the highway, the girls peered back to the final sights of the puʻuhonua.

Cacy turned to her cousin, who looked deeply concerned about what the Man had shared. She kept tapping the red button of the Digital Data Pad as if at any moment they would be attacked by the Queen's henchmen. Cacy tried to cheer her up and pointed out the window. Far down below on their right side was the rich blue ocean and the black coastline of lava rocks.

It was a beautiful day, unlike the deep clouds they had seen all day yesterday. Heading along the long winding roads of Highway 11 for over an hour, their parents all fell asleep, but Kiara and Cacy remained alert and energetic thanks to the magic drink provided by the kahuna and the priests. Soon the view changed and they looked at the moonlike surface of the steep smooth lava along the road as they approached the entrance to Hawai'i Volcanoes National Park. Traffic slowed as cars from both directions neared the familiar welcome sign. They watched as vehicles slowly entered lanes leading to the front gates. The recent news about them had created a huge sudden interest among tourists and locals, all hoping to see the spot where their adventure first started.

It was a sad feeling they shared as they passed the entrance sign of the volcano park and continued on to Hilo. They thought about the wondrous magic and adventure they had experienced in the park, as well as their Menehune friends. Both knew that if they ever returned, it just wouldn't be the same. Out on the left side of the van was the same scenery of lava fields that had mesmerized them the day before. They gazed out to see the solid black landscape stretching miles toward the misty horizon. Standing out in the middle of the desolate land was a figure dressed in bright red and orange. It was Pele.

"Stop the van!!" Kiara shouted to the driver. It startled him and woke up all the parents.

"What's wrong?" they all said, overlapping each other.

"Stop the van. Cacy and I need to get out," Kiara insisted.

"Why you no wait till we come to a nice bathroom to make shi-shi?" Kiara's mom inquired bluntly.

"No, it's not that!" Kiara said with embarrassment. "We need to go out in the lava field, but you all stay here in the van. We'll be right back."

The driver slowed down and made a U-turn, pulling alongside the lava field. Cacy and Kiara got out of the van and excitedly made their way about one hundred yards over the ropy overlays of lava rocks. Their parents and the driver kept careful watch from inside the van. Sometimes the girls disappeared from view when dipping into a low area and back in sight coming over steep mounds. Dried skeletal trunks of petrified ʻōhiʻa trees twisted high among the black rocks. Large broken branches were scattered everywhere like the bony remains on an ancient battlefield. When they reached Pele, the Fire Goddess smiled and motioned with her hand for the girls to not come any closer.

"I wanted to see you two one last time before you leave this island." The goddess spoke loud and clear for the girls to hear, yet she did not move her lips to speak. She was communicating by sending her thoughts to the girls. "The Language of the Land spell placed on you yesterday by Hiʻiaka has worn off by now. You are hearing my voice in your minds."

It was an eerie feeling looking at someone not speaking but still hearing their thoughts. The Fire Goddess looked at Cacy. All the while those in the van only saw Cacy and Kiara standing by themselves. Pele approached Cacy and took her by the hand gently.

"I'm so glad you were rescued by Kiara and her ʻaumakua." She nodded. "I want to apologize for almost consuming you with lava flows. I was enraged by those two men and their dog. Sometimes in my anger, I fail to remember the innocent people. Please forgive me."

"It's okay," Cacy spoke, smiling with reassurance. "We returned the kiʻi and the curse is gone. Plus those two men who were after me and Kiara were arrested."

"I know. It's a big island, but news travels fast." The Goddess winked. She then looked at Kiara to direct her thoughts.

"As I watched you and Cacy working together and becoming closer, I began to think about my relationship with Hiʻiaka. We both have our differences, but it is also our strengths which bond us. I think it's long overdue for me to talk with her."

"That's great!" the girls exclaimed.

Kiara couldn't help mentioning the threat of their enemies coming back for revenge.

"Don't worry," Pele insisted with strong emotion on her face. "You have each other and you'll meet new friends as well." Cacy wondered if Pele knew something about the future but didn't want to reveal anything.

"Will we ever see you again?" Kiara asked.

Pele smiled. "You are keiki ʻo ka ʻāina, children of the land. Whenever you see a magnificent lava flow or the beauty of the trees and flowers, you'll always see me and my sister. Now, go over to that dead tree over there." She pointed to a tall white petrified tree several yards away. Obediently, the girls made their way along a long trail of shiny pāhoehoe. When they came to the tree they looked down near its base.

Freshly carved into a smooth sheet of lava rock was a petroglyph. They knew what it was, but the design was not like any they had seen in a textbook. Their eyes widened as they studied the abstract drawing and identified the images. It was two girls standing side by side locking hands. One had the shape of a skirt on her waist with an odd-shaped tool attached to it and the other had two pigtail lines coming from

her head. In her hand was a form of a bat. Carved above the girls was the image of a large owl spreading its wings, and below them was a sea turtle.

"It's us!" Cacy shouted. The girls turned around to look back at Pele. She was gone. They scanned the entire circumference of the field but there was no sight of her.

The girls looked down at the petroglyph, feeling a deep sense of pride and connection to the land, the ocean, and especially to the past. Cacy motioned her cousin to look at a small crack in the rock just a few feet from the images. Reaching out of the small shaded crevice was the little green sprout of an infant ʻōhiʻa tree. Many years from now this entire field would be a rich rain forest teeming with life. It was Pele's sign of allowing a new beginning.

"Give me your backpack, Cacy," Kiara said.

"Huh? Why?"

"Just do it."

After taking her backpack, Kiara handed Cacy the baseball bat and knelt down. She unzipped the pack and began to dig around inside.

"It's kinda hot to wear your jacket," Cacy mentioned as she watched Kiara comb through the bag. To her surprise, she saw Kiara take out the last ti leaf. She carefully straightened it out and laid on the ground.

"Wait!" Cacy shouted. "What are you gonna do with it?"

Kiara looked up at her and drew out her small bag of rock candy from inside her vest. "I'm keeping a promise."

Kiara placed the bag of candy on the ti leaf and wrapped it up like a hoʻokupu, or traditional spiritual offering. She then placed it next to the petroglyph and stood up alongside her cousin. For a long time the girls looked at the scene and carefully made sure to remember this exact spot. A cool breeze blew through their hair as they stood silently side by side, absorbing this special moment. The loud horn from the van signaled that their parents wanted them to come back.

Kiara turned to her cousin. "Race you!" And with that she ran off back to the van.

"Hey! Wait up!" Cacy yelled, jamming her bat into her backpack and putting it back on. She sped off to catch up.

The girls laughed loudly as they leapt and skipped over the mounds, feeling like they were weightless and flying. Their parents opened the door to allow the giddy girls to jump back into their seats.

"What was all that about out there?" Cacy's mom asked. "It looked like you two were talking to someone."

"We just wanted one last look," Cacy replied, bouncing in her seat. Kiara was just as excited.

"Listen, folks," the driver said as he turned the van around and back in the direction of Hilo. "If you're all hungry, we can stop somewhere for breakfast before going to the hotel. It's all on the police department."

Cacy didn't remember seeing any fast food places on the way to Hawai'i Volcanoes National Park and couldn't think of anywhere to eat. Kiara nudged her and winked like Old Futt. Cacy picked up on the idea and nodded in eager agreement.

Both girls sat up straight and leaned forward. Kiara answered, "There's a pancake house in Hilo a friend told us about."

The End

Glossary

'a'ā—A type of lava. It is more viscous than pāhoehoe. The surface is jagged and sharp after cooling.

a hui hou—"Till next time..."

ali'i—chief

aloha—Greetings and farewell. Also, love, peace, and friendship.

'apapane—Species of honeycreeper birds related to the finch. Endemic to Hawai'i.

'aumakua—Family ancestor spirit or guardian. They are often considered to take the form of animals.

canopy—The top level of a forest. The bottom is called the forest floor.

Digital Data Pad—Electronic device built by Kiara. It can interpret and record data of seismic activity, electromagnetic waves, sound, temperature, speed, and other environmental changes. With Pele's upgrade, it can fire blasts of electrical streams.

eruption—Term when an outburst of volcanic products occur due to build up of pressure under the crust of the Earth.

Hale o Keawe—Temple at the Place of Refuge which housed the deified bones of ali'i.

Halema'uma'u Crater—Pit crater located in the Kīlauea caldera. The crater is still active and is home to Pele.

Halo Peer—At the Place of Refuge, one of a pair of guardian statues connected to the order of Kāne.

happy face spider—Tiny yellow spider endemic to Hawai'i. Markings on the back of its abdomen looks like a smiling face,

hāpu'u—Slow-growing native tree fern that was once used for stuffing, food and medicine. As it grows, the curled fonds can unfurl to about twenty feet high and three feet in diameter. The soft fluff on the fronds are called pulu.

Hawai'i—The 50th State in the U.S.A. (1959), consisting of a chain of eight islands. The largest and youngest is Hawai'i Island and is commonly known as the Big Island.

heiau—temple or structure for worship

Hi'iaka—Hawaiian goddess of the forest, winds, and hula dancing. She is one of Pele's younger sisters.

Hilo—Coastal town on the north eastern side of Hawai'i Island. Rainfall is common due to its location and climate.

honu—General name for sea turtle.

ho'okupu—An offering wrapped in ti leaves (and tied with 'ōhi'a lehua). Often it is given for respect and thanks as a spiritual connection between both the giver and the receiver.

ho'oponopono—To put things right and just. Some families practice this to resolve conflicts peacefully.

Hummer—A brand of off-road vehicles originating from High Mobility Multipurpose Wheeled Vehicle (Humvee) used in the United States armed forces.

i'iwi—Hawaiian honeycreeper bird endemic to Hawai'i. Easily recognized for its bright red feathers and long sickle-shaped beak.

kahuna—priest

Kalapana—A small coastal community affected by lava flows from the Pu'u 'Ō'ō vent in 1990.

Kamehameha Butterfly—An endemic butterfly recognized by its red and black wings with white spots. Named after the Kamehameha family.

Kāne—Hawaiian god of creation.

Keiki O Ka 'Āina—Children of the land.

Kiei—Peep. One of two guardian statues at the Place of Refuge. Like Halo, Kiei is connected with the order of Kāne.

kīhei—Shawl. Traditionally a square shaped tapa cloak tied in a knot over the shoulder.

ki'i—Tiki image or statue.

Kīlauea Caldera—Also known as Kīlauea volcano. The two mile wide caldera is both the home of Pele the Fire Goddess and the heart of Hawai'i Volcanoes National Park. Since 1983 Kīlauea has been erupting continuously at Pu'u 'Ō'ō. Gases from active Halema'uma'u crater inside the caldera continues to rise. Steam vents, Devastation Trail and the Jaggar Museum can be accessed from Crater Rim Drive.

kīpuka—Small forest island in the middle of a hardened lava field. Molten lava would wrap around a section of a forest leaving it untouched and isolated. Over time, plants and creatures living within the kīpuka adapt and evolve.

koa—Hawaiian endemic tree prized for its hardwood. Trees can grow up to nearly one hundred feet high with trunks about 20 feet in circumference.

Kona—Coastal town on Hawai'i Island located on its west side. Its climate is not as wet and rainy as Hilo. Coffee beans grown on Hawai'i Island are commonly referred to as Kona coffee.

kukri—A curved Nepalese knife used as both a tool and a weapon.

Lahaina—Coastal town on the island of Maui. In the early 1800s, Lahaina was both a thriving sea port for whalers as well as a new location for arriving Christian missionaries.

lava—Molten rock released by a volcano during an eruption. Under the surface it's referred to as magma. A lava flow can move at various speeds and distances due to its viscosity. Hawaiian lava can flow as either 'a'ā or pāhoehoe. As it cools and hardens, new land is created.

lava tube—As lava flows downhill, its top skin can cool and harden creating a shell which covers the continuous flow. Once the flow ends a long hollow tube exists. Ancient Hawaiians often used vacant lava tubes for storage and burial.

limu—seaweed

Lono O Makahiki—Lono of the annual feast. Lono is the Hawaiian god of fertility and music. The makahiki was an annual period of peace where games and festivity took place. War was forbidden during this period.

lū'au—Traditional Hawaiian feast among friends and family. Today, it is associated with a celebration such as first birthdays and weddings.

mahalo—thank you

maka'āinana—commoner, or people of the land

malo—Hawaiian male loincloth

mana—spiritual energy or divine power

Mango Head—What Kiara likes to call her cousin.

Mauna Kea—"White Mountain" in Hawaiian. It is a dormant snow-capped volcano 13,796 feet above mean sea level. Adding its base on the ocean floor would make it taller than Mount Everest (above sea level). Astronomers from around the world use its summit for observatories.

Mauna Loa—"Long or Large Mountain" in Hawaiian. Although shorter than Mauna Kea, Mauna Loa is the world's most massive shield volcano covering over half of Hawai'i Island. It is 13,677 feet above sea level.

Menehune—Legendary race of little people living in the Hawaiian Islands. Some accounts tell that they populated the islands before the first settlers from Polynesia. They are considered intelligent and excellent in craftwork and building structures such as homes, fishponds, or temples overnight. They are friendly and playful but prefer to live in forests secretly hidden away from outsiders.

mu'umu'u—a loose gown (dress)

Nahuku—The Hawaiian name for the Thurston Lava Tube.

nēnē—Hawaiian goose. They are endemic to Hawai'i, endangered and under Federal Wildlife protection. It is discouraged to feed them in Hawai'i Volcanoes National Park or anywhere else as it can cause them harm.

O'ahu—The third largest Hawaiian island and most populated, known as the "The Gathering Place." Both Cacy and Kiara are from this island.

'ohana—family

'ōhelo berries—Endemic, bright red berries similar

to cranberries which are found in Hawaiʻi Volcanoes National Park. They are considered one of Pele's favorites. Offerings of branches with the fruit were often tossed into Kīlauea.

ʻōhiʻa lehua—An endemic tree which grows quickly over lava rock. It is easily recognized by the bright red flowers made up of stamens. A growing tree will provide shade for smaller trees and plants which allows them to grow and create a rainforest.

olonā—A prized fiber plant use by Hawaiians to make cordage for tying and stringing.

ʻŌlelo O Ka ʻĀina—The Language of the Land.

Pāoa—Pele's digging stick

Pāhoehoe—The second type of Hawaiian lava. It resembles thick, ropy masses. When cooled to a solid form, it's smooth and curvy in comparison to ʻaʻā.

Pele—The Hawaiian goddess of fire and volcanoes. She is Hiʻiaka's older sister. Certain legends tell of Pele arriving in the islands and settling at Kīlauea. She is respected by many.

petroglyphs—Images carved into rock surfaces by the Native Hawaiians.

pidgin—At times regarded as Hawaiian Creole, Pidgin English is a local dialect using both slang and mixed with words from different ethnic backgrounds. Example: "Wow. It's going to take a long time to clean up all this litter."—"Auwe. Going take long time fo' pick up all dis ʻōpala."

pohaku—rock or stone

poi—The famous starchy staple food of the ancient Hawaiians made from the taro plant. The corms are peeled, steamed, pounded smooth and watered down. Most people today eat it as a side dish when eating Hawaiian food.

pueo—Hawaiian short eared owl

pulu—Silky fibers found on the hāpuʻu ferns. They were collected, dried, and used for pillow stuffing.

Puʻu ʻŌʻō—An active vent on the Eastern Rift Zone of Kīlauea Volcano. Eruptions have been been ongoing since 1983.

snout—The best (and tastiest) part of a roasted wild boar.

tapa—Called kapa in Hawaiian. Fabric cloth made from paper mulberry tree.

ti—Versatile plant used by Hawaiians but found worldwide. Leaves can be used for things such as weaving, clothing, thatching, medicine, wrapping, and religious ceremonies.

tiki—Common name for idol carvings and sculptures of figures from Hawaiʻi and most of Polynesia.

A Note to Readers, Parents, and Teachers

The Hawaiian culture is rich with history, religion, and traditional practices that continue today. Both Hiʻiaka and Pele are revered, respected goddesses whose multifaceted stories are passed from generation to generation.

This fictional story is not intended to distort or disrespect ancient Hawaiian religion, practices, ancestors, or those deeply connected to the locations and settings herein, including Puʻuhonua o Hōnaunau and Hawaiʻi Volcanoes National Park.

As a part-Native Hawaiian myself, I have an appreciation and connection to my culture, and I enjoyed visiting and learning more about these locations during my research for this book. My portrayals of the goddesses, Kahuna, Menehune, and the locations are not meant to be the "whole picture" or "true version," and should not be construed as the general belief or view of all Native Hawaiians or the National Parks Service.

I encourage readers to learn more about Pele and Hiʻiaka, Hawaiʻi's volcanoes, Puʻuhonua o Hōnaunau, and their role and importance—both historic and present—in the Hawaiian culture. Visit your local library or bookseller and talk to your teachers, kūpuna, aunties, and uncles.

Tracing the Past at Honaunau by Dorothy B. Barrère (Hawai'i National History Association, 1994) is a very detailed and informative book. One of the many books I have on volcanoes is *Hawai'i Volcanoes National Park: Fire from Beneath the Sea* by Barbara and Robert Decker (Sierra Press, 2002). It contains awesome photos and information covering the fauna, natural inhabitants, and ecology of the park.

To learn more about our wonderful National Parks, visit: http://www.nps.gov/state/hi/. Better yet, visit and support them.

My intention was to write and illustrate an entertaining adventure for kids and adults. I realize that there are some who may be quite sensitive to the portrayal of Hawaiian gods and sacred places in a fictional novel. (Believe me, I've seen more than enough distorted and stereotyped portrayals of Hawai'i and her people on screen and in print, so I understand this apprehension.) Weaving known details with free creative self-expression and imagination, I attempted to portray Hi'iaka and Pele with respect and to highlight their humanity so that young readers could relate to them.

Above all, the story is really about Cacy and

Kiara and how, like the two cousins, we all have shortcomings and challenges in life to overcome. When we're able to put aside personal differences and work together with hope and forgiveness, we can make it through.

–Roy Chang

About the Author/Illustrator

Roy Chang is an art teacher, editorial cartoonist and freelance illustrator. He graduated with a BFA in Illustration from the Academy of Art University in San Francisco and earned his Masters in Education degree from the the University of Hawai'i at Manoa. He is also a two time Pa'i award winning Editorial Cartoonist for *MidWeek,* Hawai'i's largest read non-daily newspaper.

This story is his first novel and was inspired by a unit lesson created in 2002 for his 7th and 8th grade Fine Arts students to come up with their own two original characters, depict them in a four panel storyline and then create a hand painted "animation" cel based on their favorite scene. In doing the project himself, Cacy and Kiara were born. The following year, Chang visited Hawai'i Island to research details for his plot and settings. As a part-Hawaiian, he is very honored and proud to have learned more about ancient Hawaiian culture in the process of writing and drawing.

Previous work as an illustrator includes:

You Know You're in Hawai'i When...
Wuz da Nite Befo!
Haunted Hawaiian Nights
The Legend of Morgan's Corner and Other Ghost
Stories of Hawai'i

Children's book illustrations for BeachHouse Publishing include:

The Storm Dog of the Ko'olaus
*The Shark Man of Hana**

His favorite writers and artists include Mark Twain, Charles Dickens, Hayao Miyazaki and Norman Rockwell.

To celebrate the completion of his book, he treated himself to a new pair of Emporio Armani aviator sunglasses. Chang lives in Honolulu, but would rather be visiting San Francisco.

*received a 2005 Ka Palapala Po'okela Award of Excellence for Children's Hawaiian Culture)